Off The Path

a novel

DANIEL J. WELLS

OFF
the
PATH

DANIEL J. WELLS

iUniverse LLC
Bloomington

Off the Path

iUniverse books may be ordered through booksellers or by contacting:

iUniverse
1663 Liberty Drive
Bloomington, IN 47403
www.iuniverse.com
1-800-Authors (1-800-288-4677)

ISBN: 978-1-4917-2886-4 (sc)
ISBN: 978-1-4917-2885-7 (hc)
ISBN: 978-1-4917-2884-0 (e)

Library of Congress Control Number: 2014904716

Printed in the United States of America.

iUniverse rev. date: 03/31/2014

FOR SAUNDRA,
now and always

Prologue

She had carried the child for eight months and three weeks, and now it was gone. She faintly remembered seeing him—she *thought* she'd seen a boy—but it was a hazy recollection. She couldn't convince herself that the whole thing hadn't been a dream, or perhaps a hallucination, caused by anesthesia or the shadows that haunted her soul. Anyway, the child, named David, was gone.

The man returned the patient file to its hook on the end of her bed. Laura Adams watched as he closed his eyes and rubbed his nose between the thumb and forefinger of his left hand. "Your blood pressure is running a bit high but that isn't unusual," he paused to examine the tops of his shoes, "for someone in your ... situation." He folded his arms across his chest. Their eyes met when he stole a look at the woman covered in white bedding. She was a pretty girl, young and blond with large green eyes. He abruptly resumed the shoe inspection.

"Is my baby okay, doctor? You know," now Laura looked down to his shoes, "normal?"

The doctor cocked his head a little to the left, glanced at the door and then to a place on the wall directly above the woman's head, just below the crucified feet of a twelve-inch brass Jesus and who knew how many coats of paint.

"Yes, very much so, but"—back to the shoes—"you shouldn't think of the child as yours. You may never see him again. You know that, right?"

"Yeah, I know." She spoke very softly and without conviction. "But couldn't I see him? Just for a second, you know, through the window? Please?" She begged with those beautiful emerald eyes. In her life, they had often been enough to win the day, but not here and not now.

The doctor shook his head quickly and turned to the door. He grabbed the knob to pull the door open and paused. "I'll be back to check on you a little later. Right now, you should sleep. The baby is a ward of the court. There's nothing we can do now." With that, he stepped into the hallway and pulled the door shut.

The young woman, alone in the flat-white room, occasionally heard muted voices from the hall but could not understand the words they spoke. She was warm and tossed her feet toward the bed's right side to free them of the covers. A spear of pain immediately charged from her midsection to her brain and drove her to sit upright, rigid, eyelids pressed tightly shut, teeth clenched, breathless. *You are truly a dumbass*, she scolded herself.

When the sharp objections of her jarred and stressed parts fell to a steady, throbbing ache, Laura opened her eyes and saw her own feet. There were tiny scratches on them, and the left big toenail was a deep blue, almost black, and cracked. *Gonna lose that nail*, she thought, and she recalled through a haze that at labor's onset, she had viciously stubbed her toe against a cement parking block as she hurriedly stumbled out of a cheap motel—they once called them *fleabags*—and into the street.

Through the mist in her memory, she now watched herself, hobbled as she fell and wept, but a tall, heavyset black man lifted her in his arms and carried her gingerly to his taxi. He told her not to cry or worry; he would get her to the hospital in "plenny o' time, plenny o' time." He drove very fast, and the grotesquely lavender Detroit City Cab, with red, white, and blue "1976 USA Bicentennial" decals on each rear door, shook and sputtered all the way.

After he carefully toted her from the cab to a wheelchair beneath a bright red EMERGENCY sign, the cabbie smiled into her eyes and said only, "Good luck and God bless, little miss." He left without collecting the fare that she was several dollars short of being able to pay anyway.

Laura recalled the great fuss at the hospital when word spread of her arrival. Her picture had been in the papers and on TV, the weeping, obviously pregnant woman in black, trying to hide her face behind her arm, surrounded by a mass of reporters with their intrusive microphones and handheld video cams. Next to her picture, both the Detroit *News* and *Free Press* ran the same shot of her husband as he leered defiantly and angrily through the rear window of a Salt Lake City police squad car, obviously sitting on cuffed hands. His upper teeth were pressed against his lower lip and his cheeks puffed out slightly before he shrieked, "Fuck you! Fuck you all!" although neither paper reported his parting remarks. The headline in the *News* announced: COP KILLER CAUGHT AS BLOODY TRAIL ENDS IN UTAH.

Laura now thought of her husband and the cage he lived in. She left him in Utah after his trial and rode buses east until she was in Detroit, cloistered in a dingy, cramped motel room, another cage, waiting for his seed to make its move into this world. She went into hiding to conceal her shame and disbelief over what her life had become. She surrendered anonymity when labor started; meanwhile, her husband, the *cop killer*, the drug-ravaged thief and murderer, sat alone on death row in a Utah prison, awaiting appeals, awaiting the end.

Laura had quit the drugs and the booze, mostly, but self-pity and loathing continued unabated. Alone and frightened in her motel room, she asked God to help her, to save her, and she promised to keep the child and find redemption. She turned off the small black-and-white TV and listened all night for a response. She heard sirens, car horns, people laughing drunkenly, the periodic bark of a dog, church bells chiming somewhere far away, all the sounds of the city—but no word from God that she could hear. *Did he hear me*, she wondered, *or did he just not care?*

Eventually, Laura drifted into sleep as black night left her motel window and early daylight sneaked in. Later that day, a woman from social services and a big Detroit cop knocked on her motel room door. It hadn't taken long for someone to drop a dime and turn her in. Laura faced a hearing to determine her involvement in her husband's crime spree, and the state decided it would claim her yet-unborn child until she could be proved a "fit and worthy" mother, free of drugs and innocent of complicity in her husband's evil deeds.

While no one thought her innocent, not by any stretch, it was decided that her husband had acted alone at his heinous peak, and so the states along Billy's death ride to Utah lost interest in Laura and she escaped imprisonment. But in her native Michigan, failed drug tests and her fruitless attempts at rehab made the state's ultimate decision inevitable.

And at last the child came and was quickly taken away. She closed her eyes to the dull white hospital as the past few years of her life swirled by in a haze. Laura dropped her head to the pillow and stared up at the ceiling to await sleep. Thoughts and images floated loosely through her mind, unattached and disjointed. They glided by as though on a breeze, collected and carried away into nothingness, lost and unclaimed. She saw faces, so many different faces: some smiling, some screaming, some bleeding, some laughing. At last she saw a little boy, sitting on the floor, petting the head of a very large dog with green eyes. When sleep finally swept them away, she drifted through the clouds and into darkness, where she saw nothing. In separate rooms, Laura and her child slept. One dreamed of the night and the other of the morning.

For whether lighted over ways that save,
Or lured from all repose,
If he go on too far to find a grave,
Mostly alone he goes.

EDWARD ARLINGTON ROBINSON

Chapter One

Davie ran through a thick mist and waved his arms before him, a futile attempt to clear the haze that engulfed him. He chased apparitions that darted into and then beyond his perception. At once the mist receded, and the boy saw a naked woman as she slowly turned to face him. He knew her—he thought he did—and he ran to hold her and be embraced. She held out her arms, palms upward, and flipped rigid fingers up and down, up and down to him.

"Come to me, Davie," she whispered in a husky voice. *"Come to me, Davie."*

He stopped two steps short of the woman and froze in horror. Blood gushed from gaping slashes in each wrist and streamed across her cracked palms until it poured from ten fouled spigots that were her fingertips. Her pallid face glowed like a haunted moon, and her eyes burned scarlet from two deep holes. She dropped to her knees and whispered his name again and again, "Davie, Davie, *Davie,*" her

1

voice rising in pitch with each repetition until it was a bellowed howl. The boy turned to run, but his legs responded maddeningly in slow motion, as though filled with lead.

At last, safely away from the bleeding woman, her wailing slowly faded into a ghostly memory. Davie was again lost in the haze, where nothing was clear or tangible. He turned in every direction and spun from side to side in panic as light grew dim and all forms vanished. He twisted to his left, fell to his knees, closed his eyes, and began to pray.

Davie heard sounds, rustling leaves and rushing water and, he thought, croaking frogs. He opened his eyes and saw only shadows, silhouettes that flitted by too quickly to be recognized or seen with any clarity. The mist again withdrew, and in a new light and place he saw a woman and a man run past him, the man in apparent pursuit. The man couldn't quite catch her, and she wouldn't stop. Davie thought he knew them too and began to follow, calling out names, chasing their shapes, but he couldn't make them aware of his presence.

Their elusiveness frustrated the boy, but he trailed them until they disappeared into a depth of blackness where he could—*would*—not follow. He watched as darkness was vanquished by vague hues of blue and yellow. Gradually, Davie became aware that he was in his own bed, his reason overshadowed by trepidation, so he hurriedly sat up and looked about for a trace of familiarity, something that spoke loudly of reality and consciousness.

His heart pounded and filled his ears with a buh-*bump*, buh-*bump*, buh-*bump* in the interminable instant his eyes needed to focus and adjust. Davie spotted a six-inch plastic figurine standing atop the nightstand beside his bed. It was a baseball player, Reggie Jackson, in a California Angels uniform, a halo atop the big red *A* on his cap, a baseball bat cocked in his hands, ready and waiting for a pitch in his zone to take deep. Reggie called home runs "taters," his uncle Jack said. The boy relaxed slightly.

Turning his head toward the window to his right, Davie gazed beyond the glass at the house across the small field that bordered his home. An eerie blue light glowed from an upstairs window into the night and writhed in the shadows of a towering oak tree.

Davie stared at the blue light for a long time, arms wrapped around his knees, legs bent under the covers of the bed. When drowsiness dulled his anxiety, he lowered his head to the pillow, straightened his legs, and closed his eyes. As Davie began to doze off again, he heard his uncle Jack's voice rising in volume and urgency from just down the hall. No, the boy decided, Uncle Jack was angry.

"Don't blame me for something I didn't even know about!" the man blurted. Davie sat up and hugged his knees. Uncle Jack and Aunt Angie were arguing again.

"Oh no, not you, Jack. God knows, you know *nothing!*" Aunt Angie's voice had risen to meet Jack's decibel count. "You want to dump everything on me, so your innocent and perfect world goes on and on! Maybe it *should* go on—*without me!*" Davie heard something thump against the wall.

"Nice try, but you missed! I don't know what to say to you," Jack declared. "You won't fecking listen to me, to what I have to say. You didn't care what I felt then, and you sure as shit don't care now!"

Davie heard their bedroom door slam shut, felt the vibration even in his bed, and he quickly straightened his legs and turned onto his side. In a moment, the boy heard his bedroom door softly squeak as it slowly opened. He closed his eyes, pretended to be asleep, wishing for quiet, wishing it would all just *settle down*. In a few seconds, Davie heard the door click shut, and he listened as Uncle Jack walked down the hallway and then down the stairs. Davie thought he heard Aunt Angie sobbing, alone in her room.

Davie began to cry. It frustrated him to hear his aunt and uncle fighting. It made him feel alone and frightened; only eight years old, he was too young to truly understand what had happened down the hall. He cried quietly, embracing himself tightly under the covers until sleep mercifully claimed him. Davie fell into its arms without resistance.

In the morning, Aunt Angie woke him with a cheery, "Rise and shine, pookie!" Davie washed and dressed for school. He ate breakfast quietly as Angie moved from station to station in the kitchen, fixing his bag lunch, sipping coffee, and finishing off a cold piece of toast.

"You'd better beat it for the bus, sweetheart. And don't forget you lunch," Angie said as she handed Davie a brown sack. She leaned down and kissed him on the cheek. "Be a good boy, okay?"

"Okay, Aunt Angie, I will. You too, okay?" The boy looked up to the woman, his head tilted slightly to the right.

"I'll sure try," she said with a wan smile.

She patted Davie on the back and watched as he left the house for the bus stop. *I wish I was eight years old again*, she thought. No real worries or problems or complications that couldn't be quickly sorted and mended, *Oh, to be young*, she mused.

Angie remembered herself as a little girl, holding her father's hand as he walked her to the bus stop or riding along when he drove her to school in his shiny white Cadillac. The car smelled of cigarette smoke and his cologne, and the radio played classical music, faintly, in the background. A sweet moment, tenderly preserved in her memory, unclouded by all that followed.

Angie double-checked her makeup in a pocket mirror, applying the finishing touches to a face that really didn't need any help at all, except for the slight shadows below her eyes. She stared into her mirror and decided she'd need a little Visine to "get the red out" of her green eyes. She was only thirty-five, but this morning, after another late-night row with Jack and very little sleep, she felt much older. She was tired, too frustrated to close the widening gap between her and Jack, a rift that had started a few years ago with her own lost child and now seemed beyond repair. A few moments later, she was through the door and on her way to work.

At the end of the school day, the bus deposited Davie and several other kids a few doors down the street. They all went their separate ways, eager to get home for a snack and to exchange their school clothes for play duds. It was sunny day, warmer than might be expected for April in Michigan. Twin brothers, Robby and Ricky Goldman, told Davie to come by their house for a game of whiffle ball home run derby, and Davie said he'd try.

Davie scampered home and was surprised to see both Uncle Jack's Mustang and Aunt Angie's LTD parked in the driveway. It wasn't unusual for Jack to be home, but it was too early for Angie. Davie entered the garage and walked slowly toward the man door that led into the house. He stopped short of opening the door when he heard them speaking excitedly.

"Goddamn it, Angie, why don't you stay home and talk to me? You don't need to go back to work now. Call in sick, tell him you're busy, tell him anything, but stay with me now!" Uncle Jack didn't sound angry; he was *determined*, it seemed to Davie.

"I don't know what you want me to say, Jackson. I truly don't. Everything I have to say, I've already said, many times. I'm sorry for what happened, I'm sorry I didn't tell you, I'm sorry ... you know." Davie barely heard her last words as they trailed off. He decided he'd eavesdropped enough, so he opened the door, climbed two steps, and entered the house, carefully setting his schoolbooks on a small table in the short hall that led to the kitchen.

"Hey, wheezer, what's the good word?" Uncle Jack greeted Davie and picked him up with both hands. He pulled the boy to his chest and gave him a big hug before setting him back on the floor. Davie blushed slightly but smiled when he looked at Aunt Angie.

"Hi, Davie! Good day at school?" she asked before leaning down and kissing his forehead with a loud *smack*. She had the sniffles and her eyes were damp.

"I guess so," Davie said softly. "How come you're home so early? Did you get canned?" Davie arched an eyebrow and the woman and man burst into laughter. Both tickled the boy's ribs and he joined their mirth, however short-lived it might prove to be.

"You've been watching too many of those old movies with your uncle, young man!" Angie straightened and turned to collect her purse from the kitchen counter. "Just came home to get some notes I forgot this morning, and now I have to get back to work." She watched as Davie sagged slightly, and Jack turned and walked away, into the living room. "I won't be home for dinner, so make sure Uncle Jack eats his vegetables, okay?"

Davie smiled up to his aunt and took her free hand. He gave it a quick squeeze and then turned it loose. Angie thought the gesture touching, if not a little odd, and she again kissed his forehead before quietly walking out the door. She did not speak to Jack before leaving.

Curly, the family bulldog, waddled into the kitchen and laid claim to Davie's attention. He obliged, dropping to the floor and rolling around playfully with his slightly rotund pal.

Jack and Davie ate a tasty dinner of leftover spaghetti ("It's always better on the second day," Uncle Jack proclaimed), tossed salad, and breadsticks in front of the television. When they'd each polished off a bowl of orange sherbet, Jack poured himself a few fingers of Irish whiskey and lit up a smoke. Davie sat on the floor and worked through a set of math problems. They did not challenge his quick mind, but they were homework, and homework had to be done.

Davie occasionally glanced at Jack, who watched the six o'clock news from the couch. Davie looked down at his schoolwork, but heard a TV newscaster narrating video of Angie's brother-in-law, his father, standing and weaving slightly, side to side, his eyes pressed shut, obviously stationed in a courtroom.

Former Detroiter William "Billy" Adams, who staged a nationwide crime and murder spree that stretched from here to Utah and claimed eight lives, will tonight face justice for the last time, at least in this life, when he is given a lethal injection in a Utah prison . . .

Jack fumbled to find the TV's remote and hurriedly switched channels until a black-and-white Mr. Ed, the talking horse, wearing a huge pair of sunglasses, filled the screen. Jack looked at Davie, who was writing with a pencil across a sheet of lined white paper. *Did he hear that?* the man wondered. *Is he aware of what is happening to his biological father, the nervous-looking man standing in that courtroom on the other side of the country?*

Davie continued to work through his math problems. He'd sneaked a peek at the twitchy man on TV and felt a twinge of recognition, a slight twist in his stomach. He looked to Uncle Jack, who seemed about to say something, but only gazed back at Davie, mouth open. "You okay, Uncle Jack?" he asked.

"Yeah, bud," Jack said softly. "You okay?"

Davie nodded, smiled, and closed his homework notebook. The television was simply white noise, something in the background, until he heard Mr. Ed's deep baritone. "Hey, Uncle Jack!" Davie cried. "Let's watch Mr. Ed!"

Jack smiled at the boy and patted the sofa cushion to his immediate right. "Come on up here, porcupine," he said. "It looks like Mr. Ed is going to the beach!"

Davie flew across the room and bounced onto the couch. His

uncle grabbed him and tickled the boy's ribs until his laughter filled the room. *Mr. Ed beats math anytime*, Davie decided.

Davie and Uncle Jack watched TV while Curly curled in a plump ball on the floor before them. When a rank stench filled the air without warning, boy and man pointed fingers at one another.

"You made a stinky, Uncle Jack!" Davie shook a finger at Jack while holding his nose shut with his other hand.

"Nice try, but that silent-but-deadly beauty was all you, sweet lips!" Jack fanned at the air briskly with both hands, until Curly rose to his feet and quickly waddled toward the front door.

"Curly!" Davie and Jack called out in unison.

"Oh gross, dog farts," Davie moaned. Jack followed Curly to the door and opened it to let the dog loose into the night. "Hurry up and do what you gotta do, stumblenuts," Jack instructed the dog's departing derriere.

Jack returned to the couch, leaving the inner door open to allow spring's cool evening air to freshen the room. In a few minutes, Curly returned to the porch, business concluded, and with a single bark announced his wish to come in. Jack opened the door and Curly waddled into the kitchen, sat, and waited expectantly. Jack did not disappoint, handing Curly a Milk-Bone, a cookie for dogs. Curly dropped to the floor and went to work, stumpy tail waving contentedly.

After a little more TV and a little more orange sherbet, Jack sent Davie up to bed. "I'm gonna wait up a while for Aunt Angie," Jack told the boy, who stood on tiptoes to kiss the man on his chin.

Davie climbed the stairs, emptied his bladder, washed his hands and face, and brushed his teeth. He went into his room and changed into his pajamas and then knelt on the floor with both elbows on the bed. Davie closed his eyes, bowed his head, and clasped his fingers together.

"Dear God," the boy whispered, "thanks for all you've given me today, and for keeping everybody safe. Please help Aunt Angie and Uncle Jack to get along better, okay? Amen." Davie rose to his feet, pulled back the covers, and climbed into bed. His focus on the here and now began to wane and wander away, despite his efforts to control it. He cracked his eyes open slightly to ascertain his whereabouts. Reggie was still waiting for some belt-high cheese; to the left, dim yellow light poured into the room from the hallway.

In a moment, dreams dictated illusory circumstances as Davie grew weary and drifted off to sleep, into a sensation of weightlessness, where he floated through a sky's cool clouds and warm sunshine. He saw the earth slowly spin into a blur below as he cascaded nearer and nearer to the ground. The world seemed to slow its whirl to gently accept his descent, and a wide swath of towering trees loomed increasingly larger and closer.

Without sound or sensation, he landed on the banks of a lazily meandering river in the midst of a vast forest. Indomitable oaks and elms and firs burst from black dirt and dark green grass and climbed so high into the topless sky that Davie had to look straight up to the heavens to see their peaks. At once he was lost to another world: all control gone, all grasp of place and time surrendered, the final clutches of reality released.

He dipped his hands in the river's water, so icy to the touch, and it repelled him. Davie climbed up the bank, away from the river, and when he reached level ground he wiped his hands dry on the seat of his pants. He was now part of this world; it was no longer alien to him.

He pushed himself over a small knoll and, turning back, espied the river. It seemed to only flow away from him, no matter where he stood, no matter his vantage point, winding out into an outlying world that he had not seen and did not know. For an instant, in his mind, he tried to reverse the current so that it streamed toward him and not into the distance. He failed to conjure the illusion, so he turned and walked away.

Precious little daylight remained, and Davie fretted that he would miss his supper. He began to jog but soon broke into a full run. *There's always something,* he thought, *some unknown to overcome but never fully conquer.* And instantly he knew it was hopeless. The boy reckoned the length of the run before him. It would be dark in half that time. He slowed his gait to a brisk walk in the face of such futility.

Soon Davie came to a path that cut through the forest and led to the village where he lived. It was a shortcut that would reduce his travel time almost in half, but at a price. Here light escaped the earth long before the sun yielded its sky to the night's blackness. Davie was frightened of the forest, of what lurked in its mysterious shadows, unmoving but for a wavering sway affected by the whimsies of the wind.

"Nothin' good ever happens to little boys in there at night," his uncle had warned. "At night there are no rules, and we live and die by rules. You'd be wise to respect that, Davie, and the forest, too—'specially at night."

Davie ignored the advice, opted for the shorter route, and headed down the path, into the depths of the forest.

Davie redoubled his pace, as fast as his short legs could thrust him through the encroaching darkness. Sounds of the forest grew louder and louder; mixed with the pounding of his heart, it all seemed to echo and reverberate under the descending ceiling of the night. Davie looked about and recognized nothing. He was lost.

"Oh God, where am I?"

He twisted his head desperately from side to side, searching for something, *anything,* familiar—a tree, a bush, a boulder—some *thing* to grab and pull himself back into the world of right and reason.

He felt himself slipping away. The great oaks and elms and firs that had hoisted their limbs in salutation earlier now groped to seize and strangle him and rip his head and arms and legs from his tiny torso.

It grew completely still in that moment when day and night pass each other, light spiraling upward beyond the stars, darkness whirling and twisting downward to earth. And then all was black.

Davie stood alone on the jagged path that now ended at his feet. He listened as the forest whispered *death* in a thousand voices, all faceless. He fell to his knees in despair.

"Where am I? Oh my God, *where am I?*"

He stood and looked up to the sky. There was no response, so he fell back down to the ground, sat with his head between his knees, and wept. He felt the eyes of darkness pierce him, cutting through his very essence. Silhouettes raced silently about him, and he was terrified. Again he raised his head and yowled. "Leave me alone! Please! *Leave me alone and let me go home!*"

From the depth of the forest, Davie heard a stir and turned to see two gleaming eyes, burning in a strange greenish-gold glare, moving very deliberately toward him. His heart sank to the pit of his stomach and then heaved upward to his throat. The boy recoiled when he saw a huge head, exaggerated in size, with lips drawn back to display a hideous gatefold of white fangs and rich red rivulets that trickled down its jaw and throat.

It was a wolf—a lone wolf, massive, menacing, and malevolent. Davie had heard his uncle speak of this beast with great awe and respect. It grew strong, his uncle said, feeding on the souls of fools who wandered into the forest at night—just as Davie had done!

And now, dear God, his uncle's monster was steadily, slowly, purposefully stalking toward him! Davie could not move, could not breathe. He could only watch. And wait. Terror gripped him tightly; time held him frozen in its clutches, and thus forbade the seconds and minutes from proceeding in their relentless march toward infinity. Every living thing, every sound, was paralyzed with fear.

Davie began to clearly see the wolf's shape. It was, quite truly, a monster. Blood mixed with drool slavered from its mouth. What the boy perceived as a longing look—a *hungry* look—scorched what was left of Davie's courage and sent it scurrying for cover. He had reached the end of his short life, Davie was certain of that. He thought of his aunt Angie one last time, smiling in the glow of the fireplace, its flames frolicking in her green eyes.

A low snarl crawled from the wolf's belly and became thunder in its throat. Davie let out a feeble moan, hands clenched together before his face in a desperate plea for mercy, for life, as his chest heaved up and down in full-blown horror. He stood too quickly, tumbled to his knees, and fell forward until his nose was in the dirt. Tall grass veiled his head.

Davie sensed the beast as it loomed directly above his bowed head, and then he felt its hot breath on the nape of his neck. He dared not look up into the face of evil that would now surely tear him to shreds. He could only whimper a final appeal for mercy. Thousands of faceless voices arose from the forest, wailing, taunting, jeering, shrieking, until it sounded like the gates of hell had been thrown wide open, its occupants free to reenter this world in force.

"God, God, dear God! *Where are you?* Help me!" Davie wrapped his arms about his head and waited to be ravaged, life torn from this small body, devoured in scraps, his soul sent forever into the void. He willed himself to be small, tiny, imperceptible, invisible.

And then another deep rumble roared from the beast's marrow, immediately stilling the chorus of death in the forest. The wolf let loose a strange, rolling grumble. Petrified, confused, and lost, Davie now sensed that the wolf was laughing at him, and that they were each reeling into madness.

The cowering child slowly lifted his head, dropped his arms, and leaned back until he felt his heels dig into his back. He thrashed his arms, so tiny and frail, his only weapons in this battle with what was surely Satan himself. And then he stood.

"No! I don't want to die! *No!*"

In his mind, memories suddenly, inexplicably, swirled about. He watched as the village butcher's cleaver delivered a wicked slash to the throat of a squirming pig, its bright blood spewing into the street as its life gushed into the dirt and dust. He saw the animal fall limp and lifeless, to squeal no more. The butcher then took a long-handled knife and went to work, cutting and carving, right there in the street!

A forgotten slaughter, some distant memory long ago pushed *way* back in his mind; that was all that Davie could envision. He tried to picture his mother's face, but it was lost to him. He let his arms go flaccid and dangle at his sides. He refocused and stared into the gleaming eyes of the wolf.

"Follow me," it whispered in a hushed growl. As the great beast turned, the black unknown of the forest opened before them.

"You spoke! I heard you! *I heard you speak!*"

As suddenly as he had been trapped, Davie was now free. The wolf began to walk up the path that reappeared and stretched into the night, the glow of a golden moon lighting the way, a sea of stars twinkling in the clear sky beyond. Davie hesitated for a heartbeat and then followed the beast as it lumbered up the road.

"Who are you?" Davie whispered. "Why didn't you ... kill me?"

The wolf did not stop or look back at the child. It strode forward, and with each step, the forest trembled and opened before its huge paws. Davie peered ahead, up the road, and in time the first lights of the village flickered in the distance. A soft breeze fetched the warm breath of forever with a whisper to quell the chill and damp of night and darkness. Davie abruptly stopped walking.

The wolf took a few steps, halted, and looked back at the child. The fire in its eyes had cooled, and whatever menace Davie had seen only moments earlier was no longer there. Its mouth almost appeared to smile. The great beast shook its head vigorously from side to side, peering up the road, then back at the boy. Their eyes met for a long moment.

"I want to stay with you," Davie murmured.

Again the wolf's head jerked from side to side. It turned and glared toward the forest. A bobcat mewed and scampered back into the tall grass. There was a slight rustle in the undergrowth along the outer edge of the forest, and then it was still again.

Davie watched and turned back to the wolf. He saw slick mud clinging to the thick white-and-gray fur on its chest, dense clumps that glistened wetly in the moonlight. Davie saw the mud trickle down both forelegs and pool under its paws on the road. The wolf walked toward the village lights.

"Stop," Davie called to its back. "You're bleeding ... hurt!"

The beast continued to amble up the road, its thick fur flattened against that tremendous back. Davie ran behind the wolf, and when they were abreast, it stopped. They stood at the outskirts of the small village.

"That's my village! There! I live there!" Davie pointed to a small cottage, where light trickled from small windows. He turned to the wolf and carefully reached out to place his hand atop its head. Before he could touch it, the wolf turned and leaped into the forest, where it vanished into the night and its shadows.

Davie froze in his tracks and searched the darkness for one last glimpse of the beast. A stir came from the village, and a voice called to the child. "That you, Davie? Davie! That you out there?"

A man ran toward the boy, holding a lantern before him at arm's length. "It's the boy, *and he's safe*! DAVIE!" The man's tone descended from relief to an anger that quickly waned. "Where have you been? You scared the *hell* outta us, boy! You okay?" He grabbed Davie firmly about the shoulders with his free arm and then rubbed the boy's head briskly.

"Whatcha doin' in the forest? *In the dark!* You coulda been eaten up out there!" Uncle Jack led the boy to the cottage, where they climbed two stone steps. Davie was suddenly very weary. He was aware of the man, but Uncle Jack spoke from somewhere far away.

Davie walked to the glowing mouth of the fireplace to warm his hands, simultaneously inviting and resisting the heat. He spoke into the flames that danced madly before him. "I think I saw God in the forest," Davie said.

Jack shut the thick oak door of the cottage, pushed it tightly closed, and secured it further with a heavy iron latch. There was no anger in his expression as he faced Davie. "What did you say, boy?" Jack put his hands on his hips.

Davie looked up into his eyes and spoke softly. "I saw God in the forest. He was a wolf!"

Jack squatted and looked squarely into Davie's face. The blues and oranges and yellows of the fire cavorted as black shadows on the walls and floor—a joyful, exuberant celebration, punctuated by crackling wood and an occasional hiss as something damp succumbed to the blaze.

Uncle Jack embraced Davie warmly. He clutched the child tightly to his breast and then released him. He rubbed Davie's head with a hand mangled and scarred by his life's labors. Jack's eyes welled up as he looked over Davie's shoulder and toward his wife. She was drying her hands, very slowly, carefully, on an old and faded red apron.

"The boy says he saw God in the forest, Angie," Jack said. "It looks like God brought Davie home to us, safe an' sound."

Angie smiled, a bright splash that turned her tired face into as brilliant a sunrise as ever graced a far horizon. She squeezed Jack's battered hand gently in her own, stooped slightly, and kissed the top of Davie's head.

A large oak log cracked in the fireplace. It fell forward, tumbled against the grate, and then sizzled softly, almost a sigh. The flames flew ever upward. In silence and warmth, the man and woman held the child and each other.

After a few moments, Jack crossed the room and returned holding a well-worn Bible. He flipped through its pages until he found what he sought and he began to read deliberately. "The wolf shall dwell with the lamb," he said, his voice soft and even, "and the leopard shall lie down with the young goat, and the calf and the lion and the fattened calf together; and a little child shall lead them."

"Isaiah," Angie said. The man nodded, closed the book, and set it down on the kitchen table. She took Davie by the hand and led him to her husband, who hugged him tightly and then hoisted him onto a wooden chair at the table. Jack sat across from Davie as Angie began to ladle the evening's supper onto their plates. He sliced a loaf of bread and handed a thick wedge to Davie.

"All right, son," Jack said, "let's get some meat on your bones!"

Davie grinned and eagerly accepted the bread with a nod of thanks. He was warm and safe, loved and cherished, and the terror he had experienced in the forest was fading away. Angie placed a steaming plate of stew in front of him, and fear left him entirely.

There was a blink of light, and Davie now felt himself floating above the tiny cottage, looking down as the night grew cold and crept through the village to fill its streets, pursue the living, and overtake the dying. Davie's eyes were drawn to a gray-and-white mare that stomped restlessly along the side of the road, tethered to a post and unable to answer an instinctive urge, as old as time, to bolt and run. A chill pulsed through Davie and he felt panic. *Why am I outside?* he wondered. *How come I'm not by the fire in the cottage, warm and safe, with Uncle Jack and Aunt Angie?* The horse shook its great head and grunted, steam billowing from its nostrils.

Flame and smoke gradually became fog and clouds, a beautiful, swirling transition from fantasy to corporeality. When he realized that he was again awake and in his bed, Davie was on his left side. He blinked his eyes, looked into the yellow doorway, and chased new thoughts in and old thoughts, old dreams, out. He did not understand many things; he knew that well. There were so many, many things to comprehend. He rolled to his other side and stared at the blue window.

Chapter Two

B illy Adams's world was an eight-by-twelve-foot cell of cinder blocks and steel bars; a cold slab, suspended by two chains from the wall and covered with a thin mattress, was his bed. He had been locked within one bleak cell or another for over eight years, awaiting an end that was now forthcoming. It was the spring of 1984, Billy's last, and the season's hopes and renewals drifted far above this Utah prison, beyond his comprehension.

For now, he was alone, a prisoner in every sense, without hope or a window to the world, isolated, steel bars and concrete walls his only companions. Within twenty minutes, Billy would be given three injections, the third a lethal fireball loosed into a vein and bound to blow his soul to hell. He'd been told this would not hurt, just a little prick to the skin and then sleep. But what assurances, he wondered, were there of what awaited him when this "little prick" took its toll?

Billy Adams had hoed his own row, as his grandpap used to say. Too much angel dust had ripped fissures in his brain, and they exploded in violence and death. He didn't remember much, except an old man in a little burg in Illinois whose head Billy had blown into a shelf full of canned fruits and vegetables behind the counter in a mom-and-pop grocery store.

All Billy remembered about the old man was that he looked a lot like Uncle Charley on *My Three Sons*. There were also two dead cops in Michigan and a chick in Indiana, all murdered before he croaked the old man in Illinois, plus four others he'd dispatched in three states on his trip to see the West Coast and the majestic Pacific Ocean for the first time.

But the trail ended for Billy Adams in Utah, when the crystal meth and coke and Black Jack ran out, and his body, so disoriented by the constant mistreatment its occupant administered, simply gave up the ghost. Billy collapsed behind the wheel on I-80 and crashed into the back of a pickup truck.

When he came to, he was shackled, hands to feet behind his back, locked in a cell the size of a motel bathroom, naked. Thus began an eight-year trek through the American judicial system that would have saved taxpayers a lot of money if some cop had gotten off one good shot, or been left alone with Billy for just a few minutes.

When all attempts to spare his life were exhausted and the serpentine journey through the courts had been spent, all that could save his sorry ass was a call from the governor, who, in a recent interview, said he intended to be as far away from a telephone as was possible in 1984 when the final hour came for Billy Adams.

So Billy's last meal (fried chicken, french fries, coleslaw, and a Dr. Pepper) was wheeled away untouched, and a priest was dispatched down the hall, unwanted, shaking his head, reciting prayers with very little conviction. There would be no one there to send him off, save a half dozen or so survivors of the people he'd slaughtered. The years now became moments for Billy Adams.

Billy was very frightened of where he was going tonight. *Wherever it is,* he thought, *it can't be good, can it?* As he sat in his cell, he heard footsteps approach. He did not look up. He just stared at the cinderblock wall, seeing nothing. Two guards escorted two men in white and an old man in a gray suit into the suddenly crowded cell. The old man was a doctor, and he began to prepare and load a syringe.

"This will make it a little easier for you," he said brusquely as a he launched a clear stream of sodium pentothal from the syringe. "It'll make you a little numb."

"Fuck him," growled the taller guard. "I'd like to make him a little numb with an air hammer. What breaks did he ever give anybody?"

"Take it easy, pal. You're not the judge of this guy," the second guard said. The guards stood back, and the men in white began to prepare Billy. It was pretty simple, really. After this first needle's cocktail, they would wait a few minutes while Billy's eyes lost focus and his blood pressure dropped. Then he would take a short roll in the wheelchair, down the hall. In old black-and-white movies, they called it the "last mile," but Billy's trip would only cover about eighty feet.

Billy felt the prick of the needle in his right arm, as promised. At last, he thought of someone else: his state-appointed lawyer, Thomas Coleman, who was also a little prick. When his ride toward fate ended, his body was quite numb indeed, but his mind raced on, retracing his life, seeing the faces of his past. He wondered about the son he'd never seen and would never know. His time for wonder was ending.

The men in white lifted Billy from the chair, laid him out on a steel table, and strapped him down with thick leather belts around his ankles, his thighs, his waist, and his shoulders. Finally, his hands were slipped into cold steel bracelets.

A middle-aged white man in a tony light-blue suit entered the room and hovered over Billy. He looked into Billy's brown eyes and pointed a penlight's beam into the right and then the left. "I'm Dr. Wing, Billy. I have been appointed by the State of Utah to administer a lethal injection into your right arm, less than five minutes from now. Do you understand that?"

Billy looked straight up to the ceiling and closed his eyes. "Yeah, Doc. How long will this shit take to ... work?"

"Average time to cessation of brain activity is about two minutes," the doctor said in a monotone voice.

"Which I guess is sorta like bein' dead, eh, Doc?".

"More than a little, Billy, more than a little," the doctor said.

"Do you have a statement to make, any last words?" the warden asked.

Billy felt the cool leather strap across his forehead, and he knew at this moment that he would never stand or walk again. He thought to cry, but there were no tears. "No," he mumbled. "No statement, no comments. Just tell 'em I'm sorry. That's all."

Above and around him, the guards, the doctor, and the warden exchanged glances. The doctor shook his head slowly and then connected Billy to a small IV bag suspended from a tall metal stand on three wheels.

"I'm going to inject you twice, beginning in one minute," this doctor stated. "Please use this time to make whatever peace you might with ..." He did not finish. The doctor opened the state's sealed and approved injection kit. He removed a syringe labeled *Pancuronium Bromide* and unloaded its toxic dose into the line between Billy and the IV; in seconds, it would paralyze his diaphragm.

Billy kept his eyes closed. He felt a tear trickle down the side of his face and into his ear. *My last tear rolled into my ear*, he pondered. So many thoughts, so little time; his mind concerned itself only with what might lie ahead. There were no contemplations of the dead or the living, of God or family or country.

The doomed prisoner did not watch the doctor return to the state's death kit, pick up a syringe tagged *Potassium Chloride*, and unleash the grand finale into the IV. Billy Adams never opened his eyes to take one last look. He just stopped breathing as a cold mist swirled around him, and then he began to roll within the haze, whirling into the void, leaving life forever behind.

When Billy at last opened his eyes, he sat alone on a grimy seat in the middle of an old city bus that reeked of urine and vomit. Looking out the side window through caked dust and greasy layers of gray and black soot, he saw a woman in a long black coat walking without haste toward the sagging, rusted vehicle.

She was very beautiful, and at once he subjected her to vile degradations spawned in his tormented brain. He wondered how he came to board this crummy bus in this stinking town. He did not remember getting on. *Must have smoked some bad shit*, he decided. *Very bad shit.*

He returned his focus to the woman in the black coat. She definitely didn't belong on a crate the likes of this one, yet she climbed the three steps, dropped a token in the cylinder, and nonchalantly strolled down the aisle. The old wreck's twitching takeoff ignored what one imagined was suburban etiquette, wherein the driver waited for passengers to take a seat before jerking down the road. But the woman retained her balance and her grace as she elbowed her way past two punks and deftly sidestepped the hands of a toothless, drooling lecher.

When she reached Billy's seat near the back of the bus, she stopped and stared down at him, a little man with a folded newspaper in his lap. "Yes, this would be the one," she said cheerily. "Do you mind, sir, if I sit with you in this seat?"

Billy nodded eagerly and pressed his body tightly to the sidewall of the bus. He wondered why she had chosen to sit with him, rather than in one of the many empty seats. *She is way too beautiful for this to be real*, he thought. Billy unfolded the newspaper, lifted it before his face, and pretended to read a story about hundreds dead and thousands homeless after an earthquake in Peru.

The old bus veered madly through the city, into the smoke, through the mountains of trash and dead, discarded bodies. Packs of stray dogs prowled the streets, and Billy's frayed mind entertained a number of lascivious deeds, all shameful, all at the expense of the gorgeous woman who now shared his seat.

The bus was very noisy and hindered thought. A woman screamed at the back, but Billy did not look. He instead stole a glance at the woman beside him. She smiled back, the corners of her full mouth tilting upward suggestively. Her dark brown eyes were glazed, and the man sensed for an instant that somehow she could read his despicable thoughts. Yet she did not mind his violation of her body and soul. *She must be a junkie*, he thought, and he hid his face behind the newspaper.

"My, my, isn't that a sight?" The woman spoke tenderly, sweetly, in apparent awe of the chaotic spectacle that now engulfed the bus. The other riders danced hysterically in the aisle, and their insane laughter rang off of the walls and windows. The two punks stood atop seats and urinated through open windows onto dozens of dwarves who crazily ran into the side of the bus or under its wheels with a sickening crunch. A young nun with a pretty face fingered beads on a black rosary as a priest wearing a New York Yankees cap forcibly bent her over the hood of a Buick LeSabre and sodomized her.

"It's the most wonderful thing I've ever seen," marveled the woman beside Billy, who could no longer look into her face. He was terrified for his own sanity as it sailed further and further out of his reach and into the void.

As the savaging of humanity continued in a burned red blur outside, Billy realized at last that he had no choice. He must look at the woman, for she was, after all, his own creation, his own twisted hallucination—she and the goddamned weird apparitions in his window. The old bus lurched deeper into the mouth of absolute lunacy.

Billy carefully refolded his newspaper, placed it on his lap, and slowly turned in his seat to face the woman. He went rigid and cold as her eyes rolled out of their sockets, fell to the filthy floor, and landed with wet plops amid the cigarette butts, discarded newspapers, and pools of vomit and urine. She laughed like a crazed hyena, the scent of a fresh kill filling her widening nostrils, the taste of warm blood making the saliva run in her mouth.

As Billy sat stunned and paralyzed with fear, the remainder of the woman's beautiful face cracked and split and peeled away and then dropped to the floor in shreds. The muscles, tendons, and nerves, seconds ago concealed in beauty, now glistened with blood and pus, hanging in strips from her skull.

Billy could not move; he was too disgusted to cry out and too defeated to tremble. He could only close his eyes and pray for death to claim him, to release him from these demons that tortured his mind with horrid, fetid phantoms.

"Don't you see it, sir? Can't you see the truth, even now?" the woman asked, her head now completely liberated of flesh and blood. Her skull was a pitted, dark gray, like a charred and spent match head, and its endless evil was unleashed at last. "You had better eat something," she croaked. "This promises to be a very long journey. You never know when you'll get the chance to eat again."

Billy Adams looked at the beautiful woman with the skeletal head one more time as she ripped into the hind leg of a jackal or a very large dog with her sharp teeth. It was fresh kill, and Billy wondered where it had come from. He looked down and saw his empty left pant leg. He felt no pain and saw no blood, but he screamed anyway.

The skull ripped at the leg's flesh with jagged teeth and spat bits of bone to the bus floor. It attacked the raw meat with a vengeance. The fingerless hand, now a large red claw, offered the leg to Billy, dripping its blood on his newspaper.

"Take it, please," she implored again. "This will be a long journey, a very, very long journey, and we won't be returning here again." Her voice had become deep and guttural. She belched with revolting malevolence and affirmed the certainty that nothing, *nothing*, remained of natural life. There was only death.

"Eat hearty, my friend," rasped the skull as its red claw shook the dripping leg at Billy. "Eat hearty."

Billy sank back in his seat and looked out the window as the ravages of hell spun around the bus. From the back, a woman screamed again and again and again, but Billy did not hear her. He was screaming too loudly himself.

Chapter Three

In a room at another end of the yellow-lit hall, Jackson Thomas sat on the edge of a king-size bed and trimmed his toenails with a pair of cuticle scissors. His wife sprawled behind him, watching a small color television, its images nameless and soon forgotten. She threw her legs over the side of the bed, took a three-hop dance to the TV, and depressed the on/off button. The screen went black.

"If I find any of your toenails on the floor or in my bed, I'm gonna bop you, Jack." She waved a stiff index finger at him to support her threats. Jack looked up from his feet and into her eyes and fell in love, their earlier arguments forgotten.

"I mean it, Jack," she said. "You better not leave any lying around."

The clippings fell harmlessly into a flowered plastic wastebasket set beneath his foot to collect her discarded enemies. The tenth victim joined its fallen comrades, and Jack rose and returned the small container to the corner next to his dresser.

"Angie, have you ever found any of my toenails on the floor or in the fecking bed?" He spoke softly, without anger or malice. The woman did not answer. She searched on her dresser top, and when she found her hairbrush, she glanced at Jack and rolled her eyes.

"Well? Have you? You always make such a federal case out of it," Jack said to her softly, without rancor.

Angie sat before her dressing mirror and brushed her thick brown hair as it tumbled over her shoulders in curls that shook with each twist and turn of her head. She was very pretty. She spoke to Jack without losing sight of her own dark green eyes in the looking glass. "Because," she said with authority, "if you weren't such a sow, you'd do that in the bathroom and not in my bedroom."

Jack smiled. Yesterday Angie thought the bedroom was messy, and so she called it *his* bedroom, not *her* bedroom. He stood in front of the mirror perched atop his dresser and looked briefly into his own eyes. *They're beginning to fade,* he thought, *at thirty-fecking-seven, fading out.* Over the reflection of his shoulder he saw another image, cast back to him from Angie's mirror across the room. She lifted off her shirt, and as her black bra and its lovely contents came into view, Jack complimented himself on the perfect placement of the two mirrors.

Angie flipped the blouse into a growing mountain of discarded clothing that gathered on the floor of her closet. He watched as she reached behind her back and deftly unhooked the bra strap. She let it slip from her shoulders, and her breasts were now free of earthly restraints. Jack fell in love again as the blood in his brain rushed south. He had no control whatsoever. At last she caught him in her mirror, and her face blushed slightly and became cross.

"What're you looking at?" She covered her breasts with her right arm while pulling a tattered blue flannel nightshirt over her head with the left.

"I was just looking at you. You're still rather pretty, see, for an old broad," Jack noted, slipping into his Edward G. Robinson voice. Angie frowned and shook her head, threw her long hair behind her, and began to twist it into a rope. Jack watched it all.

"It's okay," he said. "We're married. It's among my executive privileges to watch you disrobe here in our royal chambers whilst I plot acts of physical rhapsody." He smiled at the execution of what he deemed an eloquent phrase.

"Bullshit," Angie declared. "You have no 'executive privileges' at all, so get that crazy look out of your eyes. And don't call me an old broad!"

Thus dashed, his longing smile expired, however slowly, and the blood began a hesitant surge northward. It was never sure which way to flow with *this* guy.

"I was only kidding, Ang …"

Angie jumped onto the disheveled bed and pulled the covers to her chin. "I'm cold," she whined. "Did you turn the heat down again?" She reached for the small lamp on the table by her side of the bed and clicked it off. "You know, the Republicans don't care about energy conservation anymore. You can turn up the heat and Ronnie Reagan won't mind."

"The heat is at seventy-something, I think," Jack said. "Just turn the blanket up on your side." He watched as she leaned over and fumbled with the control dial. "Oooo, it's so *cold!*" she moaned.

"I know a cure for that," he whispered lewdly.

She shivered. Only the top of her head was visible. Jack was amused by the sight but stepped to the doorway and flicked off the overhead light. He stood there for a moment to allow his eyes to adjust to the darkness, now complete but for the faint yellow glow of the hall light. He returned to bed and lay atop the covers. He rolled on top of the woman with only the electric blanket between them.

"If you lay on top of electric blankets, you'll wreck 'em," she said.

Jack spun off of her and onto his left side. He propped his head up with a pillow and began to stroke Angie's face and hair with his free hand.

"Did you lock up the critters?" she said as she shooed his hand away.

"Yes, milady, they rest down deep in the royal dungeon." Curly was a slightly fat bulldog and Cheetah a black cat. They shared an uneasy armistice in the basement ever since a late-night brouhaha rendered Angie's prized hurricane lamp into pieces on the floor. As neither animal could speak, both were presumed guilty and sentenced to spend nights in the basement—for life. To Jack, the punishment seemed unduly harsh, but he'd been overruled.

In the dim yellow night, his eyes strained to see her face, her eyes. She was so very lovely. She rolled onto her back and looked toward the ceiling. To Jack, she looked to be waiting for a movie to begin on a blank screen. "Tonight's the night for Billy," she said. "Tonight's the night they give him the injections."

She turned onto her side and propped her head up with her hand. Jack stroked her cheek with the back of his hand, very delicately. A tear pooled in each eye, a drop in the right the first to escape and roll down her cheek.

"They should have done it a long time ago, Angie," he said. "They should have done it the day they caught him."

"I suppose," she muttered, gazing blankly above and beyond Jack's shoulder. "I never really knew him, though, you know? He had those faraway eyes. I always thought he was ... unbalanced."

"He had fucked-up eyes, is what he had," Jack declared. "And you're right. He was unbalanced, mainly because he smoked enough crystal meth to kill an elephant and drank Jack Daniels like it was water. So, tonight he pays the piper, and that's all she wrote."

Angie looked past Jack and into the hallway. Teardrops finally broke down the dam and began to streak her cheeks.

"Hey, babe, don't waste tears on that guy. He's not worth it," Jack whispered as he stroked her hair.

"I was thinking about my sister, Jack. Laura was so naive, so innocent, when she met him. And he killed her, too, just as surely as if he'd shot her."

Five years ago, Jack recalled, Angie's baby sister filled a bathtub with hot water and bubble bath soap. She then slashed her wrists with a razor blade, leaned back in the tub, and bled to death. She had gone sideways, just like Frankie Pentangeli, the old mafioso in *The Godfather: Part II*.

Laura's son, David, barely three years old at the time, had found her body in a porcelain tomb of bloodied water and red and pinkish bubbles. Jack closed his eyes and envisioned Laura's eyes, sunken but open, staring into the doorway. Davie went back to his bed, and Jack could see him quietly sobbing through the night until Laura's mother came home in the morning and discovered the wretched scene.

The story recycled in Jack's memory now: the two and a half years the state allowed Laura to live in the same house with Davie and his grandmother, the extensive drug rehab and counseling, the many visits to drug-testing facilities, and then the tub. It had been too much for the boy's grandmother; she soon slipped into a depression that approached madness. She refused to go into the bathroom where Laura had offed herself, and her sanity and personal hygiene suffered accordingly until she too required treatment. She died alone in a small room in a nursing facility, the grace and elegance she'd carried with confidence throughout her life another victim of the madness. So the state reinserted itself into Davie's life, and he was headed toward foster care, or worse.

Jack and Angie, themselves childless, intervened and became Davie's legal guardians. Jack accepted the boy into their home without complaint. Davie gave him more joy than anything else in his life, and Jack came to think of him as his son. For Angie, it seemed to Jack, the boy was at times a sad reminder of something she'd rather forget entirely, but she treated him quite well, with a kindness and tenderness the boy otherwise might not have known. But Jack knew what that memory was that haunted his wife, for he carried it on his back too. It was something they needed to face, but had thus far been unable to do together.

While Jack felt no remorse whatsoever for Billy, and little for Laura, he felt great pain at the sight of his wife's tears. They made him feel helpless because he believed, however improbably, that it was his job to see that she never, ever cried—an absurd proposition. Jack understood that, but he undertook the task anyway. He put his arms around her, rubbed her back, and lifted and drew her close to him. She trembled and wept fervently.

"I know, honey, I know," he whispered sympathetically. "But it's over now, and it'll all work out for the best. It'll work out best for Davie, and that's what we have to worry about now."

Angie did not speak. Soon the tears stopped and she gently pushed away from Jack. She threw the covers back, reached to the table beside the bed, and, with a quick jerk of her hand, pulled some tissues from a Kleenex box next to her clock radio. The little cardboard box barely moved. She blew her nose, dropped the tissues into a wastebasket, and removed a few more Kleenex to wipe her eyes and face dry. She crawled back, turned onto her right side, and propped her head up with her hand.

"How much of that stuff do you think Davie remembers? You know, about Laura and Billy?" she asked.

"Jesus, I hope none of it," Jack said, "but I don't know. I'm afraid if I ask him, that crap will come back to him, you know? But he's never said anything to me about it. I just figured to wait until he was a little older to talk with him about it."

"How much older, do you think?" she asked, her brow slightly furrowed.

"Oh, I don't know." Jack thought for a moment. "Forty, maybe?"

Angie giggled a little and playfully smacked Jack's shoulder. He felt better to see her smiling, the light back on in her emerald eyes, her cheeks still wet with spent tears.

"Seriously, though," she said, suddenly somber again as she looked into his eyes, "do you think he has any genetic predisposition toward mental illness, or violence, or drug abuse?"

Angie stared into Jack's eyes intensely; the time for jokes had passed. It was a hard, straight question that Jack had thought about many times. Her college psychology classes had left her inadequately equipped to answer the question herself, and Jack could only speak to what he'd seen.

"I've never seen a single sign of meanness in him, not one," he said. "Look how good he is with Curly and Cheetah, and the other kids, and old Stan next door too. I don't think I've ever seen him lose his temper, not *really* lose it. No, Angie, honest to God, I don't believe he has any of that stuff in his nature. Zero. He is way more like *you* than he is either of his parents."

"Oh Lord, that po', po' child!" She pretended to faint and dropped her head to the pillow. Jack chuckled and tickled her ribs.

"You're a fecking nut, Angela Thomas, certified pistachio nuts!"

Whatever mirth had entered Angie's soul left her as quickly as it came, as mirth is wont to do. "I'm so tired, Jack," she said, pushing her legs back under the covers, which she then pulled to her chin. "So much sadness, everywhere we look! I wish this was a better world, you know?"

"Yeah, babe, I know. But it's the only one we've got, so far as I know," Jack said as he righted the covers around her chin, reached down, and gently kissed her forehead. "Now go to sleep."

Jack lay on his side for a while, looking at his wife, who had closed her eyes. He knew he would not sleep for a long time. Within a short while Angie began to snore quietly, and Jack's heart sighed. Eventually he sat up and spun himself around to the edge of the bed, his feet dropping to the floor.

Jack looked out his bedroom window and into the night through a six-inch gap in the curtains. Angie brought these curtains home four months ago and, as yet, had not found the time to sew on the accompanying lace trim. Jack listened as an early spring wind pushed against the glass.

Finding no solace in the window, Jack got up, walking to the door and into the hall. He decided to go downstairs and smoke a cigarette after looking in on Davie. His path to the boy's room was illuminated by a yellow night-light plugged into the wall, designed to provide safe passage from the boy's bedroom to the bathroom in the middle of the hall.

Jack poked his head through the doorway and saw Davie sitting up in bed, facing the window. When aware of the man's presence, Davie quickly wiped away a tear from the side of his nose.

"Uncle Jack! What're you doin' up?" The boy rubbed his eyes with the backs of his hands. He looked up as Jack approached the bed. "I couldn' sleep 'cause I had a dream, Uncle Jack. I couldn' sleep 'cause I was scared, so I was just lookin' out the window."

Jack sat on the edge of the bed and draped an arm around the boy's shoulders. "What were you looking for in the window, Davie?"

"Uncle Jack, 'member once, when I was littler, you told me if I had a bad dream to look out the window and ask God to come and blow it away?"

Jack remembered. It had been a long time ago, but he remembered. Jack felt his discussions with God were decidedly one-sided; God, he thought, only spoke directly with evangelists and lunatics.

"And that if I closed my eyes," Davie continued, "I could hear him doin' it?" Jack nodded. "That's what I was doin'. I had a bad dream that I wanted blowed away." Davie wrapped his arms around his knees and looked back to the window.

"What were you dreaming about, porcupine? Monsters? Spacemen? Girls?" Jack playfully pushed the boy down to his side and then pulled him upright again. Davie wore a thin smile, but it was forced. *Such a sensitive kid*, Jack thought. *So damn serious!*

"Uncle Jack," Davie said slowly, "I keep dreamin' about you. You and Aunt Angie."

Jack hadn't known the boy was aware of their sparring over an old wound, one that left both of them hurt, in pain, one they could only realistically hope to survive as individuals, but not as man and wife. It was now obvious that Davie knew something was wrong. Jack looked up from the child and toward the window. *Where are you, God?*

"You and Aunt Angie was runnin' away from me, and I couldn' catch up to you. I think maybe you was chasin' her, but I'm not sure. I think I saw my mom there, too, like she was, you know, the last time I saw her."

And there it was. It only took a short walk down the hall to answer Angie's question. Maybe God *was* out there, eavesdropping, Jack wondered. Davie's head dropped and his chin almost rested on his chest. Jack rubbed his back gently. In a kinder world, Davie would not remember his mother at all, but he did, just enough to give him nightmares.

To Jack, suicide was the ultimate act of selfishness, a devastating slap in the face to those left behind to clean up the mess, without a thought for the heartbreaks and bad dreams it triggered. Had Laura given even a thought to Davie, or her mother, or Angie? The act's cruelty was compounded, Jack believed, because you couldn't call out the dead for their misdeeds.

Jack swept the boy's strawberry-blond hair from his forehead and pushed it to the side of his head. It immediately tumbled back to where it had been. "Davie, you know Aunt Angie and I would never run away or let anything bad happen to you."

The boy stared at his feet. Jack lifted Davie's chin with a thumb and index finger and looked into his eyes. They were a deep, dark blue, almost black, and in the conflicting shades of yellow from the hall and faint blue from the window, carried an odd glimmer as tears were held briefly in abeyance to pool and shimmer. Jack, in this moment, felt deeply the fear and sadness now locked within this small boy.

"And didn't I tell you that we would always be together?" Jack spoke quietly, hoping to sound reassuring. The boy blinked.

"Tonight I had a dream about a wolf in the forest," Davie murmured quietly.

Jack looked to the window and then back to the boy. "You know," Jack said, "that dreams are just dreams, like TV is just TV. They don't necessarily mean anything, and they almost never come true."

Davie deliberately nodded his head up and down, up and down. "But it was so *real*, Uncle Jack." He turned quickly. "I think the wolf's out there right now, *watching us!*" He spoke excitedly, his voice barely rising above a whisper, jabbing a finger toward the window.

Jack scratched at the stubble of beard on his chin, wishing for a way to wring the hurt from the depths of those wet blue eyes. He knew the boy had been thoroughly betrayed by circumstance, and the man was bound never to let it strike the boy again—yet another Herculean task that he accepted without a second thought.

Jack considered Davie's father, maybe already dead, and his mother, so weak and confused that she mindlessly left the boy behind, left him to find her corpse, floating in its own mix of blood and bathwater and pink bubbles, giving him a death stare. *What a great gift she left him*, he reflected. *What a great memory.*

Davie was Jack's boy now, and Jack loved that, except for moments like this, when the boy's pain crept out and Jack felt he could provide no comfort, no solace, and no relief. Something gnawed at the man's essence and told him he'd let the little boy down when he was needed most. And so Jack felt the pain too.

"Uncle Jack, why do people run away?" Davie turned to face Jack, his arms hugging his skinny legs below the knees, eyes wide and alert, waiting for just a trickle of wisdom, a shred of insight, a simple piece of truth to cling to.

Jack rose to his feet, wished for a cigarette, and walked to the window. The cigarettes were downstairs, out of reach. He peered into the night.

"I don't know if there's any right or wrong answer to that one, Davie. I guess they just get scared, too scared to face whatever frightens them. They don't know what else to do, so they just run." Jack looked at Davie and then back to the world beyond the window.

"But you know they never really get away," Jack said, "because whatever it is that's scaring them is still there. It hasn't been dealt with. So they're like prisoners, trapped by their own fear."

Davie tilted his head to one side, absorbing the man's words and trying to fully understand them. "But how come they *run*? Why don't they just stay and fight if they can't get away anyway?" he asked, his eyes pinched nearly shut.

Jesus, Jack thought, *why doesn't the kid ever ask simple questions, like who won the Cy Young Award in 1968, or the World Series in 1956?* Now he *really* wanted that smoke. "It's just not that easy," Jack said. "Sometimes people run and they're not even sure why or what from. They just get frightened and confused, and so they run away."

The boy crawled to the edge of the bed, dropped to the floor, and padded to the window. He pointed into the night beyond the windowpane. "See that house, over there, across the field?"

Jack squinted and then nodded. "Sure. That's the Gibbons's place. They've lived there for a long time, longer than we've been here. They took care of the critters once when we went on vacation. Remember?"

The boy nodded his head. "Ev'ry night I look out the window at their house, and I can see that bright blue light near the top," Davie said, tapping softly on the glass. "It's inside, I think. Can you see it?" The boy turned, looked intently at his uncle, and then climbed back into his bed.

Jack nodded his head affirmatively. Old Lady Gibbons was a strange bird who kept a 300-watt blue light bulb burning in their upstairs bedroom. She'd read in the *National Enquirer* that blue lights were good for her arthritis, and ever since, a blue glow emanated from the second floor of the old house beyond the small field. She swore that it eased her miseries.

"I want us to be like that light," Davie said, "'cause it's always there, ev'ry night."

Jack stood at the foot of the bed and looked down at his nephew. Davie was too small, too vulnerable, to have to feel so much or to be told that, one day, that blue bulb would burn out. Jack circled the bed, sat next to Davie, lifted his legs, and stuffed them under the sheet and blanket. Jack then pulled the official Major League Baseball bedspread to the boy's chin. A Boston Red Sox emblem sat squarely upon Davie's throat. Jack despised the Bosox, so he tugged at the quilt in search of a less offensive team logo. The Chicago Cubs appeared. *Christ*, Jack thought, *it's no wonder the kid has nightmares.*

"Davie," said Jack, still fidgeting with the bedspread, "just think of me as your personal Kmart blue-light special. Even if the Gibbons's bulb burns out, I'll still be around. Okay?"

The boy lifted his head from his pillow and looked into Jack's eyes. "Aunt Angie too?"

Jack turned slowly to face the window. He closed his eyes for a long second and listened for the wind. It was very, very quiet. "Sure. You and me, Aunt Angie, Curly, and Cheetah too. I promise."

Davie let his head fall back to the pillow. For a moment, he looked unsure, even doubtful, to Jack, in whose eyes tears were contained with some effort.

"Sometimes I get scared that it's all gonna get blowed away," Davie whispered hoarsely, "that God's gonna make a mistake and blow it all away by accident."

Tears welled in Davie's blue eyes, his efforts to suppress them less successful than his uncle's. Sorrow came to Jack as he rubbed the child's head. He forced his eyes wide open and shook his head slightly, as if to shake out the melancholia.

"God doesn't make mistakes, son." Jack tried to sound convincing. His voice was a little huskier. He wished to assure himself as well as the boy. "Only people make mistakes. And we won't, I promise." Jack crossed his heart with his right thumb.

"Okay, Uncle Jack," Davie said, wiping away a small stream that crept down his cheek with the back of his right wrist. "I love you a lot, you know." With that the boy lunged up in his bed and wrapped his arms around the man's neck.

Jack held the boy closely to his breast and his heart. In this room where blue light from across the way sought entry and yellow light from the hall sought release, the two players embraced warmly in the glow. Reggie Jackson looked on from the nightstand, his Louisville Slugger always at the ready, just in case.

"I love you, too, sweet pea," Jack said gently. "Okay? Now you have to get some sleep, knucklehead. How would it look for a kid to have bags under his eyes?"

Jack kissed Davie's forehead. The boy smiled and dropped his head back to the pillow. Jack tugged again at the bedspread until the Detroit Tigers emblem roared back at him, leaving half of the bed uncovered.

"If you're quiet—and I mean *really* quiet—I'll let Curly out and he can sleep up here with you tonight. But you've got to go straight to sleep. Is it a deal?" The boy flashed a warm smile. Cheetah would have to remain in confinement; the cat always bolted straight up the stairs and, inevitably, jumped on the bed, walked across Angie, and woke her up. She would not approve.

"I'll send Curly up directly," Jack said in a conspiratorial whisper, "but in the meantime, you get ready to fall asleep as soon as he gets up here. Okay?"

"Okay, Uncle Jack," Davie said with a nod.

Jack gave the boy's head a final rub and then stepped into the yellow hall. He made his way downstairs and gingerly opened the basement door while he guarded the narrow opening with his left foot, wary of one of Cheetah's mad bursts for freedom. Sometimes the cat slept against the door, and he was always there in the morning when Jack opened the door to free and feed the animals. But tonight the cat's guard was down, and he was somewhere in the darkness below.

"Curly," Jack whispered. "Curly, you old fart! Get your fat ass up here!"

In a few seconds Jack heard some commotion at the foot of the stairs, followed by clumsy feet and the clicks of claws as the dog made his ascent. Curly squeezed through the small opening and sauntered into the kitchen. His stubby tail wagged and his eyes were alert as Jack dropped to one knee and gave the dog's head a thorough scratch and massage.

When Jack heard Cheetah scamper up the stairs, he hurriedly spun and closed the door. "Sorry, Cheets, this isn't total amnesty." The cat loosed a furtive cry of protest from behind the door. Jack returned his attention to the dog. "Okay, lard ass, drag your old butt upstairs and go sleep with Davie. And for cris'sakes, be quiet," he said to the dog's meandering rear as Curly trotted off and climbed the steps, one at a time.

Curly slowed to a slinking crawl as he passed the first door on the right—the bedroom where Angie slept. Once safely past, he made a mad dash for the end of the hall.

The cat moaned again, and Jack opened the door. "Feck it. All for one ..."

A flash of black darted out of the basement's darkness and disappeared into the living room. Jack found his cigarettes on the kitchen counter and fired one up. He sat alone at the kitchen table and smoked as the wind pushed against the windows.

Chapter Four

The cigarette was half gone when Jack's drifting thoughts came to Angie. She was slipping away, he was sure of it. *A guy just knows when he's losing hold of a woman,* he thought. His spirit sagged under the weight of his suspicions, but he could not escape their force, the crushing and impending certainty. She was so pretty and he loved her so much. It wasn't fair.

Maybe I'm overreacting, he thought. Maybe she was just going through some woman thing, a symptom of early menopause or some kind of marital crisis point that one day would simply disappear. Maybe she needed vitamins, or maybe it was just a phase, like when his mother started taking *guitar* lessons, for God's sake, in her late fifties. Angie was only thirty-five.

She was a victim of all that Oprah bullshit, *that* was her problem. And all those fecking tabloids they displayed at the supermarket checkout counter with headlines about becoming a "TOTAL WOMAN IN 30 DAYS" and "ELVIS LIVES IN A MARTIAN LOVE CASTLE!"

But that was all bullshit, and Jack knew it. The space between them had been widening for over four years, almost imperceptibly at first, but now a yawning gap that threatened to swallow and destroy their marriage. Jack looked at the cigarette stub still burning in his left hand.

Shortly after Davie moved into their home, Jack was called into his supervisor's office at the Ford plant. Something happened to Angie, Jack was told, and the supervisor did not know what, only that she'd been rushed by ambulance to the emergency room. Jack left work and raced to the hospital, charging nearly breathless into the ER.

Angie had suffered a miscarriage, a nurse informed Jack, but she was going to be fine. "You can see her in a few minutes," the nurse said. "Just wait here and I'll come get you soon." Jack stood dumbfounded and cold as the color left his face. He'd had no idea Angie was pregnant. He began to question himself. *How could I not know? How could I not know?*

After several endless minutes, the nurse returned and led Jack back through a labyrinth of curtained rooms, medical machinery, rolling beds, and people in wheelchairs. The nurse stopped, pulled back a white curtain, and there was Angie, lying flat on her back in a light blue hospital gown, weeping softly. Jack took her left hand in both of his and kissed it gently. "Oh, baby," he whimpered, "what happened?"

Angie raised his hands to her mouth and kissed them. Her other arm was attached to an IV tube that dangled from a plastic bag of clear liquid, and an air line delivered oxygen to her nose. "I lost our baby, Jack, and I'm sorry I didn't get to tell you I was pregnant. I just found out …" Her voice trailed off and was swallowed in a burst of sobs. She closed her eyes and turned her face away from Jack.

"When … how long … when did you find out?" Jack spoke in a whisper, and it took all of his self-control to contain the emotions that surged through him. "I'm so sorry this happened to you, Angie. Jesus, please don't be afraid, don't turn away from me. I love you. You know that, right? Please, don't think I'm mad at you, or disappointed, or anything like that." Jack was holding back a tidal wave, but the tears were working their way past his defenses.

Angie turned back to face Jack, her eyes swimming in grief. She felt ashamed, but not for the reason Jack suspected. "I didn't tell you," she forced the words out slowly, one at a time, "because I wasn't sure I wanted to *keep* it." Angie threw her left arm up to cover her face. She wept, gasping loudly between sobs, pale arm in stark contrast to her reddened face.

Jack stood, bent at the waist, hovering over her with his mouth agape, eyes bulging. Tears streamed down his cheeks. For timeless moments, he forgot to breathe or to blink or to comprehend the thoughts that raced through his mind. He kept his stare on the woman in the bed before him, cowering under a white sheet. She wept uncontrollably. For an instant, Jack did not know who she was.

When her sobs slowed and then quieted, and his breath and some of his senses returned, Jack said, "What do you mean, if you wanted to keep it?" His voice steadied and grew agitated, almost threatening. "What do you mean, Angie?" He put a hand on each of her shoulders, shook her slightly, until she looked up and into his eyes.

"I was afraid, Jack," she whimpered. "I was afraid the baby would be crazy, like my mother, or a junkie, like my sister, or just *wrong* in the head!" She began to cry again. "I was trying to get right with it, you know. That I was gonna *keep* the baby, Jack, I swear that to you …" She gasped, sucking in air quickly, hoping it would bring her the strength to continue, but it did not. She collapsed and again began to weep.

Jack released her shoulders and stood straight. He bowed his head and remained quiet until Angie had settled down, out of tears. She yielded to exhaustion. At last, he fell to his knees on the tiled floor, never taking his eyes away from hers. "You should have told me, Angie. You should have told me. I could have helped you. I *would* have helped you. Don't you know that?"

"I'm so sorry, Jack. Please forgive me. I didn't want to hurt you or worry you, and I always knew in my heart that I was gonna keep our baby. I just needed a little time, that's all, and I would've told you. I'm sorry, honey." She reached out and caressed his face.

Jack rose to his feet, pulled a straight-backed chair from the corner, and sat next to Angie's bed, holding her hand. He kept his head down, eyes on the floor. They were quiet for a long time, each lost in thought, searching for words that eluded them like whispers in a hurricane. At last, Jack looked into her eyes. For a moment, they shared a great emotional surge of hurt and disappointment, but neither spoke.

Eventually, a doctor and a nurse joined them, speaking words neither husband nor wife really heard. Angie was finally discharged. They drove home mostly in silence, except for Jack asking every few minutes if she was okay. "No," she finally muttered, "not so much." Jack saw her force a wan smile, and his heart sagged.

Davie spent the night and most of the next day across the street with neighbors, unaware of anything that had taken place. Jack stayed home from work and served Angie snacks and meals in bed. They spoke no more of the lost baby—not that day or in the years that followed. They grieved thoroughly but separately, and this was now the chasm that lay between them as man and wife.

Jack understood that this gap needed to be breached, and soon, if their marriage was to be saved, but he did not know how to accomplish the task. His efforts to approach her ended in misunderstandings, and then arguments, as she either resisted or misinterpreted his efforts. They had waited too long, it seemed to Jack, to clear away the shadows between them. She went to work and was too often late coming home. Jack began to fret that Angie was having an affair with her boss, Peter Brookings, a smarmy lawyer whom he had never trusted. These suspicions slowly festered until they began to seethe, muddying the connection, the *intimacy*, that Jack and Angie desperately needed to reestablish as man and wife.

She's getting away from me, Jack thought, drifting out farther and farther, out to sea, into space, into the void, and there was no stopping it.

When the last orange glow died in the glass ashtray, Jack rose and mounted the stairs, his back slightly slumped. He walked dully to the end of the yellow hall. Davie was sound asleep, an arm draped over Curly's back. The dog looked up and panted twice before laying his wide head across his paws. Jack listened to the wind swirl beyond the blue window, and then turned and headed back up the hall.

Once inside their bedroom, he paused to let his eyes adapt to the darker environs. He listened and knew by her breathing that Angie was fast asleep. He stepped cautiously toward the bed and sat on its edge. Angie's left leg was stretched out across his half of the bed. Jack looked at the side of Angie's face, puffed slightly in sleep, and he fell in love. He was hopeless.

Jack wanted more than anything at that moment to talk to her, to hold her in his arms, to feel her warmth and softness. He wanted to tell her that he understood and that everything was going to be okay. It was something that he had to do, so he nudged her leg.

"Angie. *Angie!* Wake up, honey," Jack whispered. She moaned faintly. He pushed into her thigh again, a little harder, then again with still more force, until she groaned and opened one eye.

"Wha's a matter? Wha's wrong?" A small hand darted from

beneath the electric blanket and scratched at her left cheek, then disappeared, leaving sparks of static electricity to pop in the darkness.

"Nothing's wrong, angel. I just wanted to talk to you, that's all," Jack said softly. "Can we talk for a little while?"

She tossed onto her other side. "Wait till morning?" Aggravation was thinly veiled and her voice was thick with sleep.

"No. I need to talk to you *now*, tonight. I feel ..." Jack let the thought die in midair, a casualty of his apprehension that he would lose her attention and she would fade off to sleep again.

"What?" she murmured. "Why don't you go to sleep?" Angie coughed and flipped onto her stomach. Jack heard her breathing change slightly, and he knew that she was dozing off again. What was *she* dreaming of, he wondered. He pushed her butt down, into the mattress.

"Angie, for cris'sakes, I said I need to talk to you!" There was too much urgency in his voice, more despair than he wanted to reveal. He needed her now, but he didn't want to beg.

She lifted her head and looked at the man sitting on the edge of her bed. "What do you want, Jack?" She was awake now and rolled onto her back. "Are you mad at me or something?"

He closed his eyes tightly. *She won't understand. I've made a mistake. This is the wrong time,* Jack chastised himself. "No, no, no, no. I'm not mad at you," he said. "I'm just feeling a little ... out of time, that's all."

Angie's hand again flew out from the sanctity of her covers to shield her mouth as she coughed. "Honey," she whispered sweetly, "will you get me a glass of water? Just a little one?"

Jack opened his eyes and looked down at the woman as she pulled the blanket up to her nose. She returned his gaze briefly, but she was not fully alert. She shivered, and a chill ran up the man's spine.

"Did you turn down the heat?" she muttered. "I'm cold. Could you turn it up, just a little, just this one time?"

She shook, and a pleading look filled her eyes. Damn, they were so pretty! Jack always fell for this ploy, without fail, and he was sure that Angie knew it. He stood up. "Yeah," he sighed, "I'll turn up the heat, and I'll get you some water, but don't fall asleep on me while I'm gone. I'll only be gone for a minute."

She opened her eyes wide to assure him that she would, indeed, be conscious when he returned. "No, I won't. I promise," she said.

Jack peered down at her, into those green eyes flecked with gold, and he was gone again. He walked briskly to fetch the water and crank up the heat, but in his haste and distracted state he did not clear the doorway. He rammed the two smallest toes of his right foot into the jamb.

"Ah, mother-*father*! Sweet *Jesus*! God bless America!" He danced on his left foot into the yellow hall, just beyond the door, as Angie giggled under her electric blanket. Hearing this, he hobbled down the corridor in shame, angry with her and at himself. *What's so fecking funny about broken toes?* he asked himself.

Jack entered the john, spun the faucet knob, and let cold water flow while he pulled a paper cup from the dispenser glued to the cream-colored tile beside the mirror. As he waited for the water to run cold from the tap, he looked at his face in the mirror. *You look eerie in the muted yellow light*, he told himself.

Jack filled the Dixie cup, shut off the water, and limped into the hallway. He stopped at the thermostat. It was set at sixty-eight degrees, and Jack turned the dial up to seventy-two. He envisioned Jimmy Carter, out of a job and down in in Georgia, sadly and slowly shaking his head. It was 1984, and Reagan and the Republicans now held sway. Turning away from Jimmy and the thermostat, Jack reentered the bedroom and paused at the foot of the bed.

"Angie?" He whispered her name expectantly, listened to her breathing, and knew she was asleep again, all of her promises lost and forgotten to slumber and dreams. Jack set the paper cup atop his dresser without looking. It toppled over, and the cold water splashed across the dresser's edge and down to his still-throbbing toes.

"Oh, for shit sakes," he mumbled, leaving the water to soak into the carpet and the woman to sleep peacefully. Jack descended the stairs and walked into the kitchen. He sat at the table and lighted a cigarette. It was dark and quiet but for the sound of the wind, now thrashing through the trees beyond the window. He heard the furnace kick on and a few seconds later felt warm air pour across his bare feet.

His mind wandered in and out of the room, tracking shadows he had once known as dreams, chasing them through the darkness. Cheetah pawed at the closed basement door and mewed softly. The cat now wanted to return downstairs, probably to eat or use his litter box.

"Cheets, don't you know? There's no way in and there's no way out," said Jack, smoking in the dark. When he finished the cigarette, the man stood and rigidly stepped to the basement door. He opened it and the cat raced past him, only a sound, sailing down the stairs. He left the door open and turned away.

Jack returned to the kitchen table and flicked a match to ignite another smoke. He watched as the hot ash left orange trails in the space between his lips and the glass ashtray. A small veil of blue-gray smoke floated over his head. He closed his eyes and listened to the wind as it pushed against the back door and pawed at the kitchen window, begging Jack to let it in.

Chapter Five

As March became April, rain and drizzle flushed the snow and ice abandoned by winter down gutters and into drains while the earth absorbed what it could. The rest was left to pool on neighborhood lawns or overflow into the streets.

Nineteen eighty-four began like most years in Michigan: cold and snow-covered, bleak and gray, with a chance of spring, sunny and hopeful, its warmth and renewal a promise that all awaited eagerly.

It was now early spring or late winter, depending on how one looked at things. Buds were just beginning to appear on some of the trees, and in the washed-out, dully brown lawns, sporadic patches of bright green grass sprouted amid the bleached remnants of the past summer's glory.

Eventually the dreariness of February and March ran off the cold shoulders of the community, and a warm spring sun brought out the eternal hopes of April's fools. On Saturdays, broken sticks and twigs were mustered and picked up in bundles and bags to be burned or hauled away by the huge scoop buckets of county collection trucks. Seeds and bulbs were buried in the soft, soggy topsoil to attempt the regeneration of the living, even while the fallen were being removed.

Fathers pulled bicycles down from garage rafters or up from basements so that their children could ride through large puddles that lined the streets, their arms waving little hands recklessly above their heads. Thus, winter was swept and raked and drained away, forgotten until its inevitable reprise.

As April advanced, leaves appeared on the tall oak trees that lined the neighborhood and hid houses from the main streets and freeways that fed the suburbs into Detroit each morning and pumped them back home at night. Jack did not participate in this seasonal rebirth and felt little of this spring or its optimism. He slipped into a lethargic funk and felt like something constricted his soul and squeezed life and hope out of him in small but steady doses. He struggled mightily with his own flagging spirit.

Angie spent less and less time at home with Jack and Davie. She called nearly every night to announce a new emergency—late work at the office, a date with friends, someone who needed her help. Jack listened to her as a cyclone of emotion twisted within; sometimes he lost control and ugly arguments followed, punctuated by an abrupt slam-dunk of the phone into its cradle on the kitchen wall. With each call he imagined another dram of his essence and spirit hurtled into the void via the microcables of his telephone.

Jack and Davie ate their dinners without her too many nights, then retired to the family room and its long, blue sofa, where they watched TV—each with his head nestled on opposing arms of the old, comfy couch, their legs alternately entwined or engaged in horseplay.

On this Thursday morning, Jack left for his job at the Ford plant before Davie woke up, before Angie stirred, before the sun pushed night away in the eastern sky. Automotive workers in and around Detroit often referred to the Ford Motor Company as "Ford's," as in, "I work at Ford's" or "He's been at Ford's for twenty years." It had a familial feel to it. Ford somehow could be connected with virtually everyone in the area, surviving the most vicious union-busting battles in American history. Ask any UAW member about "The Battle of the Overpass," almost fifty years past, and you would still get an earful.

Detroit was a blue-collar town and, feast or famine, damn *proud* of it, too. In the wealthier suburbs, like the Grosse Pointes, Birmingham, and Bloomfield Hills, many moneyed families were only two or three generations removed from someone who came up from the South or crossed the ocean from Europe to work on the line in one of the auto plants. In this way, at least, there existed a common bond.

On the last afternoon in April, Davie changed out of his school clothes and walked next door to the Koski house. Stan Koski was a widower in his mideighties and a resident of Bull Run Way since the 1920s. As Stan's vision began to fail and eyeglasses proved less and less effective, Davie became Stan's designated reader and a valued companion to the old man. In turn, Davie honed his reading skills and benefitted from Stan's gifts as a living dictionary, historian, philosopher, and social commentator. Davie particularly enjoyed listening to the old man opine on the ups and downs of the Detroit Tigers.

"If Sparky Anderson had one more brain, he could start a rock garden," Stan might say on Tuesday. The next day, after a victory, it was, "You know something, son? Sparky's going into the Hall of Fame someday. He's *so* sharp." The next day, "Sparky, if you had one more brain, it would die of loneliness." *Mr. Stan sure sees a lot for a guy who can barely see the end of his own driveway*, Davie thought.

Davie knocked three times on the front door, and Katie Ralls, who lived across the street, opened the door. She and her husband, Terry, were good friends of Jack, Angie, and Davie. She wore a bright pink-and-white floral apron and a light blue do-rag on her head. She smiled brightly at Davie. "Hello, big man! Have you come to read to Stosh? He was just asking about you, so he'll be happy to see you."

She swung the door open, and Davie stepped into the house. It smelled of furniture polish with a twist of lemon, and a heavy dose of freshly brewed coffee. Davie walked quietly into the living room, where Stan Koski sat in well-worn black leather chair, his feet propped up on a matching ottoman, warmed by the moderate heat emanating from an old brick fireplace. He wore tattered brown moccasins, khaki pants, and a blue flannel shirt.

At first, Davie thought that the old man was asleep. His thin, white hair was pushed straight back, barely covering the crown of his head, and stray strands dangled over his ears and forehead. Stan had a handsome face, although well lined with the avenues and creases of a long life, and soft brown eyes, when they were open. His hands were folded across his lap, the gold band on his left hand casting a faint gleam in the low flames of the fireplace.

"What's the matter, boy? You never see an old man before?" Stan flashed a surprisingly full set of white teeth ("And they're all mine," he'd be quick to tell you) at Davie, who had straightened abruptly when the old man suddenly came to life. Stan reached out for the boy with his left hand. "Come here, son. Stand close so I can see you," he said.

"Hi, Mr. Stan, how are you doin'?" Davie stepped toward Stan, and the old man wrapped his arm around the boy's shoulders and gave him a hearty squeeze. Their eyes met in the glow of the fire, the young and the old, tomorrow and yesterday. Katie entered the room and set a mug of coffee on the table next to Stan, and then handed Davie a can of Coca-Cola.

"Do you two boys think you can stay out of trouble while I finish fixing Stan's supper?" she asked brightly.

"I don't have much choice," Stan said, "but Davie here might have other ideas."

Davie chuckled and shrugged his shoulders. "I'll be good, I think," he said, and he took a long draw from the can of Coke. Stan laughed and Katie shook her head, muttering, "Men!" as she strolled into the kitchen.

Davie sat on the floor, cross-legged like a tiny guru. The fire felt good, not too hot. It was just right. Stan coughed for a few seconds and pointed to a stack of small logs in a brass log-holder. "Put one of those logs on the fire, okay, son? And be careful! Take your time. Don't want to burn this old place down."

Davie climbed to his feet, slowly pulled open the screen, lifted a small log from the stack, and delicately placed it on top of the glowing embers at the center of the small fire. He closed the screen and returned to his spot on the floor. "You want me to read the paper, Mr. Stan?" the boy asked, looking up to the old man with his head tilted slightly.

Stan reached over and patted the boy on the back. "No, not today, son. Let's just sit here for a minute and enjoy the fire." Stan stared into the flames that began to rise and consume the log Davie had just placed on the grate. "Davie," Stan said, his voice soft and a little hoarse, "I appreciate you coming over here and reading to me. I enjoy your company, and I'm proud that you're my friend."

"Me too, Mr. Stan," Davie replied, looking up at the old man.

Stan leaned back in the chair and let out a long sigh. "I've been around a long time," he said, "and I can tell you for a fact that good friends are as scarce as hen's teeth. When you have a true friend, you've really got something, you know?"

A confused expression came to Davie's face. "Hen's teeth? Chickens have teeth?"

The old man laughed, which led to a wheeze and then a coughing attack. His eyes teared up. He pulled a handkerchief from his shirt pocket and wiped at his face. Davie stood and handed Stan the coffee mug. Katie peeked in from behind the kitchen's swing door.

"Everything okay, boys?" she asked, a lilt in her voice.

Stan waved the hankie in the air for a moment, collected himself, and said, "Yes, darlin', we're okay. Get to work in there; I'm getting hungry."

She stuck out her tongue and gave Stan the raspberry, which gave Davie the giggles, and retreated into the kitchen.

"That's what I mean," Stan said, pointing an index finger to the kitchen. "Katie is a dear friend. What would I do without her? She comes over damn near every day to look after me. She doesn't have to do that, and neither do you. So thanks, son. I mean it." The old man dabbed at his eyes with the hankie and then cleared his throat. Davie, back in the lotus position at Stan's feet, reached up and rubbed the old man's knee. He wasn't sure what to say.

Davie thought of his aunt and uncle, arguing in their bedroom at night, arguing in the kitchen when he came home from school. *Maybe it's my fault. Maybe they're fighting about me. Are they gonna split up and leave me? Should I ask Mr. Stan what he thinks? He'd know what to do, what to say.* Davie turned his gaze to the fireplace and watched as the log he'd set on its grill begin to flame and crackle. For just a moment, he thought he saw the green eyes of the wolf glaring, even brighter than the fire, and the outline of its massive muzzle and head lurking in the light gray smoke. And then it was gone. Davie felt the fire's warmth on his face, and he lowered his head.

"All right, all right," Stan said softly. "That's enough of my ramblings, right? Why don't you go home now, do whatever it is that eight-year-old boys do these days, okay? I think I need a nap before dinner." He leaned forward and rubbed Davie's head. The boy stood, took Stan's hand, used it to pull himself up, pressed his head against the old man's chest, and hugged him with both arms. Stan squeezed back tenderly.

"Okay, off you go," Stan whispered. "Be good and mind your aunt and uncle. And do your homework!" He waggled a finger at Davie, who smiled and turned toward the door. He paused near the kitchen and called out, "Bye, Katie! Thanks for the Coke!" He waited until he heard her reply.

"Okay, babe. Say hello to Uncle Jack and Aunt Angie for me, okay?"

The boy turned to give Stan a quick wave, but the old man's head was bowed and he appeared to have gotten a quick start on that nap. Davie left, closing the door quietly behind him. As he walked across the Koski front yard, he was pleased to see Uncle Jack's Mustang in the driveway. Curly was sitting on the porch, tail wagging fiercely, as Davie climbed the steps and entered the house.

Jack and Davie played catch for a while in the backyard as Curly jogged back and forth between them. When it started to rain, they took shelter under the protective shield of the open garage door and barbecued Ball Park Franks—just like the ones they sold at Tiger Stadium. They munched hot dogs and spooned warm baked beans from paper plates balanced on their laps as they sat in lawn chairs under the aluminum canopy.

"Want another dog or some more beans there, wheezer?" the man asked as he raised a can of Stroh's and downed its final warm swallow. He belched wetly and the boy giggled. Jack leaned back in the lawn chair, disregarding an angry metal squeal and unable to see that its back legs were beginning to buckle under his weight. Jack spun his torso slightly and tossed the empty can in a high arc toward a thirty-two-gallon rubber garbage pail positioned in the corner of the garage. The can hit the wall behind the pail and fell into a burgeoning population of empties. Curly, lying on concrete behind

Davie's chair, followed its flight. An empty beer can was not what he was waiting for.

"That's a trey in any league," Jack said. He stabbed a slightly charred dog from the grill with a fork and offered it to Davie.

"No more for me," Davie said. "I'm all fulled up. You gonna eat any more, Uncle Jack?" A thin line of ketchup missed its intended target, trickled from the corner of the boy's mouth, and then rolled down and under his chin.

"Who are you, Bela Lugosi?" Jack chuckled as he grabbed a roll of paper towels from the rack beneath the coal pan of the barbecue and handed a sheet to the boy. Davie wet the towel with his tongue and then wiped his chin vigorously until the ketchup was gone and his skin was clean and pink. He handed the towel back to Jack, who crumpled it into a ball and tossed it on top of the hot coals. It smoked slightly, then vanished in a brief but brilliant flame. Davie raised his chin for inspection.

"You're clean," Jack said. "That was a good look on you, though, Count Chocula." He gave Davie's hair a tussle and they both snickered. They sat back and looked into a gray sky and a descending mist. Jack ate half of the hot dog in two bites, sans bun, and then handed the rest to Curly. The dog ate it without mercy.

"If a dog eats a hot dog, is the dog a cannibal?" Jack asked Davie, who turned to look at Curly as the bulldog finished off the treat.

"I don't think it's the same thing, Uncle Jack," Davie decided.

"Pull my finger, quick!" The boy obliged, and Uncle Jack cut the cheese.

Davie pinched his nose between two fingers and chuckled happily. "Gross!" the boy moaned.

"Beans, beans, the magical fruit," Jack sang cheerfully.

"The more you eat, the more you toot!" Davie answered, and then doubled up in laughter as the man tickled at his ribs.

"Hey, horsefly, if it stops raining, you wanna shoot some hoops?"

Davie looked at Jack and then to the western sky above the Rallses' house. It looked menacing, and the rain gave no indication of relenting anytime soon.

"I don't think it's gonna stop raining for a while, Uncle Wheezer," Davie said.

"Okay, Sonny Eliot, Channel Four weather expert and local wise guy, if you say so." Jack stood and ambled to the rear of the garage, where he inspected the garbage pail and reckoned that at ten cents a pop for deposit, he was stockpiling a small fortune in empties. He opened an old refrigerator positioned nearby and plucked out another brew while taking a quick inventory of the dwindling supply within.

"Do you want another can of pop, boss?" he asked the boy.

"No, thanks. I'm okay," Davie replied.

Jack slammed the door shut on the old fridge—if you didn't slam it, the damned thing wouldn't stay closed—pulled open the aluminum tab, and returned to his chair. Curly waddled outside and sniffed at the lawn until he found his sweet spot. Nature's business concluded, Curly returned to his place behind the boy.

"Well, what about the Tigers? Are they on TV tonight?" his uncle asked.

"No, they're off today; home tomorrow against the Red Sox. No TV though," Davie answered.

Jack took a long drink from his beer and withdrew a cigarette from the open pack in his shirt pocket. Davie was leaning forward in his chair, craning his neck to peer into the line of shrubs that served as a barrier against the outgrowth of the neighboring field.

"What're you looking for, hoss? See something in the bushes?" Jack attempted to light his cigarette by pressing its tobacco end down on a hot coal. He leaned back perilously in the chair and its legs buckled a little further with a slight creak. When the cigarette began to smolder, Jack put the filtered end in his mouth and puffed frantically until a cloud of smoke hovered above his head.

"I was just lookin' for Cheetah," Davie said. "You know how he always hangs around when we eat out here, waitin' for a handout?"

"Yeah. We should give him a bell and a cup next Christmas and let him set up out at the mall," Jack replied.

"I haven't seen him since after school, when he was over by the Johnsons', playin' with little Jessica." The boy's eyes slowly scanned the bushes. Then his gaze dropped to his feet.

"He's probably holed up someplace nice and dry, waiting for the rain to quit," said Jack as thunder cracked in the distance. Moments later, the rain intensified. When Jack saw Davie shiver slightly, he climbed to his feet. "Let's go inside and watch the tube. It's getting too cold out here for humans. Cheets will be along soon. I'll leave the garage door open, and he'll cry by the door when he gets home."

The boy rose, folded his lawn chair, carried it over to the side of the garage, near the refrigerator, and leaned it against the wall. Jack did the same with his chair and decided the barbecue coals would burn out harmlessly of their own accord. He turned and followed Davie and Curly into the house. Jack heard the telephone ringing and hustled to the kitchen to answer it, not sure whether he'd heard the first or the tenth ring.

"Yeah, yeah, I'm comin', I'm comin'," Jack muttered as he snatched the phone from the wall and spoke into it. "Hello?"

"Hi, sweetie, it's me." Angie sounded bored, and Jack grew immediately tense, anticipating bad news.

"Let me guess," he said. "You're gonna be late again." He looked at the microwave, and the green LED lights of its digital clock read 7:12 p.m.

"I have to prepare a brief for Peter's case tomorrow. Don't know for sure yet, but I shouldn't be too late," she said.

Peter, Jack thought. *Fecking Peter.* The name stung him, and he felt his cheeks growing warm. "Is Petie there to help you with his briefs, Angie?"

Angie exhaled a sigh of weariness into the speaker of her phone. "No, Jack. He's in his office, and I'm in mine, okay? What is your problem, anyway?"

"When are you coming home?"

"Probably nine or ten or so, just soon as I get done," Angie snapped. "The longer you play Joe Friday, the longer it'll take."

Jack fell silent. He wanted her home, yet he was angry with her. He missed her, longed to touch her, but felt a need to punish her, to let her know he was still in control—in control of himself. It all seemed so blatantly one-sided to Jack. She called; he simmered.

He said no more into his end of the line. He feared the edge he knew she could find in his voice. She knew how to turn it against him. He imagined that she enjoyed doing this to him, but maybe not. Maybe she was completely unaware of it, and this notion frustrated Jack even more.

"Jack? Is Davie ready to go tomorrow?" Angie's tone softened. The man did not speak. He was staring through the kitchen window, toward the trees that lined the backyard, seeing nothing.

"Jack? Leave the front porch light on for me, okay?"

Jack paced the ten feet of freedom the phone's accordion cord allotted him. He peered at the floor, walking briskly in a circle, a trapped animal seeking release. The cigarette in his left hand dropped an inch-long ash into the carpet, but Jack didn't notice.

"Yeah, whatever," he finally mumbled.

"Thanks, sweetie," she said, her voice falling to a whisper. "Listen, I've got to go. I'll see you as soon as I can. Give my love to Davie."

"Okay. See ya." He closed his eyes. "Angie ... I ... uh ..." It was too late. He heard the phone click into silence at her end. Jack clumsily returned the phone to its cradle, not looking at it. When it finally clicked into its perch, he turned and walked away.

At the other end of the disconnected telephone line, Angela Thomas put the handset back in its cradle and pushed the phone away from her on the desktop. She then stood and turned to face her boss, Peter Brookings. He moved quickly toward her and pressed against her, until her back was flat against the wall. He caressed her sides, slowly working his way down, along her hips.

Peter leaned into her and kissed the side of her neck, up to her ear, back down again. His hands never stopped feeling, rubbing, groping, as she leaned her head back and moaned softly. He slid his left hand under the waistband of her dark gray slacks until his fingertips reached the elastic band of her panties. He continued to probe softly, gently caressing her warm, soft skin, until she took his wrist and lifted his hand out and away.

"No, no, Peter. Not here, not now. Please." She gently pushed him back and began to fuss at her clothing, straightening her outfit.

He pushed his hair back and chuckled nervously. "Sure, babe; okay. Guess I got a little carried away. You're hard to resist, you know?" His face was flushed and his forehead glistened under a thin coat of perspiration. "Are we still on for this weekend?" he asked.

Angie reached out and adjusted Peter's tie, pulling it snug into his starched white collar. "Yes," she whispered. "So long as Jack stays home, and he said he's going to. If he does come with us, then I'm afraid it's off." She stepped away from Peter.

"Okay, then," Peter said. "I'll hope for the best."

Angie worked at her desk for another two hours, then put on her overcoat, collected her purse, and left the office. She walked to her car in a light, misting rain and drove into the night. Her heart was racing, and her thoughts weren't far behind. She was rushing toward something she wasn't sure she could control. Angie had crossed a line;

she was certain. But thus far, the right or wrong of it was still too ambiguous for her to perceive the potential consequences. She hadn't consummated the deed, and so she still believed she could jump back to marital fidelity—if she chose to.

Angie twisted a knob and the windshield wipers came to life. As they slapped away the rain, oncoming headlights danced in blurs and streaks. She tensed her shoulders and leaned forward, struggling to acquire a clear view of the road ahead.

Back at home, Jack stared at the phone and tried to picture Angie doing the same at the other end of the line. Yet another conversation that he now regretted. He turned and saw Davie standing in the doorway to the living room, his hands stuffed into his pants pockets, eyes down.

"Wanna watch TV, Uncle Jack?" The boy spoke softly and raised his blue eyes to the man. Jack smiled and winked an eye, swallowing the emotions the phone call pulled up from his gut. He crushed out his smoke in the glass ashtray on the kitchen table.

"Sure, sweet pea. What's on?"

The pair withdrew to the family room, assumed positions at each end of the long couch and, after a brief search for the remote, clicked on the set. Davie dozed off during *The Eight O'Clock Movie*, which was *White Heat*, just as James Cagney opened a train valve and steamed the bejesus out of an accomplice who called him by name during a robbery.

Jack drifted into sleep as well, shortly before Cagney stood atop a burning tower and announced, "I'm on top o' the world, Ma, top o' the world!" As the flames engulfed Cagney, the front door opened. Angie noisily slammed the door shut and switched on the light that illuminated the front hallway and most of the couch.

"Hi, kids," she said wearily. She dropped her purse on the dining room table, peeled off her jacket, and hung it on a straight-backed chair. Curly emerged from under the kitchen table, tail wagging, and dashed to Angie, who gave his butt a quick pat.

Jack rose slowly, feeling in the cushions of the couch for the once-again-missing remote. "Where is that freakin' thing," he grumbled before locating it and clicking off the TV.

"Hey, sleepyhead," Angie said to Davie. "How ya doin'?" Davie rubbed his eyes and then stretched his arms above his head, which he tilted as Angie kissed his cheek.

"You'd better head up to bed, little dude," she said. "Big day tomorrow—we're going up north, remember?"

Davie squinted and recalled the arrangements. Although tomorrow was only Friday, Angie's excuse for taking him out of school for the day was to beat the traffic jam heading out of the city at the end of the workweek. Angie was opening the cottage north of Gaylord, near the wee village of Vanderbilt, left to her by her father. Most people waited until the Memorial Day weekend getaway to open for the season, likely to extend into October. Angie's "opening" mainly meant unlocking the door and making the beds.

It was a fairly modern house, with most of the comforts of home, nestled against a small, manmade lake. They called it *the cabin*, sometimes *the cottage*, but it was really neither. "Ask Daniel Boone, when you see him," Jack would say, "what a *real* cabin looks like."

To Michiganders, the trek north to spring and summer haunts was universally known as "going up north," distance or direction notwithstanding. Jack opted not to go, citing too much work at the plant to skip a Friday. He really wanted to punish Angie for her absences from home of late, but his efforts did not outwardly faze her. He sought to rebuke, but was instead further frustrated. The logic of it all eluded the man, even as it overwhelmed him.

"Hi, Jackman," Angie said cautiously, but he did not respond. He crossed the room, opened the front door, and peered through the screen of the outer door. He listened to the wind rustle through the upper branches of the tall oak trees.

"Thanks for turning the porch light on for me," Angie said with great sarcasm. The driveway and porch had been very dark when she pulled her silver LTD up to the garage, beside Jack's Mustang. Jack turned, stared toward her, and belatedly switched on the amber-toned porch light. He pushed open the screen door and stepped outside.

The rain finally stopped, but a cool breeze persisted, carrying large drops of water from the leaves of the trees and scattering them haphazardly to the earth below. A three-quarter moon lit the sky amid a smattering of stars as the last huge, black clouds rumbled off into the east. Jack began to whistle in long, shrill notes that carried with them no particular melody. He mimicked the bosun's whistles he'd heard aboard US Navy troop carriers, like the one that took him to Vietnam, what now seemed like a lifetime ago.

Angie sat on the edge of the couch, took off her shoes, and pulled off her black, knee-high nylon stockings. Davie stopped at the head of the stairway leading to the bedrooms and called down to the woman, "Aunt Angie, did you see Cheetah out there anywhere when you was comin' in? He didn't come home for dinner."

"No, I didn't see him, honey, but he's okay," Angie assured the boy. Her voice was flat and indicated no concern for the missing cat. It was spring, and she assumed he'd picked up the scent of a lady cat somewhere or other, and that he'd be home in due course. She had forgotten about making that trip to the veterinarian wherein Cheetah was given forced celibacy. Jack said that Cheetah was being "modified" when Davie asked why the cat was headed to the vet's. Cheetah lost the spring in his step and the lilt to his strut *that* day, Jack believed.

"But what if he got lost or somethin'?" Davie asked.

"Cats don't get lost," Angie said with certainty. "They've got a great sense of direction, and if that fails, they just use their noses and smell their way home." She stood and ascended the stairs, meeting the boy at the top. She gently took his shoulders in her hands and spun him around, nudging him down the hall toward his bedroom.

Davie submitted, but after three steps he stopped and again turned to face Angie. "What if he's hurt?" the boy asked, head crooked to the side.

"Davie," Angie groaned, losing patience, "Cheetah's okay. Cats have nine lives, remember?" She gave him another slight shove down the hall.

"How do you know how many of 'em he's got left?" Davie kept walking but turned his head and looked over his shoulder at the woman following him.

She smiled and waved her left hand through the air. "Oh, he's got plenty left, dinkus. Don't you worry about *that*. Besides, Uncle Jack's out looking. He'll find Cheetah."

By now, the boy and his aunt were entering Davie's bedroom. Angie watched as he pulled off his blue sweatshirt with the maize University of Michigan block *M* on its chest, then the light gray jeans, and draped both over the backboard of his bed. He tugged a set of pajamas out from under his pillow and began slipping into them.

"Don't forget to brush your teeth and say your prayers," Angie instructed. "Then go straight to bed, okay? We've got a long drive tomorrow, and you're my navigator."

Angie could make the trip blindfolded, but she felt that titling Davie would make him feel more involved and less likely to fidget. She would unfold a Michigan map in his lap and Davie would announce each little town they passed as they traveled north up I-75. It was not a visually exciting stretch of highway by any means; glaciers had leveled off Michigan as they melted and receded some fourteen thousand years ago, so any diversion along the way was appreciated.

"Okay, Aunt Angie," Davie said. "See you in the morning." She bent down and kissed his forehead as she pulled back the bedspread. She watched as Davie padded off toward the bathroom, and then she turned toward the faintly blue light in the window in Davie's room. She looked out and saw Jack targeting a flashlight, its beam scanning the perimeter of the neighboring field.

She turned and left the room, walked down the hall, and began to undress as she crossed the threshold of their bedroom. She thought of the man with the flashlight and how the light, when pointed to the heavens, seemed to shine on forever. She wondered how far it really went.

Angie walked around their bed, came to another window, peeled back the curtain, and looked for the man with the flashlight. When she did not see him, her spirit sagged slightly, and she stepped back until she felt the cool edge of the bed against the backs of her legs. She sat down and, for a moment, felt very sad and alone because she could not see the light and she could not see the man who held it.

Chapter Six

In the outer darkness below the bedrooms, moonlight found the man with the flashlight, still whistling and occasionally calling to the cat. "Cheetah," he said in a gruff whisper. "Cheets, you dipshit! It's too damn wet and cold for this shite! *Cheetah!*"

Jack followed the edge of the field until it reached the line of oak trees that marked the end of his backyard. Here began about ten acres of trees, wild shrubs, and assorted unkempt horticulture. An old lady who lived somewhere in Ohio owned the small forest. Jack suspected she had a family member or two drooling at her back door, waiting for the old bat to hit room temperature so that he or she could tear down the trees, sell the land, and build a condo or some other moneymaker. Jack said a little prayer for the dear lady's good health. Why she held on to the woods, he hadn't a clue.

Jack ran the beam of his flashlight along the ground in the woods, seeking the illumination of the cat's pale-blue eyes, but found only scattered piles of leaves and twigs and a rusty can of Old Milwaukee beer.

"Cheetah, goddammit, hustle your fuzzy ass over here!" But there was no sign of the cat.

Jack decided to walk the outer reaches of the woods one more time, hoping Cheetah would eventually hear or see him and come home. If not, he would leave the garage door open all night and the fecking cat could bloody well sleep out there.

When he found himself at the left end of the house, he aborted the search. He was sure Cheetah was warm and dry somewhere, maybe even relaxing in the shelter of some neighbor's garage. "Cats," he grumbled. Jack shut off the flashlight and walked back toward the house. He circled around to the front, walked to the end of the driveway, and stopped. Deliberately, he scanned neighboring yards and driveways, trying to detect any sign of the cat. Nothing.

Jack ambled up the driveway, reentered the house through the front door, shut off the porch light, and closed and locked the door. He turned the porch light back on, just in case Cheetah needed a guide light. He'd read somewhere that cats really couldn't see in the dark; that was why they had long whiskers.

Jack leaned against the wall in the hallway as he stepped out of his sodden sneakers. He peeled off the socks, picked up the shoes, and headed into the kitchen, where he wrung out the socks in the sink. He wondered what Angie would think of this tactic. He placed the shoes on the floor in front of the heating vent and dropped the socks onto the shoes. Satisfied that they might be dry by Sunday—Monday tops—he switched off the kitchen light and left the room.

As he headed to the stairway, Jack spotted the bulldog beneath the dining room table, the stumpy tail wagging briskly. "Curly," the man whispered, "you old fart. That's a great job of hiding, Houdini. Come here."

The dog cautiously emerged from his sanctuary. Jack bent and scratched the dog's ears. "Don't worry, old fat ass, no lockup tonight. You hang around down here and listen for Cheetah, okay?"

Jack placed his right hand under Curly's jowls and raised the dog's head until Curly's eyes met his. The dog's tail swayed from side to side like a hyperactive pendulum. "If you hear Cheetah, come and get me, okay? Cheets is in the bush tonight. 'One in the box and one in the bush, boss,'" Jack said in a nasal twang, mimicking a guard from an old movie about a southern chain gang.

Certain that the dog understood his directives, Jack gave the furry head a final rub, stood, and mounted the stairs. The dog watched the man's climb. When Jack was out of sight, the dog returned to his spot beneath the table and lay down. Within moments, Curly was fast asleep.

Jack completed the climb and paused to look into the bedroom. He spotted Angie's form in the darkness, already in bed and likely asleep. He whispered her name, lingering for a moment in the doorway. When she didn't respond, he turned and continued down the hall to check on Davie. The boy stood on tiptoes at the window, gazing down into the night. When aware of the man's presence in the doorway, he turned to face his uncle.

"I saw you lookin' for Cheetah," Davie said. "You didn't find him, did you?"

"No, but I'm sure he's okay, son." Jack tried to sound reassuring. "Cats do funny stuff in the spring, you know? Nature calling, you might say." *But not for Cheetah, not anymore,* Jack thought with empathy.

Jack entered the room and sat on the edge of Davie's bed. The boy left his post at the window and remounted the bed. "When was the last time you saw him, porcupine?" Jack asked. "Did you see him after school?"

Davie nodded his head. "Yeah. He was over at the Johnsons',

playin' with Jessica Johnson. She was playin' with a ribbon her mom gave her ... said she was gonna make Cheets look like a Christmas present."

Jack pulled the official Major League Baseball bedspread up over Davie's legs and torso. "A bow, huh? Too bad she didn't just drop him down the chimney. Then we'd all be warm and dry," he said.

Davie smiled faintly and let his head drop to the pillow. The boy's concerned expression made Jack wish his search hadn't been fruitless.

"Listen," the man said quietly. "If you promise to go straight to sleep, I'll take another walk around the house. Maybe I'll find him, but you gotta go right to sleep ... and no more looking out the window. Deal?"

"Okay, deal," Davie said.

Jack watched Davie turn onto his right side and face the blue illumination that crept through the window. Jack patted the boy's butt, rose, and left the room. He went back down the stairs and put on the wet shoes, leaving the socks behind. Grabbing the flashlight and windbreaker, he went out the front door. He put on the blue jacket with the Ford patch on its left breast and made his way to the garage side of the house. He stuck a cigarette in his mouth and lit it with both hands cupped to block out the wind.

Jack figured to check this side and then once again follow the edge of the field back to the woods. A squat, gnarled tree that Jack could not identify by species hung over the side of the garage, where the ends of its branches reached past the gutters and gently tapped at the roof in rhythm with the wind. He paused and made a visual sweep of the area, left to right, and then back again.

Jack studied the hovering tree and wondered why he didn't chop it down. *Damned pain in the ass,* he reckoned. *Gotta stand on a ladder and get scratched all to hell at least twice a year, scooping leaves, twigs, and, once, a dead squirrel out of the eaves trough.* Jack continued to sweep the area with the flashlight, taking several deep pulls from the cigarette, his eyes now accustomed to the dark. He could separate forms from shadows, but he saw nothing. Jack took another drag and threw the butt into the wet grass. It hissed briefly as its orange glow was consumed. Turning back to the twisted branches of the unnamed and unwanted tree, Jack ducked to avoid its reach. And then he saw the cat.

The pulse of his heart froze before it seemed to drop into the pit of his stomach. Blood drained from his face, leaving it chalky and cold. When his mind was fully cognizant of what it was seeing, it jump-started his heart. Cold blood pumped back into his chest and arms and throat until it settled and pooled behind his eyes.

Cheetah swayed stiffly in the cool westerly breeze. One end of Jessica Johnson's gold Christmas bow had tangled around a knotty branch that reached out from the trunk of the tree. The other end of the ribbon disappeared beneath the black fur of Cheetah's throat. The cat's eyes, now oddly translucent, bulged from their sockets and stared down lifelessly at Jack as the wind pushed the rigid body back and forth, very slowly, toward the field and then back to the man. The protuberant eyes turned the man's stomach, the blue of life gone, replaced by a pallid blankness that he knew was death.

Jack dropped to his knees in the wet grass, still mesmerized by the sight of Cheetah dangling in the breeze. Finally he pounded the turf with the flashlight. The plastic lens cap broke loose and the batteries flew out, leaving only the hollow casing, which Jack tossed into the night.

"Ahhhhh, *shit*! Cheetah, god*dammit* ..." He coughed in fits and spasms until he caught his breath.

Jack felt the cold rainwater on his face as he forced himself to his feet. He wiped his hands on the front of his pants and attempted to dry his face in the crook of his left elbow, but the vinyl jacket resisted. He ran his hands over his face. They left muddy streaks along his jaw and cheeks.

Jack pried back one of the tree's outer limbs until it snapped and hung helplessly splintered, doomed to dry and shrivel, cut off from the lifeline of the trunk and roots. He snapped off two more branches until he could reach Cheetah and the ribbon without interference. He heard Bob Dylan singing "A Simple Twist of Fate" in his mind as he lifted Cheetah carefully in his left hand. Jessica's decoration, tangled in the branches, had apparently tightened into a deadly noose when Cheetah struggled to get free. The cat was very cold and inflexible now, but a little slack in the ribbon made untying the noose a simple matter.

"Goddamn it," Jack muttered, "why didn't you have *hands?*"

He took Cheetah down and squeezed the dead black cat tenderly to his chest. He freed himself from the entanglements of the tree and walked to the garage. With the cat nestled in his left arm, he grabbed a long-handled shovel and pulled it down from the support hooks that suspended it against the wall. Jack then removed a black Hefty garbage bag from a box on the shelf. He left the garage and made his way to the opposite side of the house, along the perimeter of the yard, until he stood at the rim of the woods.

Jack placed Cheetah delicately atop the plastic bag on a small mound of leaves, stepped under the large oak tree at the center of wooded barrier wall in his backyard, and began to dig. The evening wind blew the day's rains from the overhanging leaves and branches of the great oaks, down onto his head and shoulders and back. Jack was oblivious to the cold shower.

Jack continued to shovel away the soft black earth until he hit the small roots that fanned out from the trees. He first doubled and then tripled his efforts, the steel blade of the shovel cutting through the tree's arteries, deeper into the ground. Jack began to feel violent rage rise within him as the roots grew progressively thicker, stouter, and more resistant to his labors.

When the shovel blade hit a baseball-sized rock, he nearly fell over, cursing the trees and the earth and the skies. He fought off the desire to wrap the shovel around the trunk of the nearest oak tree, feeling dwarfed in the long shadows the oaks cast in the moonlight.

Finally, satisfied that the grave was deep enough, he tossed the shovel aside and bent over Cheetah's remains. The man gingerly picked up the dead cat and tried to shape the stiff form so that Cheetah might appear to be sleeping. Jack worked to close the lids over the protruding pale eyes but could not. He wrapped Cheetah in the black plastic, carefully folding and rolling until the bag was spent, and he had some assurance that Cheetah might be spared some measure of the indignities of death. Jack then tenderly placed Cheetah in the hole.

With his hands, Jack scooped up the earth and covered Cheetah, and wished he had a proper coffin. When the hole was filled, he gently patted the soil down, stood, and looked about until he eyed a fallen tree limb. He picked it up, broke off the ends and offshoots, and made a fairly straight stick of about two feet in length and perhaps an inch in diameter. Jack then retrieved the shovel and used its blade to pound the marker into the ground at the head of the cat's grave. He squatted and stared down at the black mound.

"Good-bye, old friend," he said hoarsely. "You were a great cat, the best ever. See you on the other side."

Jack instinctively crossed himself without thinking and rose to his feet. He turned away from the makeshift grave and walked about six feet until he stood directly in front of the towering oak. He pictured the smug face of Death on the fat trunk of the tree. With both hands holding the shovel like a baseball bat, he assumed an open stance and took a swing—a Mickey Mantle home run swing—at the face on the tree.

The shovel's handle splintered, and the vibration of the blow surged through his hands and forearms until it was expended in his shoulders. The blade rang out dully upon impact and sailed into the woods. Jack followed its flight but lost it in black shadows. He heard it land with a muted *clang*, and then he heard another sound.

From a place just beyond where the blade landed—approximately twenty feet from his right flank—he heard a low, throaty growl, very steady, ominous, and threatening. It paused to take in air and then resumed its roll, a little louder, a little fiercer. Jack froze in his tracks. He began to very deliberately step back, eyes glued to the spot where something—some *thing*—snarled, out of sight, in the dark.

Jack was startled. He had never seen or heard anything bigger than a raccoon out here, and now he had visions of Lon Chaney Jr., in full *Wolfman* fur, bursting from the shadows to rip his throat out while Warren Zevon absurdly howled out "Werewolves of London."

Jack continued his retreat until the heel of his left foot hit something and he lost his balance. This sudden stumble, coupled with an urgent adrenaline rush of fear and confusion, led him to fall on his ass in the wet grass of his backyard. He was out of the woods, which were now dead black, as if a curtain had been drawn over them.

"Holy shit," he said. The beastly sounds were gone and all was very still. "Holy shit," he repeated, rising to his feet but not taking his eyes from the trees. He still carried the shovel handle at port arms. "What the fuck was that?"

When there was no answer, Jack turned and walked hastily toward the house, a thousand thoughts and emotions conjuring to brew trouble in his heart and soul. "Must be losing my mind," he groused.

As he trudged through the wet lawn, he shook off the apparitions of the woods, lifted his head, and looked at the moon. Small gray clouds sailed just beneath it, outlined by the black sky, the trail end of the storm front. When he was twenty feet from the sliding glass door wall, a portal from the rear of the house to a small patio, he looked up. Jack let the shovel handle drop from his grimy hands.

On the second story of the house, illuminated eerily by a yellow backdrop, encroaching blue light, and a three-quarter spring moon, Jack saw Davie's tiny head and shoulders, quivering slightly. He watched the small boy bow and turn away from the window, leaving the empty glass to reflect only moonlight to the man below.

Chapter Seven

Jack stood in the moonlight and looked up to the empty second-story window. Davie knew; he had seen Cheetah's funeral, and now Jack faced another trip up the stairs that could really only end one way. Jack dilatorily trudged around the house and reentered through the front door.

In the small foyer, he kicked off his soaked shoes, peeled away the windbreaker, and let it fall to the floor. In the kitchen, he rinsed most of the mud from his hands and face and dried off with paper towels. He turned and mounted the stairs, very deliberately, searching his brain for words that might ease the boy's pain and preserve some of the hope that accompanied the innocence of youth.

Jack stood on the threshold of the boy's room and found Davie lying in bed, flat on his stomach. His back shook convulsively, and Jack heard sobs muffled by the pillow in which the boy's head was buried.

"Davie. Davie, it's okay, son," Jack said gently. "Just let it out, let it go. It's okay." He approached the bed cautiously and sat on its edge. He rubbed the boy's back tenderly and waited, his mind still tracking down comforting words that were nowhere to be found.

"I'm sorry, son. Cheetah didn't suffer ..." Jack was pretty sure that this was a lie, but he was also certain that Davie could not possibly have seen from the bedroom window how the cat met his desperate end. Jack figured that the cat's death had in fact been a mad frenzy, in which each panic-stricken thrash and lurch of his body and flailing legs had served only to draw Jessica's golden ribbon, now a hangman's noose, tighter around his throat.

"Cheetah didn't suffer, and he's in a better place now," Jack said. "He's in heaven, chasing butterflies in the sun, or maybe batting around a ball of yarn in God's living room. He was a good cat, and you know that God takes care of good things, right?" *Jesus*, he thought, *is that another lie?*

Finding words was a struggle for Jack as he pushed down his feelings. He wondered if he would ever forget the sight of the black cat swinging in the breeze at the end of the golden ribbon tied by little Jessica Johnson, the harmless act of a child. He wasn't sure he believed his own words about a caring God. For just a moment, each and every sadness he had ever known surged through his spirit. He was sad for Cheetah, but he was crushed for Davie. His body went limp, and Jack struggled to regroup and recollect himself.

Davie rolled over onto his left side and faced the man sitting on the edge of his bed. His eyes were red and his cheeks glistened, but he was no longer crying.

"Cheetah *was* a good cat, wasn't he!" Davie exclaimed, a statement rather than a question, and the man nodded.

Jack cupped the boy's face in his hands, and it was very warm. When he noticed the contrast his muddied hands made against the flushed face of the child, he withdrew them. "He was a *great* cat, Davie," the man said, "but I guess it was his time."

Jack cursed himself. *Why can't I think of something to say to comfort this poor kid?* It was strange, but all he could think of was Ward Cleaver, trying to explain to Wally and the Beaver why they couldn't keep Captain Jack, their pet alligator. Jack wished the gator had died; then maybe he could have copped a line or two from Ward to use now. But he drew a blank.

"I wish you didn't have to find him, Uncle Jack. I kinda wish that nobody had, you know? Then we never woulda known," Davie said. He sighed. "We coulda thought that maybe he had just run off and that maybe he was happy someplace else. 'Cuz I know you loved him, too, an' I know that he loved you too, 'cuz he was a good cat."

The boy's sorrow again rolled down his cheeks and chin, down his neck until it disappeared under his pajama top. Jack's sagging spirit stirred in his belly, and he straightened to look at the little boy. He wondered whether Davie was thinking about the cat or his mother, dead in the bathtub. *It would have been better if she'd been left unfound,* Jack agreed. He reached out and softly caressed Davie's face with both hands.

Jack recited:

> *He prayeth best, who loveth best*
> *All things both great and small;*
> *For the dear God who loveth us,*
> *He made and loveth all.*

Jesus, he thought, *where did that come from?* It was Coleridge, he suddenly remembered. He hadn't thought of that gem in years, but there it was, high school English lit, Mr. DeBard, many years ago.

"Are you okay now, Uncle Jack?" Davie gave the man a confused look.

"Yeah," Jack mumbled, fighting a flurry of emotions precariously harnessed behind his eyes. "I'm okay, horsefly. How's about you?"

Davie turned his torso slightly, dropped onto his back, and rose up on his elbows. "I'm all right," he said, "but did you see a wolf in the woods?"

The man rose to his feet and peered down at Davie. "Well, I *heard* something," Jack said, "but I didn't *see* anything. Have you seen something in the woods?"

Davie looked to Jack and then to the window. "I saw a big wolf in my dreams, and I think he's out there, watchin' us. I thought I saw his eyes in the woods when you were buryin' Cheetah. I don't know what the wolf wants, Uncle Jack," Davie whimpered as tears began to stream down his cheeks again, "but in my dream, I thought the wolf was God." Davie now gazed directly into Jack's eyes and said, "Did the wolf kill Cheetah, Uncle Jack?"

"No," Jack stated. "The wolf is just something you saw in a dream. It's not real." Jack worked to convince himself that what he'd heard was probably a dog; until now, he hadn't connected Davie's dream with the malevolent noise in the woods. He felt a twinge in his gut and thought of the old horror movies he and Davie watched on TV. For just a moment, he heard the creepy organ music they played when Boris or Bela was up to no good. Jack looked out the window and decided he was being silly. *It was just a dream,* he thought, *and what I heard was a big dog.*

"It's okay to cry," Jack finally said, bobbing his head slowly. He rubbed the boy's head, then crouched and gave him a hug. Davie wiped at his face with the sleeve of his pajama top. "But like the lady said, 'Tomorrow is another day.'"

Davie nodded in mute agreement and lowered himself onto his

pillow. Jack pulled the bedspread up to his chin. "I'll already be gone for work when you get up in the morning, pookie, so you have a good time up north and take care of Aunt Angie for us, okay?"

"You take care of yourself too, Uncle Jack," Davie said. "Why doncha come up after work? We could go fishin'!"

"Well, we'll see," Jack said. "You go to sleep now, okay? Hey, I love you."

"I love you, too, horsefly," Davie whispered, a twinkle back in his blue eyes. Jack chuckled. He had come up to console a little boy, a two-ton boulder on his back and a knife in his heart, worried for his wife and his marriage, saddened by Cheetah's cruel end, dreading Davie's reaction, and he'd found a small measure of comfort. Jack turned and left the room.

He went into the bathroom and undressed, leaving the wet and soiled clothing piled in the bathtub. *That'll surely piss Angie off,* he speculated, but he left the soggy heap in the tub anyway. He'd forgotten that he would return here to shower in just a few hours, before Angie was even awake.

Jack again washed his arms, hands, and face over the sink, dried off with what had been a pink guest towel, and then removed his brown bathrobe from a hook on the inside of the bathroom door. As he tugged it on and tied off the waist cord, he studied himself in the mirror on the medicine cabinet above the sink. He stared into his eyes as they reflected back. After a few moments, he closed his eyes and turned away.

Jack walked down the yellow hallway toward the stairs, pausing briefly at the bedroom door to look in on Angie. She was curled up with her back to the doorway. Hearing the long and deep rhythm of her breathing, Jack knew she was sound asleep. There was no point in waking her up to deliver the news about Cheetah.

Downstairs, he grabbed a fresh pack of cigarettes from a carton on the refrigerator door and shuffled into the family room. He pulled a wooden rocking chair out from the corner and twisted it until it faced the large glass door wall and its view of the backyard and woods. Jack opened the drapes and sat in the rocker. He was bone weary, but knew that sleep would not come easily tonight.

Curly sauntered into the room and joined the man's vigil, lying at Jack's feet and blinking up at him. Dogs had a special sense for human misery; Jack was certain of it.

"Curly Q, there will be no more prison time in the basement, you old sot. Your sentence is hereby forever rescinded, and I grant you a full pardon." Jack leaned forward and rubbed the dog's head and upper back. Curly's stubby tail wagged slowly. Jack wondered if the dog knew about Cheetah or shared his feelings of loss and frustration. "Just how much do you really know, fist-face?"

The dog gazed up at the man and blinked. His mouth dropped open, his tongue rolled out, and Curly began to pant steadily. He licked Jack's outstretched hand and then rested his head on his forepaws with a low grunt.

Jack wondered what else was out there, waiting. He sat smoking and rocking and talking to the bulldog. Occasionally he stared past the glass and into the darkness for answers as the world tumbled by indiscernibly and swirled ever onward. The last of the rain clouds chased the dawn toward the east, and, from infinity, tiny stars blinked and flickered.

Chapter Eight

On the first afternoon in May, Jack drove away from the Ford plant and headed west on Michigan Avenue. The radio blared out an oldie by the Kinks, and Jack rolled down the window to let in the warm spring air. It was a sunny day, blue skies with scattered white puffs floating by, and rush hour traffic was already building.

Jack set out for home but decided to stop for a beer or three along the way. Angie had taken Davie up north, so the house stood empty, save for Curly, who wouldn't begrudge Jack a brief respite. Jack had had enough of emptiness, so when he neared the Avenue Bar, he steered into the right lane, slowed the car, and looked for a place to park.

When he at last eyed an open spot, he pulled the car alongside the curb and stopped three feet from the rear bumper of a '79 Buick Electra. He was on the outskirts of a sagging community, a now-forgotten, former suburban servant of the City of Detroit.

Where automobile plants and parts suppliers had once flourished, there now stood dirty, gray buildings, largely deserted, most of their windows long ago shattered by rocks and bottles tossed from the street, their innards gutted by scrappers and scavengers. This little town that hunkered in the shadows of Motown had thrived during World War Two as the home of huge defense plants, churning out the machinery of war that was shipped overseas to vanquish distant enemies. The "Arsenal of Democracy" was a title well-earned and, having succeeded in that end, was no longer needed.

The defense plants shut down and the automobile plants steadily followed suit. Those few people who remained were as old and gray and vacant as the buildings that surrounded and imprisoned them. It was a modern urban ghost town, all signs of life gone save for a few wandering ragpickers and the derelicts who occasionally left the alleys and buildings in search of one more bottle, one more jolt, one more high.

At night, the old gave way to a few younger occupants, who supported their habits through various nefarious activities at the expense of what civic pride remained, ensuring death to a community where damned few stopped to visit, and even fewer chose to stay.

The Avenue Bar had once been jammed to capacity during shift changes at the factories, but it now sat ignominiously between the boarded-up shell of a vacant Food Town Supermarket and the former law offices of Murphy, Crandall & Ross. Murphy and Ross had long since taken dirt naps; Crandall nursed a bad heart and a choking case of emphysema in an Arizona nursing home and would rejoin his partners in the fall, in even warmer climes.

In the street, cars driven too fast wove between and around one another, responding to each intrusion of space with a blaring honk and angrily thrust middle finger. Rush hour was heating up, and the masses renewed their daily flight from the city. While most cars were down in the nearby, ditch-like freeways, Michigan Avenue remained a busy alternative between Detroit and its wealthier western suburbs. Drivers jockeyed for position and escape.

Jack parked perhaps sixty feet from the bar's entrance. He rolled up the window, opened and locked the door, and got out of the car. He looked down at his feet as he walked to the bar, carefully avoiding the many cracks that riddled the sidewalk. *Step on a crack, break your mama's back.* The old bell in the spire atop the First Methodist Church just up the street tolled three times. Jack checked his wristwatch; it was 3:22.

Jack pushed open a peeling, dark-green door and stepped into the saloon, pausing momentarily to allow his eyes to adjust to the bar's cavernous darkness. As his vision gradually adapted, Jack eyed a fat man who was pushing himself and his faltering stool away from the bar with pudgy hands.

"Hey, Jack! *Jackson!* Sit and I'll buy you a drink! Where the hell have you been, my friend? Wait a minute," the fat man said, shaking Jack's hand vigorously. "I must answer the urgent call of nature." The fat man, whose name was Pentz, staggered as his great weight settled to his feet. He belched and strode down the narrow aisle. Jack nodded and smiled as the fat man turned and toddled away, and then seated himself on a stool at the end of the bar nearest the door.

Around the half-square bar sat three other men in various stages of inebriation. Jack smiled at the girl seated behind the bar on a wooden stool, looking up at an old RCA TV perched on top of a cigarette machine. Veronica, or Ronnie, was ten or so pounds overweight, and her bottle-blonde hair was slightly unclean, tied up in a long ponytail. What scant makeup she wore did little to complement her hazel eyes, but she could have been very pretty with a little effort, Jack decided.

She was watching *I Dream of Jeannie.* She held up her right index finger to let Jack know that she would be there directly and, when Major Nelson tripped over an ottoman that Jeannie had just blinked into the room and fell on his ass, she laughed. She stood on the lower rung of the barstool, aimed a heavily duct-taped remote at the TV, and clicked it into the eerie green world where one could no longer see its images.

"Hi, Jack," she said cheerily. "Wanna beer?"

Jack nodded. The girl opened a cooler door beneath the back bar, extracted a longneck bottle of Stroh's, and addressed the men who lined the long, straight section of the bar. Jack sat at its elbow and overlooked the room. "I don't know why you guys don't think that show's funny," the girl said.

Dorsey, a tall man perched at the left end of the trio, looked up from his beer and smiled at the girl. "I keep watchin' and waitin' for her top to fall off. Now *that* would be *funny*."

The girl shook her head and removed a spent beer bottle from Dorsey's hand. "You want another one?" she asked through a long exhalation. Dorsey reached into his pocket and pulled out a folded stack of bills. He extracted a ten and dropped it on the bar, waving his left hand above his head in a circular motion.

"Sprinkle the infield, sweet pea," Dorsey ordered, "and don't forget Pentzie. He's in the can."

The girl grabbed the bill and nodded. Dorsey turned on his seat without rising and faced Jack, who sat five stools down to the tall man's left. "Hey, mushnuts, where in the hell *you* been lately?" Dorsey leaned over empty stools and extended his right arm. Jack had to stand and reach out to take the tall man's hand.

"Same old shit, Dorse," Jack said. "Just workin' and workin' some more. You?"

"Same old, same old, Jackie. Hey, honeybuns," said Dorsey, his attention now swiveling toward Veronica, "Don't forget a brew for the Jack o' Diamonds here." Dorsey again circled the air with his left hand.

"You know ten bucks ain't gonna cover this, right, Dorsey?" Veronica said, hands on her hips. The tall man dropped another sawbuck on the bar. The girl drew two mugs of beer from the tap, pulled two more bottles from the cooler, and distributed them to the four men at the bar. She then lifted a bottle of Dewar's from the back counter and poured two fingers' worth into the fat man's glass.

From the unlighted hallway a voice said, "May your skies be ever blue." The fat man Pentz emerged from the shadows and mounted his stool. Calvin, the black man at the end of the group, lifted his bottle in salute to Dorsey. The other man, a short, thin fellow, rapped on the bar three times with the bottom of his mug. He was rapidly losing his war with male pattern baldness, as the thinning comb-over atop his head attested.

The bar had no windows to the outer world, so the men were left to assume that the skies were indeed blue. The front door opened slowly and an old woman crept in cautiously. She shut the door gently and turned to enter, her face squinting as her old and dim eyes struggled to adjust to the dark.

"It helps if you're part mole," said Dorsey.

The old woman did not acknowledge the comment. She carried a bundle of artificial flowers, red and blue and an odd shade of orange. Jack swigged beer directly from the brown longneck bottle and did not look at the old woman. He was hardened to the street people who frequently wandered into bars and stores, pestered car drivers at stoplights with greasy rags, and panhandled on the sidewalk. It was just something you got used to, like the weather. Sometimes you slipped them a buck or two, sometimes you ignored them, but you *never* made eye contact or really looked at them.

"Hey, lady," Dorsey called out amiably, "where'd you get the horseshit flowers? Those orange ones look just like my ex-mother-in-law's hair." The tall man looked to either side to find a laugh but was denied.

The old lady handed him a tattered business card. Jack looked on, his face expressionless, as Dorsey read it out loud.

"It says, 'I am deaf.'" Dorsey looked at the woman's face briefly, his eyes slightly squinted. Jack drank more beer and lit another smoke. "'I made these pretty flowers and sell them for one dollar each. Any donations would be appreciated.'"

Dorsey handed the card back to the woman and returned to his bar stool. Jack studied the old woman's face and eyes. She wore an eager expression and a smile left ugly by time and her life. The few teeth she had were a dull brown, and a dark blue bruise underscored her left eye. The right eye wandered helplessly, unfocused and undirected in its watery socket. Jack turned from the old woman and fixed his gaze on his bottle of beer.

"Beat it, you old retread," Dorsey mumbled, head bowed over the bar. "If anybody's gonna piss away my dough on booze, it's gonna be me."

Veronica angrily slapped the bar in front of the tall man with both hands. "Dorsey, you're a real sensitive asshole, you know that? Why don't you leave the old lady alone?" She spun around to face the cash register, extracted two one-dollar bills and handed them across the bar to the old woman. Veronica picked two blue flowers from the bundle the old woman offered her and propped them up in an empty mug among the liquor bottles that lined the back bar.

"I think they're pretty," she said. "They'll give the place a little color."

Dorsey swigged greedily from his beer, belched loudly, pointed to the black man on his right, and declared, "If we get any more color in here, we can make a Tarzan movie."

The black man slowly turned his head and faced Dorsey, feigning anger. He grasped the neck of his beer bottle and turned the bottom up slightly, careful not to spill any beer. "Bitch, you shoulda been born on some got-damn plantation." He smiled and shook his head. "A Tarzan movie." The man snickered, still twisting his head from side to side.

The old woman gave Calvin an ugly grin and skipped erratically toward his end of the bar. He stopped giggling. The woman had misread his mirth as another sale. She offered the motley bouquet with short thrusts of anticipation and invitation. "Git the fuck away from me wi' that shit!" Calvin scowled at her. "I ain't buyin' none o' that shit." He shooed her away, flapping both hands, wrists stiff. The woman's unpleasant smile faded from her tired face, and she bowed and circled clumsily away from the bar.

"Nice, Calvin, real nice. You guys got a lotta class," said the girl behind the bar, shaking her head. Jack kept his attention on Veronica as she sat down on her stool, pouting and wishing she were elsewhere, anywhere at all. She turned and faced Jack, and when their eyes met, she smiled, and so did he. They remained locked on one another, Jack's anger and disappointments and frustrations with Angie lost to the moment. The possibilities he imagined within Veronica's smile were alluring to him now, showing him another door, another way out, here in this dank old bar in a forgotten part of town.

The old woman approached Jack, ending his moment with Veronica, and he handed her a five-dollar bill. When she offered him a bouquet, he shook his head and said loudly, "That's okay, you keep 'em." It occurred to him that speaking loudly to a deaf woman was like shouting in English to a Martian. The old woman smiled and repeatedly bobbed her head.

The fat man Pentz leaned forward on his stool, and it squeaked under the strain. This was followed by the unmistakable sound of a very loud, very long fart, greeted with hoots and catcalls and a general outcry of bemused disgust.

"Pardon me, ladies and gentlemen," he announced, "but I calls 'em like I sees 'em."

Dorsey vigorously waved the air with his right hand. "Pentz, you shit ass, how many times do I gotta tell you? Nobody wants to hear big band music anymore!"

The three men at the bar's center laughed as the fat man extended his arms outward, the palms of his hands facing up. Jack watched the old woman as she covered her nose and mouth with the sleeve of her grimy coat and made her way to the door. Dorsey made an elaborate gesture with his right hand, shaking the index finger as if to say, "Watch this!" The bar's patrons silently watched and waited.

When the old woman's hand reached out to the door handle to pull it open, Dorsey called out, "Hey, lady, you dropped your *money!*" The old woman gave no indication that she'd heard the tall man. She tugged the door open just far enough to get out, stepped into the light of the outer world, and shut the door behind her.

Veronica shook her head as the door closed. "Dorsey," she scolded, "has anybody ever told you that you're a real horse's ass?"

"Ahhh, once, maybe twice." He shrugged his shoulders. "Skip the sermons and bring me another beer, okay?" He dropped a five spot on the bar and spun his stool to face the fat man. "Hey, sweet lips, I hope the concert's over," he said.

"One never knows when the urge to strike a discordant note might be felt," said the fat man, smiling. Pentz lifted his scotch on the rocks and drained what was left of the amber fluid, wincing as he replaced the glass on the bar. He waggled a pudgy finger over it in a circular motion as the girl glanced his way. Jack absentmindedly tapped a cigarette on the bar, staring at it until his eyes lost focus. He then flicked his lighter open and fired up, exhaling a cloud of blue smoke.

"Just make sure you keep them notes down there," Calvin commanded the fat man. The girl set a Budweiser in front of Dorsey, refilled Pentz's glass with ice and scotch, and walked to stand before Jack. She stuck each thumb in the corresponding front pockets of her jeans and pitched her head back. Her breasts bounced beneath a tight black sweater, and Jack watched a tiny silver cross pitch outward until its chain lost all of its slack. As the cross dropped to rest in her cleavage, he raised his eyes to meet hers and was embarrassed for his curiosity. She smiled, leaned forward, and kissed him lightly on the lips.

"I wish you would take me far away," she whispered, inches from his mouth, her warm breath caressing his lips, her hazel eyes very beautiful and captivating. For just a moment, they were all Jack could see, and he wanted to jump in and get lost in whatever stirred within. She stayed close, and her steady breathing warmed his face. Jack let the moment thaw his spirit entirely, a welcome reprieve.

"Me too," he whispered softly without moving his eyes, and then he mouthed the words again, "*Me too.*" Jack dropped his gaze to his hands, to the gold band on his left ring finger. "Better just bring me another Stroh's, Ronnie," he mumbled, and her heat began to fade away from him as quickly as it had taken him. Veronica shrugged, smiled wanly, and turned away.

Jack tipped his bottle up and finished the beer as she retrieved another. He eyed his compatriots along the bar. Despite the jokes and crudities, an undercurrent of sadness always lingered, a certain unspoken dissatisfaction. They shared a forgotten corner of the world where they could feel isolated for a while, safe from further damage. In time they would walk away, leave the bar behind them, temporarily fortified until the next time reality clubbed them right between the eyes. And then they would come back.

"Hey, Stymie," cried Dorsey, waving his bottle in the general direction of Calvin. "I hear they found a cure for sickle cell anemia."

Calvin, his graying head still bowed, looked sidelong at Dorsey. "You be careful, now, homes," he warned, shaking an index finger at the tall man.

"They call it—hey, I'm serious here, dipshit," Dorsey said to the small man on his immediate right who had already began to chuckle. "They call it *work!*"

Calvin stared down at his hands atop the bar; the small man chortled. Finally, Calvin clenched his fists and brought them down heavily on the bar top, knocking over an empty bottle of Bud in the process. It rolled off the bar and shattered on the floor at the girl's feet.

"*Jesus H., Calvin!*" She spun and strode off angrily in search of the broom and a dustpan.

"Got-damn Dorsey," Calvin snarled, "I'm gonna fix your honky ass!" With great deliberation and suspense, he reached into his jacket pocket. Dorsey leaned back slowly and rigidly. "*Once and for all,*" Calvin announced dramatically. With a great flourish, he pulled a pen from his pocket. The small man tittered nervously. "I'm gonna go write your name and number on the wall in the ladies' room. Then they can find out for themselves what a little prick you really is!" Calvin intentionally brutalized the Queen's English for effect.

By now all the men were laughing, including Dorsey. Calvin rose to his feet and strutted toward the unlighted hallway that led to the restrooms. Pentz stood, raised a chubby finger, and announced, "Don't bother, my pigmented friend. That's common knowledge throughout the free world!"

The men all laughed, even Jack, now into his third or fourth beer; he'd lost count. The girl cleared her throat in mock disgust as she emptied the dustpan, the shards of glass tinkling into the trash can, her anger over the plight of the old, deaf flower woman now forgotten.

"Give the rest of these bums one too, Ronnie," said Jack, pointing down the bar. The girl took the twenty he slid her way and returned to the cooler to repeat the ritual. Finished, she rang up the damages and brought Jack his change. He pushed it into the well that ran along the inside of the bar.

"Hey, Ronnie," called Calvin, waving a twenty of his own, "how's about givin' us all a shot of Black Jack?"

"*Black* Jack. That figures," said Dorsey.

"Pour one for yourself too, babe," Calvin said.

"Ahhhhh, what the hell," she said to no one in particular as she took six shot glasses from under the bar and lined them up in a tight row. Ronnie poured the shots and the banter flowed, neatly lubricated by the beer and the booze. A large cloud of cigarette smoke lay motionless over the room. From the street came muffled reverberations as cars continued to hurry away: to home, to families, to empty apartments—to wherever commuters fled when they left the city. It was Friday, and traffic grew heavier and more insistent in its exodus.

The girl and the five men lifted their glasses as Dorsey announced, "To Chesty Puller, wherever you are!" All six drained their shots and slammed shot glasses onto the bar. They did not notice that they were being left behind to fend for themselves, and they did not care, so they joked and laughed and drank and smoked. It was their private world, and they did not need the one outside. It would be there waiting when the time came for them to leave.

The barroom dialogue was abruptly interrupted. A car horn blared in the street, immediately followed by a long screech of rubber skidding on cement, and then a solid thump as something bounced off the outside of the bar's front door.

"What the hell was that?" asked the little man as the rest of his companions rose in unison and rushed toward the door. Jack got there first and quickly jerked it open. On the sidewalk at his feet, grotesquely twisted and misshapen, lay the old woman. Her artificial flowers were scattered about the street and sidewalk. She did not move. A white Chevy Impala peeled away and was immediately lost in traffic.

Dorsey bent over the old woman and tugged lightly on her right shoulder. She fell back without resistance, head bobbing. A thin line of blood ran away from her hair and into the cracks in the cement, through the cigarette butts and trash, until it pooled in the dirt where a chunk of sidewalk was missing.

"Damn it, *goddamn it*," Dorsey yelled, "call EMS, Ronnie! Call nine-one-one!"

Another vagrant, pushing a rusted shopping cart filled with rags and empty bottles and cans, grabbed Jack by the elbow. "Who da fucks is dat?" he said in a raspy voice. "Who da fucks is dat?" His rheumy eyes rolled slowly from Jack to the old woman, and then back to Jack. Jack did not answer. He looked down at the woman.

Pentz was turning very pale. Jack bent at the waist and leaned over the woman, across her body from Dorsey, and took her wrist between the thumb and first two fingers of his right hand. He saw blood trickle from her nose, her ears, from the corner of her lazy eye, and he blanched. Dorsey stared at the old woman as if waiting for her to wake up.

"Too late," said Jack, standing. "She's gone."

Calvin watched the blood stream away from the woman to form a small red sea in the middle of the sidewalk. He rushed toward the street, doubled forward, and vomited on the hood of a red Toyota. The little man began picking up the blue and red and orange flowers.

"It's too late, it's too late," Dorsey repeated mindlessly. He held her throat gently in his long fingers. There was no pulse. She was indeed dead, dead and gone. The tall man put his hands over his face for a moment and then crossed his arms over his chest, embracing himself.

Off the Path

"Goddamn," he said. "GODDAMN! Why do they let old, deaf women walk around by themselves? Goddamn it!" No one answered. Jack took off his Ford windbreaker and covered the old woman's head and shoulders.

"She shoulda been in a home someplace for deaf old ladies that ain't got nobody to take care of 'em," Dorsey moaned. "She shouldn'a been walkin' around loose! *Shit!*" Dorsey was now screaming at the cars that darted past. No one stopped or even looked. No one cared.

After minutes that no one measured, an ambulance showed up, followed by a police car. The men on the sidewalk told what little they knew and were dismissed. The cop returned Jack's Ford jacket, and he walked up the street. He found himself at the next block before he realized that he'd passed his car. He doubled back and tried not to think, tried not to think of anything at all. But he felt sick inside just the same. Up the street, the church bell atop the First Methodist Church pealed five times.

Chapter Nine

The setting sun turned the western sky a vivid pink as it fell into the horizon and left the heavens in a cascade of peaceful, melding shades of salmon and fuchsia, through lavender, and into the deep purples and dark blues that signaled the day's final retreat. Directly above, a smattering of stars could be seen, and the moon, large, yellow, and nearly full, was on the rise.

Terry Ralls sat on the top step of his cement porch, sipping beer from a can and listening to a portable radio perched on the window sill behind him. The Tigers were losing to the Boston Red Sox, and Terry Ralls was not amused. "Jesus, boys, it's Bahh-ston, c'mon already!"

Terry took another pull from the beer can, stood, and peered at the house across the street. He wondered what Jack Thomas was doing. Often, one of the two men strolled across his lawn and the street to join the other for a little beer and small talk. They shared a love of baseball, and the Tigers in particular, and cold beer was okay too.

Terry stood and spotted Jack's car, parked haphazardly at an off angle in his driveway. He reckoned that Jack had stayed perhaps a bit too long at the Avenue Bar. Curly was asleep on the Thomases' porch, stretched out on his right side, legs extended straight. The inner, wooden front door was open, but looking through the screen door, the house appeared dark and still. Terry walked his eyes back across the lawns and sat back down on his porch.

Terry surveyed the street he'd lived on for over fifteen years, noting the trees that had grown tall and those that were gone. The street was named Bull Run Way after the Civil War battle, the first major fight of that war, during which well-to-do citizens of nearby Washington, DC, rode out in carriages to picnic and watch the Union Army vanquish the Confederates. It hadn't worked out that way: the rebels had home-field advantage, and the Yankees were routed, dispersed, and chased out of Virginia—for the time being, at least.

Bull Run Way transformed but little in Terry's time, other than the new house across the street and two doors north, which replaced an apple orchard some five years ago. It currently sat empty with a *For Sale* sign out front, another victim of the struggling local economy. *Last up, first down*, he pondered.

He looked in the other direction at the oldest house on the block, the Koski house, a white, two-story Gothic from another time that didn't match the rest on the block. Terry could see the outline of Stan Koski, long widowed, rocking slowly in the shadows on his porch, where he could be seen most every night when it wasn't too cold for his old bones. Terry waved when he thought the old guy looked his way, but there was no response. *Probably can't see this far*, Terry thought, and he considered strolling over there for a visit. Stan's thoughts on the plight of the Tigers were always highly entertaining.

Behind Terry, another screen door opened with a slight squeak, and a woman poked her head through the break. "How're the boys doing, babe?" she asked.

"They're losing three to one in the fifth. Petry can't find his ass with both hands tonight," he said, slowly shaking his head.

"Well, fear not; it's early. I'm going upstairs to read—gonna be out heah long?" She put a thick Southern drawl on the last line and then batted her eyelids.

"I don't know, sugar … little while longer, I guess," he said, turning slightly to face the woman in the doorway. "Will you bring me another beer before you go up?"

The woman stepped fully outside and playfully rubbed the top of Terry's head. "You'd better call 1-800-I'M BALD, or start combing your hair different, maybe over to the side. You know, a comb-over. Getting a little thin up here. Some gypsy woman might start reading fortunes off the top of your dome."

Terry grabbed her behind the knees in the crook of his arm. She didn't resist as he pulled her down until she was seated on his lap. He then wrapped his arms around her and gave a good squeeze. "Easy, big fella! Fragile merchandise!" She kissed his forehead, then his nose, before resting her lips on his, kissing him softly, tenderly. "Ya big ape," she whispered.

"Katherine, have I told you lately that I love you?" He stared into her hazel eyes, their noses touching at their tips. In the background, Tigers' announcer Ernie Harwell's voice rose in tone and excitement.

"Parrish swings … it's a high fly ball to deep left center field … and that one is LOOOOONG GONE! Three-run homer for Parrish, and the Tigers now lead, four to three!"

"Well, that was a tender moment. *Was*," she sighed, and then shook her head and began to rise. Terry held on. "You want that beer, Skippy? Let go of me!" She feigned anger, but Terry knew she wasn't mad, not really. She kissed him on the nose again, and he let her up.

"If they don't win, you can just keep your big butt out here *all night*," she warned.

"Oh, really? And if they win?" He arched his left eyebrow and formed a leer.

"Dahlin'," the Southern belle had returned, "you just climb those stairs and come see me sometime, heah?" Katie turned and walked away with an exaggerated sashay, her hips swaying from side to side, right hand on her waist. Terry watched. *It was a beautiful thing*, he thought, *a beautiful thing. What did I ever do to deserve her?* He shook his head and smiled.

Terry stood, picked up the radio, and switched it off. "Sorry, boys," he advised the Tigers, "you're on your own tonight. The South has risen!"

He shut and locked the screen door behind him; old Stan Koski would have to wait for another night. Terry turned to find Katie standing at the foot of the stairs, pulling her pink T-shirt over her head.

"Well, Scarlett, I do declare," said Terry, now a Southern gentleman.

✫   ✫   ✫

Across the street, behind that screen door, as the last lights crept in and out of the room, Jackson Thomas sat in a rocking chair and faced the large glass door wall that overlooked his backyard. He sipped Irish whiskey, smoked cigarettes, and tried not to think of all that had happened. He felt himself spinning downward in a maelstrom's descent, as powerless as a tiny spider, caught in a funnel of water, sucked down a drain, lost forever.

But was it that *dramatic*, he wondered, or just circumstance? *Maybe I take this shit too seriously.* He got up and opened the front screen door, and Curly sauntered in and sat on the floor next to Jack's chair. The dog looked up at the man, now also seated, and tilted his head.

"We're the only ones left, Curly." Jack scratched the dog's head. Curly yawned and flopped down. "Does that mean yes or no?" Jack asked.

Curly did not speak. Instead, the dog dozed off, content to leave life's riddles to someone else. Jack, however, felt no such relief. He drained the last of his whiskey and closed his eyes. From the kitchen, he phoned Angie at the cabin. They spoke briefly as he paced the length of the phone's accordion cord, and then he ended the connection.

After several moments of self-flagellation over his fumbled words, Jack called her again. She told the man that she loved him, and that she and the boy would be home Sunday. Angie sounded different in a way that Jack interpreted with hope in his heart, for the first time in a long time. He wasn't sure why, but he felt it; he was *sure* of it.

Jack refilled his whiskey glass and returned to the rocker. He Jack was exhausted, physically and mentally. He was confused, and all efforts toward reason evaded him, zigzagging like leaves in a brisk breeze. He missed his wife. There were too many leaves in life, he decided: green in spring, brown in death, and all the colors in between, hanging tall in the highest oak trees, autumn's flourish of colors their last gasp, to then die and flutter to the ground, swept up, blown away, raked, collected, or burned. *Do we live for one season,* he wondered, *when our colors are at their most robust, only to fade and wither and disappear?*

Jack briefly considered driving up to the cabin to be with Angie, but it was late, and a long drive for a man who'd been drinking for several hours. He took a sip of whiskey, replaced the glass on the end table, and closed his eyes. Sleep soon overtook him, effortlessly, stealthily, thoroughly. His chin dropped to his chest, but he continued to rock in the chair, very slowly; back, slight pause, forward, slight pause, back, and so on. The chair creaked weakly at each restart.

In sleep, Jack entered another world, "not of sight and sound," as Rod Serling would have described it. At first his dream was foggy, and then at once it burst into a dazzling midday sun. It was very still, and Jack, although unaware, was no longer Jack, as his senses slowly returned.

Apples lay rotting in tall grass under a hot mid-September sun. Ants carried them away in tiny shreds and yellow jackets tried to suck them dry. Those few apples still on the trees clung desperately to branches, wary of the inevitable fall to earth. Squirrels scampered in and out of this pathetic orchard and stole apples. They sampled in quick nibbles and rushed away to store the fruit in a secret place, long forgotten by winter's return. Jack was now as a boy, not quite a man. He sat on an oak stump in the shade of the oldest and tallest apple tree and stared at the squirrels foraging in the grove.

An old hound named Massa stretched out in the shade of the youngest apple tree and occasionally snapped at flies. They buzzed his ears, bit his back, and generally annoyed him. Tiny blue clouds filled Massa's dark brown eyes, robbing him in pieces of his sight, and his legs twitched of their own accord. He'd quit running off squirrels a long time ago, and the little bastards knew it. An apple fell from a tree, landed beside the boy, rolled a few feet down a gentle slope, and came to rest in tall grass.

The boy saw his father, hacking, chopping, and slashing with an ax at the huge stump of an oak tree, cursing softly in the twilight. His father struggled to clear the trees and expand his little orchard, but these giant oaks had proven formidable foes. His mother walked out of a thick mist and into the hot sunshine of the grove.

"That old oak tree ever gonna give up the ghost, Rafe?" the woman asked. She was smiling, her hair the color of mahogany in the last light of afternoon. She was very beautiful, her green eyes filled with speckles of gold, cast randomly throughout like tiny flower petals in a gentle breeze. The boy remembered that gold dancing in the woman's eyes as she sat before the fireplace on a winter's night, and the flames, reflected in an emerald sea, were so lovely.

His father, shaking his head, walked away from the stump and into the mist. He'd marched off two springs ago with General Pickett to win the big war up north and left a gold locket with the woman to remember him by. He never returned, except in the haze.

The boy's father had fallen in a cornfield in Pennsylvania at a place called Gettysburg. From the fog he now reappeared, staggering, his hands pressed against a gushing hole in his chest, his eyes wide with fear and shock as life poured through his fingers and cascaded to the dirt at his feet. And then he dropped to his knees and was lost, swallowed by the mist.

Word came some weeks after the battle that his father had died honorably with his comrades and was buried with them near the cornfield. His mother, sullen and silent after the news from Gettysburg, sat in the small cottage and stared at the locket, reading its inscription again and again:

ALWAYS IN LIFE

YOURS TO BE

Her eyes were lifeless and the gold speckles were gone, the sea of green flat and still, and then she was only a memory. They were both gone, into the fog, but sometimes the boy saw them as they once were. He could sometimes make the mist come and go, if he sat still and thought about it very deliberately. But he couldn't make it stay, and he couldn't enter into it either.

Massa labored slowly to his feet and began to lumber toward the boy. Each step brought him new miseries. The sun was at its crest and was unmercifully hot as katydids screeched from high atop trees in the forest. The dog reeled slightly, dizzy from the heat and exertion, and lost his way. The boy watched as the dog fell forward, his legs collapsing beneath him. The boy rose slowly, and then he ran to the dog, calling his name.

"Massa! Massa! Easy, boy, easy!"

The dog staggered and fell, sprawled in the dying grass amid the rotting apples and ants and yellow jackets. His eyes were now entirely a pale blue, filled with the skies and oceans he had never seen. Massa could faintly hear the boy's gentle voice, soothing him from somewhere in the distance, as the old hound slipped nearer the void.

The boy buried Massa at precisely the spot where the old hound surrendered his life. The boy did not cry outwardly. There were no tears in his eyes, nothing there to give, but he felt a crushing sadness in his heart. He knew that Massa had gone into the mist.

Jack walked down the dirt road with his great-grandfather's musket and never looked back. He walked north and joined Lee's army in its retreat, backward with honor, into Virginia. He saw many men fall, and himself sent three Yankees into the mist with the old musket.

The gold locket was in a front pocket of his well-worn butternut coat, near his heart, when a Minié ball found the boy near Appomattox. He fell on his back and lay motionless for several moments before mustering the strength to sit up slightly and look at the wound. His bowels were leaping, squirming, twisting out of a gash in his stomach, and there was no way to put them back. The boy was now a dying man, a gut-shot soldier. He took the gold locket from his coat pocket and squeezed it with the last of his strength. Vapors surrounded and swallowed him whole as he stared into the sun and let himself die.

In his fist, clenched forever in death, was the gold locket.

ALWAYS IN LIFE

YOURS TO BE

Jack awoke and gazed through the door wall as the real world refocused. The dream and its mist faded away. Jack could not recall a time in his life when he'd dreamed with such detail, such clarity. Would he remember this dream tomorrow, or in two weeks? He sat for a long time, slowly rocking, wondering what it meant. *There was not a glimmer of hope in that dream,* he thought, *not one flicker.*

His sleep had been ephemeral and brought Jack no rest or relief. He wanted to go upstairs, collapse into bed, feel Angie's warmth, and absorb it with his own, but that sanctuary was empty, and what dreams awaited him there? The rocker continued to squeak toward the dawn.

✫   ✫   ✫

Next door on Bull Run Way, Stan Koski swayed slowly back and forth on an ancient, straight-backed rocking chair that creaked and teetered uncertainly, all part of its well-worn comfort. The porch moaned softly with each forward roll, a muted protest. Stan came out to the porch most late afternoons, as weather permitted, rocking slowly into the twilight. A small radio on the table beside Stan brought the Tigers' game to the porch, beside a cup of tea that had gone cold hours ago.

Though Stan was an old man, well into his eighties, many in the neighborhood still called him "Stan the Man." Few of them remembered Stan Musial, the *true* Stan the Man, but Koski did. *What a sweet stroke that guy had,* he thought. *Saw him play in Cincinnati once, against the Reds, and they don't make 'em like that anymore, no sir, guys swingin' from their heels and hitting .250—and making ten, twenty times the dough that Musial made!* He shook his head and would have spit into the evening if his mouth weren't so dry.

His wife, Hildie, always called him Stosh, but she'd been gone for nearly thirteen years now. God, how he loved that woman, even still! Why had he been left behind, to hang on to life for so long after Hildie had gone on to her final reward? It frightened him to think that perhaps he had no final reward coming, that *this was it*. Maybe all he'd been entitled to in life was Hildie, that one glimpse of beauty and love for all of eternity, the rest of time to be spent tottering alone on the old porch, forgotten. He hated such thoughts, but he had no real choice. He was too wise to be optimistic, and far too old to be hopeful.

Stan wrapped a faded and tattered blue blanket around his legs in defiance of spring's chill and looked to the west. The blue sky turned a stony gray that moved steadily toward the porch. In a few minutes the sun would be gone, and late shadows would move in until they in turn were consumed by the night.

The porch upon which Stan sat and rocked was attached to the front of a house built shortly before World War One, "the war to end all wars," when what was now a neighborhood had been mostly an apple and pear tree orchard. The Koski house faced west, and from here Stan could sit and watch the sun set every night, a steady descent into a high tree line of oaks and elms and maples a mile or so away, before it was gone, leaving an old man alone in the dark.

Stan's thoughts tonight ambled unhurriedly back in time. The man who'd built the house, a doctor named Sutcliffe, died in Belgium at a place called Belleau Wood. Stan had gotten as far as France, briefly, but there his WWI adventure ended when the armistice was declared. "I didn't even get to Paris," he often complained to Hildie.

"Just as well," she'd reply. "Those mademoiselles would have never let you go!" She overestimated his prowess in *chemins de l'amour,* and he loved her for that too.

Now the old man fondly recalled the first time he'd seen Hildie. He and some friends had gone to a church picnic at St. Agnes (long gone; now a nursing home). It was late April and everyone was outside, basking in the birth of spring, the death of winter, and the first real warmth since the war ended the previous November. A band of local musicians played atop a stage of straw bales beside a grassy green knoll as young couples danced and mingled below.

Stan was not a dancer, so he shied away from the crowd. Young, single girls queued up under the pink-and-white umbrellas of freshly blossomed cherry trees that filled the air with a sweet, inviting scent. It was warm and it was spring, and the sun smiled on a tiny spot in its world, briefly at peace.

And then Stan saw Hildie. She was the most beautiful vision he had ever seen, with hair the color of black walnut and eyes so blue they could break the heart of Satan himself. He rose to the occasion with unprecedented self-confidence and danced with her in the gloaming, his heart leaping beyond shyness and into elation. She forgave his awkwardness, he thought, but she had, in fact, not even noticed it, and in her eyes twinkled all of Stan's dreams, afloat in calm, blue seas.

Stan realized, as they swayed together in a spring breeze, that there was nothing else in all God's universe. Eternity waltzed in three-quarter time as Stan and Hildie fell in love. They were married four months later, and it lasted over fifty years, most of them in this house on Bull Run Way, both knowing that there could be no finer thing in life.

They created two children together. The first, a boy they named Michael, after Hildie's father, died on some godforsaken hill in Korea, a place so pitiful that it was known by a number instead of a name. The second, a girl named Rose, after his mother, shaved her head and joined the Krishnas in the sixties, and Stan hadn't heard from her since Hildie's funeral, thirteen years ago come July. He thought of Rosie often, but had not a clue how to reach out to her, or even where she was these days.

Ever since Hildie's passing, the old man spent the better part of every day rocking back and forth on this sagging old porch, just dreaming of his Hildie, of cherry tree blossoms in spring, and missing her so very much. Losing his son had been a crushing blow, which he and Hildie fought through mostly together; however, each endured moments of deep grief that they kept to themselves. Stan knew that Hildie sent Rosie money on a regular basis, but he said nothing of it. What was there to say?

Autumn came to the porch earlier each year, it seemed, arriving as a chill in the old man's bones that finally drove him into the empty house to sit before the fireplace, alone in the orange glow of a blaze that never truly warmed him. He felt so alone, and life had become little more than a dull throb in his tired heart. When you lose the love of your life, he understood, there was nothing left to do but wait, and so he waited.

Stan's eyes followed the sidewalk that split his yard from driveway to porch, but his failing sight could see only as far as the Thomases' house next door. *Left my damn glasses in the house again,* he thought. He knew that the world stretched and sprawled much further beyond, but it was now out of sight, out of his grasp.

Stan gazed past clarity and into the blurred outskirts of his vision. There he saw the silhouette of a woman, a young woman, he thought, as she briskly walked toward him, and the streetlight at the end of his driveway enveloped her like a ghostly halo. There was a slight sway to her gait, a *lilt,* as if a band played a delicate waltz in her ears for her private and personal enjoyment.

Suddenly, Stan sat up straight and went rigid as the rocker stopped its roll on the porch. All of the old parts—his legs, the chair's, the porch itself—moaned softly. *Jesus,* he thought, *she walks just like Hildie did, the same way!* He rubbed his weary eyes, his heart now pumping with a fervor not felt for many years. He looked again to the west, but she was gone.

Stan Koski peered above and beyond the lawns and trees and into the evening sky. He stopped breathing when he again saw the young woman swaying up his walk and toward the porch. Stan carefully, slowly, pushed himself up from the arms of the old chair.

"Hildie! Hildie! Oh Lord, Hilda, is it really you?"

The young woman was at the foot of the porch steps when she looked up into the pale brown eyes of a lonely old man. She did not speak. She merely smiled with a radiance that seemed to relight the entire horizon.

"Hildie, my honey," Stan whispered hoarsely, "I have missed you so ... please ... *please* ... come to me ..." His words trailed off as he reached out to touch her, to hold her, to again sway with her as one. He was certain that he smelled cherry blossoms, tantalizing him sweetly. And then she was gone.

The old man stumbled down the steps, grabbing at air that just moments ago had been his Hildie. He staggered and fell to his knees, looking desperately to the west, instantly cold, a silly old fool in the damp grass. Stan picked himself up slowly, pain stinging his legs. He heard and felt his tired joints as they strained to lift him one more time. He climbed the three steps with great effort and sat back down in the chair.

Stan Koski stared wistfully into the heavens above, then again to the west. He slumped in the chair and bowed his head. He did not rock. He looked to his knees, at the wet, green grass stains on his pants, and cursed them softly. If only these old bones had been a little quicker, a little *younger*, Stan might have held her again, if only for just an instant.

"Dear God," he implored, "I would cheerfully give you my every breath just to hold my lover for *one more moment!*"

Stan Koski ignored the persistent throbbing in his chest and closed his eyes tight. Why did she have to die first? Why had he been left behind and alone for so very long? He had been abandoned here, and he did not know what he waited for. At Hildie's funeral, a priest assured Stan that he and Hildie would one day be reunited on God's golden shore, but that had been a long, long time ago. He wondered if maybe this, this *now*, was all that there was.

The old man sat still as tears made their relentless, hopeless journey from his tired heart to his fading brown eyes, pushing their way out, running down his cheeks through the deep creases that a long lifetime had left behind. He saw the world now through a membrane of loneliness and despair, and a bottomless ache engulfed his core like a storm at sea.

Stan remained motionless until he slowly opened his eyes, raised his head, and looked into the sky before him. A lone white cloud cut through the darkness, drifting nearer and nearer. The old man righted himself in the chair and was mesmerized.

"Is this another phantom, Lord," he said, "or am I losing my mind?" He spoke quietly, still peering into the sky. The white cloud glided surely until it hovered above the street in front of Stan's house. He remained paralyzed and asked no further questions of God, who thus far had been silent, apparently unstirred by the old man's pleas.

A mist slowly descended until its outer edge rested on the porch's top step and spread open. Stan sat frozen in his chair. There, within the cloud, shrouded in gold and silver so bright that it stung Stan's eyes, stood Hildie, just as she had been on that spring day in 1919. She beckoned to him with her hands, seduced him with a smile that carried a promise of forever in her embrace. He smelled cherry blossoms and heard a gentle, swaying waltz that played somewhere within the cloud.

"Come to me, Stosh," she sang sweetly, "and we'll dance through eternity, just you and me. Come to me …"

The old man stood up straight. At once he was no longer old, but young and vibrant, full of hopes and dreams. All the pain and dullness and loneliness swept away like dry dust as the last breath of this life left his body. He rode a wisp of smoke into the brilliant illuminations of the cloud, and they were as gone as the sweet scent of cherry that wafted into the night.

Chapter Ten

Some two hundred and fifty miles north, night settled on a "rustic cabin" with central air, a microwave, two telephones, and satellite TV. Davie switched off the lamp on the night table just about the time the lights went out for good on Stan Koski. Davie had grown close to Stan, performing small tasks and errands for the old man, and his much-appreciated service as a reader. Davie would be deeply saddened to learn of his friend's passing, but for now, he was blissfully ignorant.

He sat up, weight on his elbows, and looked out the window, where moonlight shimmered on the small lake beyond the glass. Across the room, the door opened with a faint squeak, and a woman's head poked into the opening.

"You okay, Davie?" Aunt Angie whispered sweetly.

"Sure, Aunt Angie," the boy replied. "I'm okay. You?"

"Finer than frogs' hair," Angie called back as she crossed the room and approached the boy's bed.

The boy giggled and dropped onto his back. "Frogs don't have hair," he stated emphatically.

"Sure they do. It's just so fine," she was now over the boy, tickling his ribs, "you can't *see* it!"

Davie laughed as he squirmed and half-heartedly struggled to escape Angie's funny fingers. She leaned down and kissed him on the forehead. "Try to get to sleep soon, darlin'. Maybe tomorrow we can go fishing or something."

"Gonna rain tomorrow," the boy said with certainty.

"That's not what the weather guy said, smarty-pants," she said, straightening the bedcovers.

"Aw, he doesn't know his butt from third base," Davie replied.

Now it was her turn to laugh. She straightened and dramatically slapped her hands against her hips. "Now where did you ever hear *that* one?"

"From Mr. Stan. It's what he calls," Davie paused, squinted, and said slowly, "a 'co-loco-kwee-lis-a-lim.'"

Angie sniggered and covered her face with both hands. "I believe the term is *colloquialism*, young sir. That's a pretty good one too, I must admit." She bent down and kissed him again. "Go to sleep, just in case it *is* a nice day, okay?"

"Okay, but it's gonna rain," he said confidently. With that, he rolled onto his side and closed his eyes. Angie smiled, shook her head, turned, and quietly left the room, closing the door behind her.

The door clicked shut, and Davie again looked out the window. The moon was almost in full bloom now, and it cast a faint pallor in his room. He thought of big fish lurking in the lake's waters, waiting for him to cast a worm in just the right spot. He could make out the edge of the short pier that cut into the lake, maybe twenty feet in length, from which he would launch his attack. He wished Uncle Jack were there. *He'd take me out in the rowboat, and we could go get the really big ones.*

But Uncle Jack was home, alone, and that thought brought a twinge of sadness to the boy. Davie examined the corner to the right of the window and saw a baseball and two gloves on the floor, and a Louisville Slugger bat standing upright, leaning, waiting for someone to play with, another reminder of his uncle.

Something was wrong, and Davie knew it, but youth kept comprehension out of reach, out of sight, beyond his grasp. Those times the boy, his aunt, and his uncle spent together were increasingly rare, and when they did occur, a certain tension pulsed between the man and his wife. Davie closed his eyes and pressed their lids tightly shut.

"God, if you can hear me, make it better, okay?" Davie whispered to the window.

He opened his eyes, and the moon darkened as a cloud passed, casting the lake away and dimming the natural light in the room. For an instant, Davie thought he saw two bright emerald eyes, burning from the darkness near the lake, watching him. He sat up in bed, too frightened to move to the window and look closer. He chose instead to lie flat, pull the covers up and over his head. When it remained quiet for several moments, Davie slowly lowered the covers and peeked toward the window.

There was nothing, only the branches of the trees alongside the house, swaying in the breeze, and soft moonlight reflected by the lake. Davie kept vigil until sleep retrieved him, and he wandered into that peaceful territory between consciousness and slumber. In a turn of time immeasurable to the boy, he became aware that he was sitting on the bank of a river, watching it lazily roll by and away. Crickets and cicadas and bullfrogs sang their discordant tunes, cicadas hitting the high notes while bullfrogs handled the bass.

Over a short time, their noise became a song, faintly familiar to Davie as he kicked off his shoes and socks and dropped his feet into the cool water. "Boy, I wish I had a fishin' pole," he said to the river. From his right Davie heard the sound of oars slapping at the river, and he saw an old wooden rowboat draw near, its dull red paint flaking to reveal water and weather-worn wood. On its left bow, in a neat script in faded white, were the words *Queen Hilda*.

Davie smiled when he saw the old man aboard, steering the craft toward the bank, a battered sailor's hat on his head. It looked old enough to have been left by Gilligan on the island, assuming he wasn't still there, screwing up everything he touched.

"Davie boy!" the old man in the boat called out. "The man says he wants to go fishin', so c'mon aboard, bud! I got two poles, a bucket o' worms, a jug o' iced tea, some cheese sammiches, and all day to do nothin'!"

"Mr. Stan! What're *you* doin' here?" Davie blurted as he stood and caught a tattered rope that the old man tossed his way.

"Pull me in a little and hop on," Stan Koski instructed. "Don't forget your shoes!" Davie did as instructed, climbed aboard, and took a seat on the bench near the stern, and soon they were one with the river. A vivid sun highlighted a brilliantly blue and cloudless sky, and a cool breeze kissed their faces. It was a perfect day, they both agreed.

"What say," Stan said as he turned and rubbed the boy's head, "we go over by Gopher Island and cast our lines there? Bet we hook a few big ones!"

"Yeah, that sounds good," Davie said. "We caught that big ol' catfish there, 'member?"

"What I recall is how good that fat rascal tasted with cornbread and corn on the cob!" Both chuckled at the memory. Stan Koski reached into a small Coleman cooler under the bench he sat upon at the center of the boat, pulled out a well-traveled hat, and handed it the boy. The Detroit Tigers' white olde English *D* sat proudly on a bed of dark blue and felt right at home on Davie's head. He didn't care that it was two sizes too big, and only his ears held it up.

"Thanks, Mr. Stan. Now we're ready!"

"You betcha!" Stan exclaimed. "Off we go!" Stan took the oars and lazily rowed toward the middle of the river, its waters oddly calm and flat, not another vessel in sight. Davie found two fishing poles and separated them from a short-lived entanglement they had engaged themselves in. No matter how careful and meticulous one was, such things drew together in tangles, like Christmas lights left neatly alone in their boxes in attics and basements, only to confound all once again come December.

"It's a day like this you've really got to appreciate, Davie," Stan said with conviction. "It's not every day when everything is just this *right*. You really gotta *grab* life when it gives itself to you like this!"

Davie nodded his head. He didn't always understand everything the old man said, but he always tried to file it away for future reference. He reckoned that one day these pearls would behoove him, help him understand life as it whirled through and around him.

Gopher Island was a half mile or so downstream, and the old man seemed in no hurry to get there. "Davie, have you ever heard the expression 'time marches on'?" asked Stan.

"Sure; Uncle Jack says that all the time," the boy replied. "He says it means you can't stop the clock, like you're a football team with no more time-outs."

"Yeah, that's about right," Stan said, slowly working the oars. "Except, even if you *had* a time-out, you couldn't *use* it, you know what I mean? The old referee in the sky has lost his whistle, and so the game goes on whether you're ready to play or not." Stan tried to rub away a dull ache in his lower back without success.

Stan looked at Davie, who tilted his head slightly to the side, a perplexed expression on his young, unblemished face. The old man dropped the oars into the boat, and the vessel drifted almost imperceptibly in calm waters. The river seemed at a virtual stop, as if someone had hit its Pause button.

"Remember when I told you about my Hildie," Stan said, "and how she passed? How hard I fought against that! But no matter what I did or felt or said, or how hard I prayed, I couldn't stop it, couldn't even slow it down, not by a whisker. When the Lord puts something in motion, no matter how contrary it is to us, that's it, and nothing short of a miracle will change it."

Davie felt sad for the old man. "I wish *you* coulda had a miracle, Mr. Stan, I wish *you* coulda stopped the clock. I know how much you miss Missus Hildie." He turned and looked down, into the deep blue-and-green mysteries of the river. For an instant, the boy thought he saw a woman's face smile up to him, but he blinked, and she was gone.

Stan took Davie's small left hand in his large right hand and gave it a fond squeeze. "I know, son, I know. But we gotta accept things as they come to us, because it's just like this river. It's always going *somewhere*, and it's never the same. Where we are now will be a long way off an hour from now. It will look the same here, in this spot, but the river will be *completely different*, ya know?"

Davie nodded and looked into Stan's brown eyes. They had paled since Davie had boarded the rowboat, and now Stan Koski looked much, much older. Davie could see *through* the old man to the trees and grassy banks beyond. "Are you okay, Mr. Stan?" the boy asked.

"Yeah, boy, I'm okay," Stan said, his voice now a little hoarse. "But my ride on the river's getting near the end the line."

"No, it's not!" Davie cried out. "You gotta long ways to go, lots more time on the clock!" He stood and pointed ahead, upstream. "Look ahead, Mr. Stan. You can't even see the end of the river!"

An unseen finger released the Pause button and the river began to move, slowly at first, then steadily picking up speed. Stan Koski picked up the oars, but changed his mind and set them back down, two dull thuds against the hull of the old boat. They seemed to be gliding faster down the river, all control lost, and Davie grew frightened.

"What's goin' on, Mr. Stan? What's goin' on?"

"Everything is fine, son. Don't be afraid," Stan assured the boy. "Take my hand. I promise, everything is fine. Look, up ahead, upstream—do you see that?"

Davie peered through the old man's right shoulder and eyed a reddish-orange glow in the distance. The banks of the river had disappeared, faded away, and with them all the noises and songs of nature were stilled. Fear left the boy, replaced by a wonder at all that he saw and sensed. *Funny*, he thought, *it smells like cherry blossoms.*

"Almost time for me to get off, Davie," the old man called out, "but there's still a whole lot of river for you to ride down!" Stan grabbed the boy with both hands and lifted him up and toward the front of the boat. "Look, son, look! Do you see her?"

Straight ahead of the timeworn, faded red rowboat sat a gleaming silver sailboat, its intensely gold sail flapping in the breeze. At its bow stood a beautiful woman in a sky-blue dress, her left hand on her hip, black hair flowing behind her, waving with her right at the boy and the man.

"Davie, this is the end of the line for old Stan. Don't be afraid, and don't be sad. Stay in the boat and it will take you home," the old man said. "I'm proud to have known you, son. Keep me in your heart, and someday, a long, long time from now, but sooner than you'd believe, we'll go fishin' again. Okay?"

Stan stood as the wind turned brisk. Davie, filled with awe and not a little panic, threw his left hand up just too late to catch the old Detroit Tigers cap as it flew off his head. It vanished as Davie reached out to reclaim it. When he turned to the bow again, the old man and the beautiful woman were together on the sailboat. They waved to Davie and then turned to face one another. They locked in a tight embrace and shared a long, deep kiss, and the years melted away from Stan Koski. In a heartbeat, they were a young couple, dressed in old-timey spring finery, waltzing across the deck of the sailboat.

The silver sailboat with the gold sail was soon alight, and then it vanished into the reddish-orange horizon. They were gone. The old red rowboat lunged forward with a violent pitch of the river, and Davie fell back until his butt hit the bench and he rolled, "ass over tea kettle," as Mr. Stan would say. He hit the back of his head on the bench at the stern and, although it didn't hurt, he blacked out.

When consciousness returned to the boy, his eyes opened to the familiar sight of the moon splashing against the flat black lake beyond the window. A light breeze worked the branches of a nearby tree, and they gently tapped against the glass. Davie continued to stare out the window for several moments.

"So long, Mr. Stan, and Missus Hildie too," he whispered as a tear trickled down his cheek. "Save a spot for me on your boat, okay?" Davie closed his eyes and was sad. *But how can I be sad?* he thought. *How can I be sad for Mr. Stan now?* Davie smiled benignly for his friend, and in moments, sweet sleep retook him.

Outside Davie's bedroom window, a great wolf walked slowly from the edge of the lake, its bright green eyes observing everything, its ears pricked and sensitive to the sounds of the night. It ambled deliberately until it could see its own beastly features staring back from the window. The wolf cocked its head, momentarily transfixed, and when satisfied, it sat in the grass. A delicate breeze played against its fur, and it waited.

Chapter Eleven

At the other end of the house, Angie sat at a round oak kitchen table (perhaps the only true rustic in the place) and poured cabernet into a large glass goblet. She took a healthy drink and wished she had a cigarette, but she'd given up the habit over four years ago when she was briefly pregnant. She wore a faded blue T-shirt with MICHIGAN embossed across the chest, flecks of the stamped letters long ago lost to wear and the washing machine. It was several sizes too large and originally Jack's, who forever lost claim to it one cool night in Virginia. She completed the ensemble with dark gray sweatpants and white socks. It looked good on her because, as Jack always said, "You happen to be a very pretty girl."

Angie thought of Davie, just down the hall, and of Jack, some four hours south on Interstate 75. She stood and walked to the kitchen drawers, pulled them open one at a time, and rummaged for a smoke the way a hopeless alcoholic searched under couch cushions for a long-stashed bottle. Somewhere, she thought, Ray Milland was laughing, stuck in another *Lost Weekend* in a black-and-white world.

What in the hell am I doing? she wondered. *Really, you're ready to smoke old, stale ciggies, put away only God knows when?* She shook her head and drank more cab. *Not bad,* she thought.

The phone rang with a sharp trill. Angie jumped a little and grabbed the receiver before the first ring had finished its demand to be answered.

"Hello?"

"Hi, babe, it's me," Jack said softly.

"Jack," she said tersely, "why are you calling so late?"

"I was just thinking about Virginia, those cabins we stayed in on the Skyline Drive. Do you remember?" His voice was husky and carried a slight slur. Angie deduced that he'd had more than a drink or two, but he was reasonably coherent. He had never been a mean or a sloppy drunk, but rather one who stepped lightly between melancholia and bliss, as circumstances dictated.

"Sure, I remember," she said, a little tension gone from her tone. "Skyliner Cabins, wasn't it?"

"Yeah, that's right. We saw a bumper sticker that said 'Virginia Is for Lovers,' and just like that, we took off." Jack paused and inhaled slowly. "We were gonna go to Virginia Beach, I think, but that cabin was far as we got."

"Those were much simpler times." Angie sighed. "When we could still go and do crazy stuff like that on a whim."

"You mean we can't anymore?"

"Well, it *is* different now, isn't it," she said, the edge back in her voice, "with Davie, and work, and everything else?"

"Davie would love it there," Jack said, a bit more excited now. "Lots to do, lots to see, and there was a great ice cream joint there too."

"As I recall, we barely got out of bed for three days, except to eat at that restaurant ... what was it called? The Skyliner Inn?"

"Yeah, everything was Skyliner in that burg, but it was cool." Jack chuckled.

"Yes, it worked," Angie said, and then it was her turn to pause. "But that was a long time ago."

"Gone but not forgotten," he said softly, melancholy Jack rising to the occasion.

"You sound tired, Jackson. Maybe you ought to get some sleep," Angie said, her tone softening.

"Yeah, sure," he whispered hoarsely, and then cleared his throat. "Okay, babe, I'll see ya when I see ya."

Before she could reply, he'd hung up. Angie sat for a moment and stared at the phone. *Shit. I could have done that better.* She took a long drink of wine and leaned back in the chair. One day, very soon, she thought, she would break his heart once and for all, and that would be that. *Without passion there can be no romance,* she told herself, but there were many things about him that she would miss. She hated doing it, but she'd persuaded herself it needed doing, and so that was that.

She drank more cab and thought of Virginia and cigarettes and making love in a tiny cabin in the Shenandoah, with no phones and no TV. She smiled. So much had come and gone in the years since that trip, but that was a good memory, recent tensions now set aside, other memories pushed away. She wished they could go back to Virginia, try it all again. She stared into the bloodred wine for a long time, until her eyes lost their focus.

The phone rang and again she jumped as it crashed into the quiet kitchen. She grabbed the receiver, figuring it was Jack.

"I hope you're still awake." It was not Jack. It was the man she called her boss—Peter Brookings.

"Of course I am," Angie said. "Where are you?"

"Less than an hour away, I think. I stopped for gas and a bathroom break. You need anything?"

"Yeah, can you get me a couple packs of Salems?"

"You're smoking? Since when?" he said with shock and a little indignation.

"Since as soon as you get here, okay?" She felt herself getting irritated. "It's fine, Peter. Just get them for me, okay?"

"All right." He sighed. "Your wish is my command. See you soon."

"Thanks. Don't forget to look for Froggy," she said.

"I won't," he said, and then he rang off.

Angie refilled her wine glass. *I have plenty of wine*, she thought. She would put Peter in the guest room at the end of the hall, opposite her bedroom, as far away from Davie as she could get him without dropping him in the lake, and explain his presence in the morning as "just a friend who needed a place to stay." She figured that the boy was still too young to understand exactly what was going on, and in truth, she wasn't so sure herself. How she might keep Davie from telling Jack about Peter's presence in the cabin, however inadvertently, remained a problem. *Then again*, she thought, *if I go through with this, it won't really matter at all.*

She and Peter had been flirting for a couple of years, as sometimes will happen in an office environment. It had not, to this point, gone beyond the recent kissing and what they called "heavy petting" in cheesy novels. *Jesus, I'm in high school*, she thought, *in the backseat of a Chrysler LeBaron with Dean … what was that guy's name? Fuller? Muller?* She stood and walked to the counter, by the sink, and turned on the clock radio.

It warmed up for a few seconds and then blasted out the sax solo from Men at Work's "Who Can It Be Now," so she quickly reached for the knob and turned it down. She thought of Jack sitting at the old upright piano in the basement as he banged out some Beatles tune. He hadn't played in a long time, she reflected, and here and now, in the middle of the woods, alone in the kitchen with a glass of wine, she missed it. She missed *him*. *Christ, it's getting more confusing by the minute,* she thought. *If I sleep with Peter tonight and miss Jack when I wake up in the morning, where am I?*

Angie continued to work on the wine as the minutes passed and Peter motored closer up I-75. "You've Lost that Lovin' Feeling," the old Righteous Brothers classic, moaned on in her head, while Ray Parker chased ghosts on the radio. The wind picked up outside, and Angie turned to the window over the sink. She saw the trees just beyond waving slightly. *No,* she thought, *I still love Jack, but where is that … what's the word? Longing? Desire? Passion? Have I lost it to familiarity? And is that a bad thing?*

Her mind wandered effortlessly between what was in the *past* and what had *passed* with Jack, and what was about to pass, here, and very soon. In her head, the blindfolded lady on the scale held two swaying trays, and Jack was now winning the day, but narrowly. The phone again interrupted sharply, and she snatched the receiver.

"Hello?" she said softly.

"Tell me I didn't wake you up," Jack whispered.

"You didn't wake me up." Angie couldn't help herself; she was happy to hear his voice.

"What are you doing?"

"Drinking wine and thinking about you," she said and giggled a little.

"That's a common combination, I've been told."

"Oh really?" Angie laughed. "Who told you that?"

"I think it was Curly."

Angie let out a snort that made Jack chuckle at the other end of the line. "Jackson Thomas, you are a silly, silly man," she said tenderly.

"I know, babe, I know," he said. "I can't stop thinking about you, and us, and you know … I guess I'm a little worried—a lot worried—and it's made me act like an ass." He paused. "I'm sorry about what happened, you know, how I fucked that up." Several heartbeats passed between them. "Am I losing you?" he said at last.

Angie sighed and drank more cab. She drained the glass and refilled it. She was on the spot, confused, uncertain, and unsure what to say. Jack sensed this during the interminable pause that now settled between them, and so he changed his tack.

"I'm sorry; I shouldn't have said that," he said. "Maybe I've had a few too many."

"It's okay, honey. I know, me too …" Her words trailed off, sent south down the phone line, where they died somewhere around Flint. She inhaled and again wished for a smoke. "Jack, let's talk when we get home. Try not to worry; I love you." She'd said "I love you" automatically, without thought, with a touch of sadness, but she *meant* it. She closed her eyes. She could see him, pacing in the kitchen, back and forth, the telephone's accordion cord walked taut and then falling slack as he retreated, back and forth, back and forth.

"Do you want me to come up now?" he asked.

"No. You've been drinking, haven't you? Please don't drive tonight, Jack. Promise me you won't," Angie said with authority.

"No, okay, you're right. But," Jack said, "how's about tomorrow?"

Angie started to say yes and then remembered Peter, now just minutes away on the interstate. *The plot gets thicker,* she heard someone say. "No, baby boy, we'll be home Sunday. Let's just think about what we want to say, what we want to do. And don't worry, okay? It's gonna be all right, and you shouldn't worry. I love you. Davie and I will leave early Sunday morning, and we'll be home for lunch. Okay?" She spoke the last word brightly.

"Okay, sugar babe," he said, "but think about this: Davie could stay with Terry and Katie Ralls for a few days—you know they love the kid—and we could drive to Virginia, or *anywhere*—you know, like we used to do. We can reconnect, get it back, I *know* we can. Don't say anything right now, but just think about it, okay?"

There was a brief pause, only a few seconds, but days seemed to pass at both ends of the telephone line. In this interlude, emotions swirled; visions came and went; past and future raced toward an unseen, unknown, and uncertain destination.

"Okay, Jack. I will, I promise." She closed her eyes, and she could see his face clearly as a tear trickled down her cheek. "Now you go to sleep and have sweet dreams, okay?" She waited for a few heartbeats, trying to sense what Jack was feeling, thinking, perceiving, through the wonders of Alexander Graham Bell. "I love you, Jackson," she said soulfully, at last.

"Okay, baby, you too. I love you, you know, since forever," he said softly.

"I know, Jackman. G'night."

"Night, babe," he whispered.

She waited for the phone to click dead, but she could hear him breathing quietly on the other end. "You hang up first," she said. *Good God, I'm back in high school again, those silly and awkward phone games. Junior high school,* she thought.

"Okay," Jack said. After a moment, the phone rattled at the other end and there was a soft thump. Angie pictured Jack, fumbling and dropping the phone to the carpet. She giggled again, and whispered "Putz!" but the line went dead before her mild reproach reached Jack. Angie took a drink of wine and decided that she had better slow down. An acoustic guitar or two rang out a stream of chords, and she heard Glen Frey singing sadly. *Jesus,* she thought, *the Eagles.* "Lyin' Eyes," she groaned out loud. She rose and switched off the radio. "Are you kidding me?" she asked the suddenly silent plastic tunesmith on the kitchen counter. "Really?"

Angie sat back down and then heard a car door close in the

driveway. She cursed softly and stood again. She shut her eyes, and the first thing she saw was Jack, sitting in his rocker, looking out the door wall to the trees in the distance. She opened her eyes and walked to the door, pushing it forward before Peter could knock. He walked up the path, carrying a gym bag in one hand and a brown grocery sack in the other.

"Hi, Angie," he said, smiling brightly.

"Hello, Peter." Angie held the screen door open and stood aside to let him pass into the house. He leaned down a bit to kiss her, but she turned her head and offered only her right cheek.

"Everything all right?" he said with a tone of uncertainty, like a man who'd walked into a room where something had just happened, maybe something bad.

"No, Peter. Come in and sit down." She steered him toward the oak table in the kitchen. He dropped the gym bag on the floor, set the paper sack on the counter, and sat at the table, a perplexed look on his handsome face.

Peter was tall and lanky with light brown hair and a matching moustache. His face was long but not too thin, and his nose was perfectly straight. Not like Jack's, she thought, whose beak had known a few bumps along the way. Peter's dark brown eyes remained glued to Angie's, and she smiled weakly.

"Want some wine? I've got a nice cab here," Angie said, grabbing another glass from the counter.

"Got anything stronger? I'm getting a sense that I might need it," he said.

Angie had her back to him now, and felt his hand as it rubbed lightly against her lower back. She moved quickly to her left and opened a cabinet door, revealing a well-stocked liquor reserve. "Scotch, I presume?" she asked.

"Yeah, yeah, that's good, with a little ice if you have it." She sensed his eyes on her as she moved about the room, switching to a cocktail glass and then grabbing some ice from a tray in the fridge's freezer. The cubes tinkled in the glass (Jack called this a "happy sound"), and then Angie poured three fingers of amber liquor over the ice. She handed the glass to Peter, who accepted it and immediately took a healthy sip.

"Ahhhhh, my dear friend Johnnie Walker." He sighed. "I know him well."

Angie reached for the wine bottle and emptied it into her glass. *That went quick*, she mused and decided to grab a reload from the lower shelf of the fridge, where she'd placed four bottles to cool shortly after she and Davie arrived. She liked her wine cold, "as cold as a well-digger's butt in the Klondike," as Stan Koski would say. She opened a drawer, grabbed a corkscrew, and began the process of opening the bottle. *Here comes at least a level-two headache in the morning*, she judged.

Angie topped off her glass, corked the bottle, and sat across from Peter at the table. He watched her closely, trying to read the extant situation, although he believed this was virtually impossible with women. There was a long pause before she finally spoke, softly, slowly.

"I'm sorry, Peter, I truly am, but I can't go through with this. I have a room ready for you, but it will be just *you* that sleeps in it, and just me in my bed. I'm really very sorry ..." Angie's words straggled off, for they had nowhere to go, and there was nothing left to follow them. She lowered her gaze to her hands, folded on the tabletop.

Peter took another gulp of scotch, drew his lips back in reaction to its potency, and stared into the glass. He brought it up and took another drink. "What's gone wrong? What changed your mind?" His tone was piqued and grew a little more indignant with each word. "You know, you could have saved me the trip! I don't get it, Angie." He shook his head.

Angie rose again and padded to the paper sack on the counter.

There she found the cigarettes she'd requested, along with a six-pack of Budweiser tall boys and a bag of Fritos. Under the smokes was a big bag of plain M&M's, Davie's favorite candy. Angie took the smokes and left the rest. She claimed the ashtray from the counter (one of Jack's, it bore the Marine Corps emblem on the bottom—eagle, globe, and anchor in red with gold trim). She sat back down.

"Peter, I just can't do it," she said firmly. "I was wrong to think that I could, or that I *would*, cheat on Jack, end my marriage, destroy fifteen years of my life—and Jack's, and *Davie's*. I just can't do it. I don't *want* to do it, and I won't."

She took a drink of wine, stripped the cellophane from a pack of Salems, tore away the foil at the top, and tapped the pack on the tabletop. A cigarette presented itself, and she pulled it out. Angie stood yet again, opened a drawer, and removed a box of wooden kitchen matches. She struck one on the side of the box, and it burst into a bright flame that filled the room with its inimitable smell. Angie lighted the Salem and blew a cloud of blue smoke over the room.

"Wow," she said, dropping into her chair, a little woozy. As hard as it had been to quit four years ago, it was just that easy to start up all over again. She took another pull, drew it deep into her lungs, closed her eyes, and widened the blue cloud. Peter waved his left hand across his face, now in full cringe, fanning away the smoke. In that instant, Angie lost all remorse for jilting him. She knew with clarity that she had made the right choice.

"Well," Peter whined, "so much for 'smoke-free,' eh?" He reached for the scotch, scooted his chair back about two feet, and drained the glass. He stood and picked up the gym bag from the floor and the paper sack from the counter. He caught himself and returned the sack to its place. He removed the M&M's and dramatically dropped the candy on the counter.

"For Davie," he said tartly, reclaiming the paper bag of beer and chips. "Guess I'll find a motel somewhere." He turned for the door, walking briskly.

"I didn't say you had to go, Peter," Angie said to his back. "You're welcome to stay in the guest room tonight."

"No," he said without turning or breaking stride. "No point in that. Will I see you at the office on Monday?"

Shit, Angie thought, the *office*. "Sure, yes, I'll be there, just … you know, no more … you know …" Words again fell to their death in midair, and she oddly thought of birds that die in flight and silently drop to earth, land on the lawn, and in the morning, there they are, not a mark on them. *They just dropped dead, and that's all there was to it.*

"Yeah, I get it. See you," said Peter curtly as he opened the doors and walked into the night and its shadows. It had begun to rain, lightly thus far, and Angie thought of the little weatherman down the hall.

"Take a left at the end of the drive. There's a motel about a mile up, on the left," she said through the screen door. He did not reply.

She watched Peter get in the car, and this time, he slammed its door. He turned the key and the engine of his black Firebird Trans Am roared to life. He threw it in reverse and peeled down the drive, the car wavering and fishtailing from side to side. He just missed taking out a pine tree, and then the mailbox, before he made it to the street, where the Firebird disappeared with a roar and a screech. With every word and gesture, Peter confirmed to Angie's heart that she had chosen wisely.

There was a flickering in the sky, and a few seconds later, thunder rolled in the distance. "The angels are bowling," she heard Jack say. The rain intensified, and Angie beat a hasty retreat inside, closing both doors behind her. Because crime had not reared its ugly head up here, not *yet*, she didn't worry about the locks. She was thinking

Daniel J. Wells

about taking a glass of wine and a smoke out to the pier, if it stopped raining for a while.

As Angie turned from the door, intent on finishing that glass of wine already waiting on the table, and another smoke too, she was startled to see Davie standing in the shadows where the living room met the hallway.

"What's up, goober?"

"I thought I heard somebody talkin'," he said, rubbing at the sleep in his eyes.

"Just me and the chickens," Angie said. Davie tilted his head, confused. "Sorry, honey, just me, that's all. I was talking to Uncle Jack on the phone. He misses us."

"Yeah," Davie said with a smile, "me too."

"Me three," Angie said as she dashed over, picked up the boy in her arms, and gave him a good squeeze.

He grunted and giggled. "Hey, Aunt Angie, whatcha doin'? I ain't a baby, ya know!"

"Well, excuu-uuse me, old timer! Say, don't tell anybody, but you know what I have?" She carried him squirming into the kitchen and held him over the counter.

"Oh boy, M&M's!" he announced excitedly. He grabbed the bag with both hands, and Angie set him on the floor. He tore into the plastic and a few dozen multicolored candies flew into the air. They bounced off the counter, the table, the window—you name it.

Davie looked sheepishly at his aunt. "Ooops," he muttered.

Angie burst into laughter, and the boy followed suit. "Five-second rule," she declared and began picking up the candy from the carpet. "Better make that ten seconds," she decided.

"Hey, that's what the candy coating is for!" Davie said.

"That's right," Angie agreed, "that *is* what the candy coating is for!" They picked up the sweets, and Davie sat at the table, his feet

128

swinging well above the floor. He was eating the M&M's one at a time, savoring them.

"Boy, these are *good*," he said.

"How's about a glass of milk to chase those goodies with, munchkin?"

"Chase 'em where?" he asked, squinting.

"All the way down into your tummy!" Angie got and up and took a half-full gallon jug of milk from the fridge and poured a small glass nearly full. *Ooooh, Jack is gonna be mad at me in the morning*, she thought, *especially for stealing the coffee.* She wanted to call him but looked at the clock and decided it was too late. She picked up the glass of wine, took a sip, and longed for a smoke. *Not around Davie*, she resolved.

"You know, I really miss Uncle Jack." She sighed.

"Me too," said Davie, who had grown a wet, white moustache. "You think maybe he can come up tomorrow?"

"Well, I was thinking maybe *we* could go to *him*, you know? Get up in the morning and surprise him for lunch." She gave the boy a conspiratorial wink. "Would that be okay with you?"

Davie popped a candy into his mouth, chewed it slowly, and took a sip of milk. Lightning flashed brightly through the window for several seconds. Davie began to count, "A thousand one, a thousand two, a thousand three ..." A loud round of thunder rolled overhead. "It's gettin' closer now. Last time I got to six." Another M&M went to its final reward. "Yeah, sure, that's okay. Prob'ly won't get to go fishin' anyways," he said, and then he nodded toward the window. "Told ya so!"

Angie smiled, sipped her wine, and watched Davie as he deliberately finished his stash of M&M's. When he'd exhausted his supply and polished off the milk, Angie stood and rubbed his head. The window filled with a blinding flash of white and, before Davie could begin his count, heaven exploded with big *booms*, highlighted by an ear-splitting *crack* that seemingly blasted through the roof directly above them as deafening thunder grumbled in the night. Both jumped in startled response.

"Jeez, that was *close!*" Angie said. She walked to the window and looked out. Seeing nothing but rain drumming at the glass, she turned to Davie. "On that note, let's go to bed," she said.

Davie stood, picked up his glass, and set it on the counter near the sink. He turned to Angie and wrapped both arms around her legs. "I love you, you know," he said.

"I love you, too, Spanky," she said, bending slightly at the waist to give him a hug. "Say, how'd you know it was gonna rain?" Davie giggled and released her after a quick squeeze.

"You gotta brush your teeth again," she said to his back, but he was too quick, flying down the hallway and jumping into his bed as its springs creaked a mild protest. *Ah, what the hell*, she thought. Thunder rumbled again after a spark of light burst into the room, but the storm had drummed its way east and was no longer overhead. The rhythm of the rain waned a bit, its incessant pounding at the glass slower now, less adamant.

Angie drained the glass of wine and thought of Jack. She badly wanted to speak to him, to hear his voice. Bob Dylan whispered in her ear, gently, from far away, singing "Shelter from the Storm," as Angie rinsed out three glasses and turned them upside-down in a red rubber tray in the left half of the split sink. "You and your frickin' Dylan, Jack," she said, shaking her head and looking out the window.

She flipped off the switch and the room went mostly dark, illuminated just slightly by a nightlight in the hallway. She took one last look through the window and then went to bed, stopping briefly on her way to peek in at Davie. He was on his side, looking directly at her.

"G'night, Aunt Angie; see you in the morning." She could hear sleep thickening his voice.

"Sleep tight, sweetheart. I love you," she said. Angie gave him a little wave and turned for her room, suddenly very tired. She pulled open the curtains and sat on the edge of the bed. The sky flickered in the distance, winking at her. She thought of Jack and what she'd almost done. She missed him very much at that moment, perhaps more than she had ever missed him before. Meanwhile, far away in heaven, an angel made a seven-ten split. The eastern sky twinkled and, an eight-count later, reverberated in the distance.

After a few minutes, she rose and pulled back the bedspread. Angie slid under the covers, propped the pillow to keep her head slightly elevated, and continued to look out the window. "I'm gonna make it right," she said aloud to the glass. "I'm gonna make it *all* right." Soon, she slept soundly into the night, as the rain and its rhythm section came and went, came and went.

When she assumed she was awake, she was dreaming, and so Angie left her bed, grabbed a bottle of wine, walked out the front door, and stepped into the rain. It felt cool and refreshing, so she tilted her head back and let it wash over her, cleansing her. She peeled off the T-shirt and stepped out of the sweatpants and socks. Angie stood completely free, liberated of all guilt and restraints, unburdened of worry and fear and regret. It felt good to be naked and alone in the rain as the moon revisited to light the way.

Angie walked around the house, under a canopy of trees and moonlight, until she reached the short wooden pier that poked into the lake. She sauntered leisurely to its end, sat, and eased her feet into the water. It was very quiet, the only sounds that drifted through the night put forth by a soothing breeze that frolicked through the leaves in the trees and sent the lake lapping gently across its sandy beach. She uncorked the wine and took a deep pull from the bottle.

For a few moments, Angie relaxed in glorious harmony with the world, unfettered by a single thought or emotion, and she wallowed in it. She then became aware of something rustling in the brush behind her, and she turned to face it. Without thinking, she covered her breasts with folded arms as modesty became the first breach of the peace.

From the tall grass along the shore, Angie heard a low grumbling, steady and ominous. She rose and glared at the other end of the pier. "Who's there?" she whispered. "Who's there?"

A pair of intense green eyes flashed alive where the pier met the beach, but Angie could see no form, no body, to go with them. The throaty murmur grew to a growl and filled Angie with fright. The only unattended path toward escape and safety was the lake, to dive into its cool, black waters and swim away from those glaring eyes, but when she turned to face it, the lake's waters began to roil and churn, and she backed away toward the shore at the foot of the pier.

She was at once caught, quite literally, she imagined, between the devil and the deep blue sea—or the black, boiling lake, in this case. Angie decided to take her chances with whatever skulked on land, and so she walked cautiously toward the shore. Being naked was no longer liberating; she felt ashamed and exposed.

Angie broke into a run. As she felt herself sink into the sand, she stumbled, fell forward, and landed in the tall, wet grass at the edge of the narrow beach, flat on her back, still clutching the bottle of wine. She looked up and straight into the eyes of the moon as it sneered and laughed at her. She quickly climbed to her feet. From the slight berm between Angie and the house, the hypnotic jade eyes reappeared. *My choices are for shit*, she deduced, but she carefully and deliberately began to walk around the eyes and toward the house. Impulsively, she hurled the wine bottle at the beast, but it sailed wide right and fell harmlessly into the sand and tall grass.

After a few steps, Angie began to acquire focus on the form that went with those menacing green lamps. Whatever it was, it was huge! *Don't know of anything that big around here*, she thought, *except maybe deer, and this is no deer, that's for sure.* She kept moving, and the sinister monster stayed put, watching, unblinking, strangely quiet. Angie turned to face the house and moved quickly toward its promise of safe haven.

"Move swiftly, little one, and don't look back until you are inside," a sonorous snarl commanded from the dense shadows behind her. "Take the boy and leave this place—*at once!*"

Angie considered this good advice and scampered around the house, not even stopping to pick up her clothes. She fumbled with the handle of the screen door but was soon inside, basking in the warmth she found there, right where she'd left it. She closed her eyes, shivered, and clutched herself tightly in her own arms. She realized that Jack was sprinting toward her, carrying a blanket, calling to her tenderly, "Whatcha doin' out in the rain, sweetheart?"

When she opened her eyes, Jack was gone. Angie blinked quickly several times. As the fog of sleep lifted, she ascertained that the trees were again swaying slowly beyond her window. She was dry, back in her T-shirt, sweatpants, and socks, warm and secure under the covers, safe. Her room was very quiet, and she closed her eyes and sighed.

"Jackson Thomas, when I get home, I swear I'm gonna squeeze you till you *bust*," she announced.

Angie rolled onto her back and sleep presently called for her again. This time, it brought tender thoughts of Jack and Davie and Curly too: her *family*. "We're gonna be okay," she said, a final but *certain* notion that she grasped and held close to her heart as her lights faded and serene slumber took her away.

Outside, the flashing green eyes were cast toward the teeming waters of the lake, which calmed at once. The smirking face of the moon went expressionless and hid behind the passing clouds. A light rain continued, shrouded within a thick mist, and the sky flashed through in the west. Another storm front was brewing, its powers reforming, moving steadily with bursts of lightning, progressively thunderous, and ominously shifting eastward.

Chapter Twelve

Peter Brookings pulled into the driveway at the Lake in the Woods Motel, parked his car, hurried through the drizzle, and barged into the motel office, just as its frumpy, middle-aged manager was about to switch off the flashing *Vacancy* sign and call it a night.

"You just made it," she said without enthusiasm, sliding a registration card across the green countertop. "Eighteen bucks a night, in advance, plus a two-dollar key deposit."

Peter pulled a crisp twenty-dollar bill from his wallet and dropped it on the counter. He picked up a Bic pen and began to fill out the card. Next to *Name* he wrote, "Jack Thomas," and then he neatly printed Jack's address. He'd seen it many times on payroll checks he'd endorsed for Angie: 229 Bull Run Way and so on. In the space requiring a license plate number, he contrived six digits, confident the woman would not venture out into the rain to verify them.

"Checkout's at eleven," she said.

"I'll be long gone by then," he mumbled.

She reached behind her and took from a hook board a key attached to a large plastic fob with a dull-yellow seven stenciled on each side. A decapitated fourteen-point buck watched the proceedings from the wall above the key rack, its glass eyes oddly alert.

"Number seven, down near the end." She pointed to her left. "There's a drop box for the key just outside the office door." She let loose a phlegmy cough, bent forward at the waist, and, when it finally stopped, spit into a trash basket on the floor under the counter as Peter blanched.

"Maybe you should cut down on the Camels," he said. "Where's the ice machine?"

"Just outside the office, on the right," she said tersely, wiping her lips with the back of her left hand.

Peter took the key, turned, and left the office, letting the screen door slam shut behind him. "That's friggin' *great*," he heard the woman say with disgust. Peter collected a small bucket and scooped it full with ice before returning to his car. He got in, set the bucket on the passenger seat, fired up the Firebird, and listened to the parking lot's gravel crunch under its wheels as he slowly drove alongside the straight row of rooms.

The *Vacancy* sign flickered and went black, along with *Lake in the Woods* in bright neon, and the surrounding parking lot went largely dark. The rain had evolved to a steady drizzle in a dense mist.

When he reached number seven, he pulled into the space before its door, gathered the ice, gym bag, and paper sack, exited the car, and closed the car door with his knee. He set the gym bag on the walk and opened the room's beige door. He recollected the gym bag and entered the room, where he set everything down, save the ice, on the carpet. Peter flicked on the light switch, pulled out the key, and closed the door, locking it from the inside. He turned to face the room.

The walls were a fairly hideous shade of teal, the curtains a well-faded yellow, and the bedspread an ill-conceived shock of gold paisley on a sea of burgundy. *There's a match*, he thought. The TV looked like it was produced around the time *I Love Lucy* went on the air, including bent rabbit ears, and the small Formica table by the windows may have been even older than that.

Peter took the ice bucket and the paper sack and set them on the table. He picked up the gym bag, tossed it onto the bed, and dropped the motel key with a dull clang onto the nightstand. Above the bed was a starving artist painting. No, it wasn't even *that* good, Peter judged; this artist starved to death and *then* painted this morose New England village scene, circa 1850.

"Nice," Peter said to no one, looking about the room. "What a *dump*," he whined in his best Bette Davis impersonation, which actually wasn't too bad. Peter opened the zipper on the gym bag and felt around with both hands until he found a squared bottle. "There you are, Johnnie," he said. He carried the scotch to the table. In the bathroom, he relieved himself before locating a plastic glass, sealed in plastic kitchen wrap, by the sink. *Is it really a glass if it's plastic?* he wondered.

"Let's see if we can drink this room pretty," he said without hope. Peter choked the plastic glass with ice and then filled it with scotch. He opened the paper sack, tugged out a can of Bud, and pulled the ring tab open with a snap and a hiss. He sat in a circa-1950s kitchen chair, felt it sag under his weight as he drained most of the scotch. Then he refilled the glass, trying to numb the thoughts that were pushing to the front of his brain. It was very quiet in the room until someone flushed a toilet in number four, and the pipes groaned sequentially from room to room until the stream died with a moan at number ten, the end of the line.

Peter scanned the room and spied a clock radio on the nightstand beside the gaudy bed. Rising to his feet, a little less steady now, he picked up the radio and played with the slide buttons until it came to life. He twisted a knob until a red bar ran into some music, so he stopped the search. Peabo Bryson was crooning, "If Ever You're in My Arms Again." Peter spun the dial further until Johnny Cash was singing about "Ghost Riders in the Sky." Peter hated country music, so the search continued. *Stations are much further apart on the dial here than they are in Detroit*, he noted, slowly spinning. At last he found some classical music, violins crying to the heavens.

Peter was pretentious enough to fancy himself an aficionado of classical music, but in truth he didn't know Beethoven from Beetle Bailey. But this one sounded okay, so he replaced the radio on the nightstand and returned to the chair by the table. He drank more scotch and gulped beer from a can. His mind began to turn to rage, slowly at first, but surely, against the woman up the road in the cottage with the little boy. Great promise—great *lust*—had died a very sudden death, and he was sore. He felt inadequate again, and it chilled him to his core.

"Fucking women," he muttered.

He drank more scotch, drained the glass, and refilled it, chasing it with Budweiser that was getting warm. In a few moments, all his life's failures and frustrations rose to his throat in sour bile and threatened to suffocate him. Angie became the face of all of Peter's dissatisfactions and disappointments, and at this moment her features lost their loveliness and assumed an evil leer. His tenuous grip on reality, on sanity, was slipping away.

"Wha'sa matter, widdle Petie," said this new Angie, who spoke in his mother's condescending voice, "is your widdle petie-weetie mad at me?" She wiggled a limp left pinky finger at him and let loose a laugh, mocking him, taunting him, belittling him. "Did you really think I would fuck a little prick like *you*?" Her tone turned severe, formidable, and Peter began to tremble. It was all too familiar.

"Fuck you, you miserable bitch," he hissed. "I could have you anytime I want!"

Now the radio *was* playing Beethoven, a maestro's hands delicately, softly caressing a piano through "Moonlight Sonata," but Peter didn't hear it. Resentment filled his ears, fueled by scotch and warm Bud, and a mind too pathetic and blind to understand why the world might fail to see that he was the greatest thing since folding chairs.

Peter felt this way many times in his life: first as a child, suffering the lashings of his drunken father's belt and his cruel, berating tongue. When the old man finally died of cancer when Peter was fifteen, it became the soul-crushing jibes and humiliations layered on by his mother. When *she* eventually died after taking a header down the basement stairs (oh, there were whispers about *that*, but there was nothing that anyone could *prove*), he still heard them both, cackling within the walls of the home he'd inherited and still lived in. This dark, private monster that he worked so fiercely to contain and conceal from the world was now taking Peter Brookings into darkness.

Johnnie Walker might have been a great guy, life of the party, but his skills at keeping demons at bay were very limited indeed. In fact, his liquid namesake now helped fuel the devils that lurked deep within Peter Brookings. While Beethoven's sonata faded out and Haydn swirled in, a fiendish thing was making its way to the surface, and so Peter drank more scotch and lukewarm beer.

He pulled back the drapes, looking out the large sliding windows into the drizzle and mist in the parking lot, and he was now seething. *It's time to do something about this*, he decided. *It's time to kill the beast, and it's just down the road.* He left the table and went to his gym bag, where he removed a pair of designer blue jeans, a trendy black sweatshirt, a black windbreaker, and a pair of blue adidas shoes with white stripes at their sides. He changed out of the dress shirt, slacks, and pricy alligator loafers and into the duds from the gym bag and, lastly, the windbreaker.

A steady rain returned, and lightning flashed in outlying western skies. Peter took a pull of scotch directly from the bottle and found something else in the gym bag, which he stuffed into the back right pocket of his jeans. He pulled his wallet from his left rear pocket, stuffed it and his car keys under the mattress, retrieved the room key, and put that in the left side pocket of his windbreaker. He stopped at the table for a little more of Johnnie Walker's bottled courage, and then he walked out the door.

Peter Brookings, for all intents and purposes, was no more. He did not look like the same man. A shadowy countenance shrouded his features, wet hair dangled over his eyes and ears, and vile thoughts, heretofore unknown to a neatly dressed, well-coiffed lawyer, danced in his brain. Raised in the finery of Grosse Pointe, educated at its best schools, he never ventured beyond the boundaries of the law. Unless, of course, you counted a little speeding in the Firebird and, perhaps, the healthy nudge he'd given his mother on her way down the stairs.

The new and improved Peter stepped outside and locked the door behind him. He would leave the Firebird here and walk to Angie's house, rain be damned. Should that crone of a manager look out her window, she'd see the car and assume the snooty city prick was still inside number seven. Peter looked about for signs of life and prying eyes. Satisfied that no one watched, he moved briskly toward the road.

When the gravel parking lot ended and he reached the shoulder of the road, he looked both ways. He saw nothing, no headlights in the distance, and so he crossed. On the other side, he found the cover of trees and wild bushes just beyond the shoulder; here he could remain unseen, should a car approach from either direction.

Rainfall grew more determined to wash the man away and pounded down as he moved with purpose, back bent slightly forward, eyes wide, his adrenaline flowing like a wild, hungry animal on the hunt. As he moved, he sensed a presence to his left, where the trees thickened and formed a canopy of black gloom. Peter stopped in his tracks and listened intently for several moments, until he heard a stir and then the sounds of a scuffle. Something growled with bad intent, a low, steady snarl that rose in its throat and shattered the quiet night with a roar.

"What the fuck was *that?*" Peter asked as he stared into the black.

A pair of intense orange eyes glistened like hot coals and said to Peter, "What the fuck are *you* looking at, dipshit?"

It was his father's voice, and Peter's guts turned to liquid. He was sure he was going to soil himself, standing in the rain, terrified, alone, drunk on liquor and psychosis.

"Go do what you've got to do, you useless, sniveling sack of shit!" Its eyes flashed to burning white as the thing in the brush resumed its unremitting snarl.

Peter broke into a trot and then a full sprint. He'd run about a hundred yards when he tripped over a log and fell flat on his face. He rushed to his feet without a care for the bruised thigh muscle in his right leg or the rib in his left side he'd cracked when he landed on a large, unyielding rock. No; he only felt horror and the absolute need to gain distance from *whatever that fucking thing was in the woods!*

Finally, nearly breathless and spent, the forest rustling ominously just behind him, he looked across the road and spotted a large mailbox with a laughing frog's face, its tongue in full dangle, eyes wide and smiling. It was something Angie's mother had hand-painted on the mailbox as a landmark to first-time visitors, years ago. Angie herself dutifully retouched the green frog's visage every summer, or as time and nature's abusive ways dictated.

Peter again looked both ways, saw no headlights, hurriedly crossed the street, and took cover in the pines he found there.

Dulled by booze and the red worms that ate away and riddled his brain, Peter ignored his injuries and the excruciating pain his body was suffering. He looked at the house he'd entered just hours ago, hopes high, and saw that it was dark within. He moved with unnecessary stealth until he reached a thick, six-foot evergreen that abutted the house by the front door. There he waited and listened for any sounds from within. When satisfied that all was still, Peter Brookings shuffled to the front door.

He slowly pulled back the screen door, wary of any creaks or squeaks, and then gripped the inner door's brass knob. He turned it deliberately and was pleasantly surprised to discover that it was not locked. *Stupid bitch*, he thought. *This is going to be very easy. I'm going to take my time and enjoy this!*

"Don't forget the boy," his father croaked from the darkness. *"Don't forget the boy!"*

"Oh, I won't," Peter whispered, not looking back, not wanting to see whatever it was that went with that voice or those fiery eyes he'd seen in the trees.

Peter opened the inner door and entered the cottage. It was dark and quiet, save a dim nightlight in the hallway leading to the bedrooms and their sleeping occupants. It was just enough light to illuminate his path. He was drenched, head to toe, and water ran off the windbreaker and collected in a muddy brown puddle at his feet. Peter didn't notice but stood still, listening, allowing his eyes to adjust and focus.

After a few moments, he walked toward the nightlight. When his shoes started to squeak, he stopped, cursed softly, and carefully took them off. Peter then resumed his sly march toward death, calm now, but his senses in overdrive. Soon he stood outside a bedroom door on the right side of the hall, where he leaned into an opening of a foot or so. He could hear Angie breathing, snoring ever so faintly, obviously asleep.

Peter removed the object from his right back pocket—a six-inch, fixed-blade Buck knife, sharpened to a razor's edge—and pulled it from its leather sheath. It glistened, even in the low wattage of the nightlight. He smiled, returned the empty sheath to his back pocket, and leaned again into the bedroom. Angie's sleep sounds continued, so he pushed open the door, very slowly, soundlessly. Peter Brookings entered the room, his heart racing. He froze yet again, anxious that the pounding that filled his ears from his foul heart might awaken her and spoil his surprise, but it did not.

"There she is!" His father breathed in his brain, and Peter deliberately walked toward Angie. She was under the covers, exposed only from the shoulders up, lying on her back. It was a queen-size bed, and the side where Jack would have slept, between the door and the woman, was empty, so the killer moved around to her side until he hovered over her.

He placed his filthy left hand on her throat, and Angie awoke with a start, tried to gasp, her green eyes open wide. Peter moved swiftly, up onto the bed, and straddled her, knees pressed against her shoulders, her struggles ineffective. Sleep left suddenly and terror filled her eyes. She tried to speak but could not. He repositioned the knife in his left hand and pressed its blade against her throat, above his other hand. A thin line of blood escaped her skin from the cut of the knife.

"Keep perfectly still, or I will slit your throat like the fucking sow you are," he said, his voice guttural and deep, unrecognizable to Angie.

She began to cry, tears pooling in her eyes and then racing each other down her cheeks. When some of the tension left her, and her efforts to rise were quelled, he removed his hand from her throat, but the Buck knife remained, stinging her sharply. It took Angie a few moments to comprehend that this disheveled outrage on top of her was Peter Brookings. Her mind had difficulty fathoming what he had become.

"What are you doing?" she rasped finally.

"I'm gonna take what's mine, what I came here for, you fucking whore, and then I'm going to gut you and that bastard kid down the hall."

Absolute shock clutched Angie rigidly, its claws tearing and sinking into her soul, shredding hope and faith and whatever dreams lived within her. She felt completely powerless, entirely at his mercy, and this both terrified and enraged her.

"Please don't hurt Davie, Peter. I'll do whatever you want. Just don't hurt Davie, *please*, Peter!" Her mind was racing, searching like a computer through its database, waiting for something to pop into her brain and offer a way out, an escape. She thought of Jack and wondered what he would do, should a madman with a knife straddle him in the night. She saw Jack's eyes, black pinheads in a hazel field, alert and intense.

"Keep your head on straight," Jack commanded. "Look for your opening. Don't miss it; make it count!"

Peter withdrew the blade from her throat but renewed pressure with his right hand, and she coughed as his downward force choked her. The blood from the cut on her neck left billowing crimson shadows on the white pillowcase beneath her head. He scooted back until he sat on her upper thighs, his knees on the bed and straddling her waist.

"Shut your fucking mouth," Peter snarled. He brought the knife under the neckline of her blue Michigan T-shirt and sliced straight down its center, between the yellow *H* and the second *I*. The well-worn cotton offered no resistance to the finely honed blade. As the shirt fell away, her breasts were fully exposed. They heaved with her chest, up and down, up and down, and the monster whose crushing weight kept her pinned was aroused by the sight.

"I don't know about you," he panted, "but I'm gonna *enjoy* this!" He returned the knife to her throat and roughly squeezed her right breast with his free hand. She whimpered and squirmed, futility raging within her. She tried to quickly raise a knee, hoping to drive it into his groin and gain some small advantage, but she was well pinned, trapped under the sheet and blanket and his weight. He reacted by slapping her sharply, backhanded, and her left cheek burst into an angry red flush. Another trickle of blood ran from her mouth, and when she drew her lips back in pain, her white teeth were bathed in crimson.

"Try that again, bitch, and I'll slit your throat," the madman snarled. "I'll still fuck you, but maybe you won't notice so much." He leered at her and laughed with a soulless squall that chilled her to the marrow. With his free hand, he struggled to pull back the covers and begin the assault on his primary target. Angie, although tensed like a coiled spring, remained reasonably still, her breaths expelled in loud, short gasps.

Peter had to lift himself to free and then pull down the covers, and then her sweatpants, so his knees relaxed their pressure against Angie's shoulders. She sensed opportunity and threw her legs and hips up with all the strength she could muster. It caught him at just the right moment. His balance faltered, and as he scuffled to regain it, he was compelled to withdraw the knife from her throat.

Again, she moved hastily. With her right arm suddenly free, she fired a fist to the side of his head and made solid contact. He grunted and rolled to his right, and then he fell off the bed and landed on the floor with a dull thump.

"I *knew* you'd fuck this up, you weak little cocksucker," his father screamed shrilly in his brain. Finally, he was aware of the thigh muscle he'd injured when he tripped in the trees, and the cracked rib likewise howled in pain from his chest.

"Oh, you fucking cunt! You're gonna pay for that!" he roared.

Adrenaline fired through Angie's terrors and kept the woman on the move. She struggled to escape the remaining constraints of the covers, but she too tumbled off the bed and thudded to the floor on the opposite side. Her shoulder hit the floor hard and told her so unkindly, but she fought on, laboring at last to her feet. The nearby door opened from its other side, so she had to either pull it toward her, all the way open, or dash around it where it stood.

Neither was a viable option; it gave the madman too much time to recover.

Peter limped around the bed and beat her to the door with ease. He lashed out with the knife, and its merciless blade sliced deep into the flesh of her left forearm, down to the bone, below the elbow. Blood gushed from this injury, but she reared back and took a swing at Peter with her other hand. Again she tagged him, belting him square on the nose, and they both heard the sickening crunch of breaking bone. Now it was his turn to bleed. His nose, once so perfectly straight, lurched wildly to the left side of his face in a torrent of blood, and he bawled in pain.

There was no time for any of his rancid vitriol now. Again he slashed with the knife, and with this swing, he carved open her upper chest from shoulder to shoulder, although not as deeply as the arm wound. She cried out against the burning flush of blood.

"You sick, pathetic bastard," she hissed. Angie heard Jack again, way back in her head, something he'd said about how to disable would-be predators. She threw her right foot up as hard and as fast as she could, and caught Peter square in the balls. He sucked in several pounds of air with a scratchy wheeze and dropped to his knees. His demented eyes very nearly bulged out of their sockets, and his face turned several angry shades of red.

Angie could not get past him yet, and that fierce kick to his manhood, such as it was, left her largely spent. She was also bleeding out. Pure evil recharged Peter, and he crawled on his knees toward her as she sagged in the corner. His eyes were filled with malevolence, an insidious glow of hate and pain and rage. She chased after whatever strength she had left in the tank and tried to throw herself onto the bed. If she could do that, she thought in a blink of time, maybe she could spin to the other side and make a break for the door.

It was an ambitious plan, but she didn't have the reserves to pull it off. Peter grabbed her left ankle before she could roll across, and he pulled her toward the end of the bed. When she tried to sit up, he punched her in the mouth, and she slammed onto her back. She was fast losing consciousness, slipping away, and the demon looming above was ready to finish her off.

Through the red fog smothering her mind, she looked up to see Peter rearing back, glimmering knife clutched in both hands. He raised the blade high above his head and held it there, eyes gleaming, a demented, fanged smile breaking through the blood that masked his face. "Say good night, bitch!" he shrieked. His eyes widened wildly, immersed in a sea of crimson, the furious moment of his murderous ejaculation finally at hand.

Suddenly, a puzzled expression replaced the ecstasy on his face. The smile withdrew into its lair, and his eyes rolled up and into the back of head. He leaned back as the knife fell from his hands and landed on the bed next to Angie's right hip. Peter Brookings fell backward to the floor at the end of the bed. There was a brief gagging noise, and then it was still.

Angie fought off the vapors that sought to steal her sight and her life, and when they cleared a little, she saw Davie, eyes and mouth wide open. In his hands, still at the ready, he clutched Uncle Jack's Louisville Slugger baseball bat. He'd gathered every ounce of strength in his little boy's body, reared back, and brought the barrel of the bat into Peter's back with all he had, a swing that, back home on his nightstand, would have made Reggie Jackson *very* proud.

The home-run swing connected with the cracked rib in Peter's left side, and its force drove splintered bone into his fetid heart like a spear. Now, as life left him for good, Peter heard his father one last time in this life. "You fucking *imbecile*! What a spineless, shit-eating little turd you truly are!"

Moments later, Peter crawled to his feet, but now he stood in utter blackness. He heard moans and shrieks and the cries of the truly anguished. Something sharp pushed at his back, propelling him forward. *It feels like claws*, he thought. Before he could collect his wits, he was shoved into a luminous room, fully furnished in the style of his childhood: 1950s modern gauche, he recalled. He looked to his left, and there sat his mother.

"Well, if it isn't our little eunuch," she whined, not bothering to look up from the horror she knitted, needle clicking against needle, weaving through a string of red-eyed rats, very much alive, gnawing hungrily at her legs and her bloodied lap.

"It sure is, dear. It's Baby Shitpants herself."

Peter spun to his right and saw his father, glaring right through him as he clenched a gigantic cigar in his dagger-toothed, steel-trap mouth, foul smoke ballooning above his shriveled head. Peter heard a door slam behind him. He spun to escape, but the door was gone. Only a wall remained, mocking him from behind his mother's god-awful, putrid, flowery wallpaper.

He turned and they both began to chastise him, to criticize, ridicule, and belittle him. Forevermore, they would spew rancid rancor into his head, locked together eternally in this room, the most hopeless corner of hell, with no doors, no windows, and no escape.

"Peter, you are one big pant load; you know that, don't you?" His mother arched an all-knowing eyebrow.

"Looks like our mama's boy got the brown end of the stick again, dear," his father opined.

"Maybe he *is* the brown end, darling," said Peter's mother. "The dripping brown end, that's our Peter, Peter, little shit eater! Champagne?"

"Yes, dear, but none for Peter, of course." His father chuckled. "You *know* how he wets the bed."

"Oh, sweet Christ," Peter cried, dropping to his knees. "Oh, sweet Christ, save me!"

"Oh, don't be silly," his mother shrieked. The startled rats squirmed and squeaked. "Don't you be *silly!*"

Chapter Thirteen

Davie dropped the bat, ignored the corpse on the floor, and raced to Angie. There was blood everywhere. It filled the boy with dread and the sickening feeling that he had been here before. Her life escaped in red streams of blood that rushed to a distant sea, far away, ruthless and relentless. *This can't happen,* he thought as panic and terror surged through him. *I can't let this happen again!* His mind grew confused with flickering images of his mother, and now Aunt Angie, bleeding out before his eyes.

Angie hastily grabbed Peter's knife and sliced into the bedsheet to make a tourniquet for her gashed left arm, the most severe wound. She worked quickly, without panic, until she'd fashioned a reasonable bandage and tourniquet, the last of her strength now spent.

"Aunt Angie, lay down!" Davie cried.

"It's okay, baby," she said calmly. "Go to the phone and call nine-one-one. Tell them to hurry." The boy rushed around the bed, stepping on Peter's hand as he went, and lifted the receiver from its cradle. He pushed the buttons quickly but carefully, not wanting the delay of a misdial. It rang twice before a woman answered.

"Nine-one-one, what's your emergency?" the female operator said in a cool and steady voice.

Davie held the phone to Angie's cheek, now turning several unnatural shades of red and blue and black. "We need an ambulance and police, 148 Lakewood Drive. I've been attacked, knife wounds, need … help …" Angie lost consciousness and fell back, her head listing to the right.

"Aunt Angie! Angie!" Davie screamed. He grabbed the phone and spoke with urgency, but lucidity too. "You gotta hurry, she's bleedin' bad and she fainted! Please!"

"Okay, I'm sending help right now," the operator said, taking control. "Stay on the line. Are you hurt? Are you *safe?*"

"No, I'm okay," Davie said. "He's dead, I'm pretty sure, but please, you gotta *hurry up!*" He could hear the operator pushing buttons on the other end of the line and then issuing dispatch instructions.

Davie grabbed a pillow off the floor with his free hand and shook it until he held only its case. Angie had done a pretty good job with her arm, presuming help arrived soon. Davie now addressed the gash across her upper chest, pressing the pillowcase lengthwise against the long wound, pushing down at its center, where it bled most freely. Her bare breasts were covered in blood and their up and down heaves had become slight billows, slow to restart. Davie tried to cover them with the blanket.

"Are you still there?" The operator returned to the line.

"Yeah, but I gotta put the phone down, I need both hands," Davie said.

"Okay, but have you done anything to staunch the bleeding, to slow it down? Is your mother conscious, awake?" The operator continued to work buttons, her voice intermittently muffled as she gave information and instructions to emergency services.

"I think she fainted," Davie said. "She put a *turn-ee-quit* on her arm, and I covered the other cut, but I gotta go *now!*"

"Don't hang up the phone, son. Just set it down," the operator said, louder and with more firmness. "Help is on the way. Hang in there!"

Davie dropped the phone onto the bed and used both hands to apply pressure on the pillowcase across Angie's chest and stem the bleeding, as best he could. Satisfied with the results, he loosened the improvised tourniquet on Angie's arm, paused for a few moments, and then rewrapped and reapplied pressure there, too. He'd paid attention watching those old war movies with Uncle Jack, and, as Uncle Jack would say, you just never knew when that stuff was gonna pay off.

"Aunt Angie, can you hear me?" he asked anxiously.

She moaned feebly and tried to open her eyes, but could not. She was too weak. "I hear you, baby," she muttered. Her words were a slurred whisper, but she spoke again. "Make sure you tell Uncle Jack that I love him, and I always will. You too, and don't forget Curly."

"You're gonna tell 'em yourself," he said with resolve. "You stay here with *me*, Aunt Angie, *please!*" He stroked her healthy cheek with his hand, and it was very warm, almost hot. "Please, God, please *bring us help!*" the boy called up to the ceiling.

Angie moaned again, more faintly this time. In the distance, Davie heard the emergency vehicles' sirens, wailing a cry of hope in the night, moving steadily closer, but so *painfully slow*. Davie kept his eyes on Angie, and the boy began to pray. "Hail Mary, full of grace, the Lord is with me." He sobbed, fear and panic strangling the words, but he pushed on. "Blessed are you who bring women," he wept, "and blessed is the fruit in your womb, baby Jesus."

Angie felt herself awaken. *Close enough for jazz,* she thought of the boy's prayer. *Maybe we should go to church more often.* She rose from the bed, pulled on a white terrycloth bathrobe, and walked outside through the glass door wall at the back of the house. She didn't notice that she'd forgotten to slide it open. The lake shimmered blue under a warm sun, pure white clouds drifted by, and a soft breeze tickled her face.

Angie saw a card table perched on the beach, just offshore, and there sat her mother, wearing a floppy white straw bonnet, and her father, topped with a Tigers cap tilted at a jaunty angle. Two martini glasses with green olives, plus an iced glass pitcher full of their beloved "joy juice," were joined by a deck of cards atop the table.

"Your mom's kicking my butt at gin rummy," her father said behind a glowing smile, eyes twinkling.

"Again," her mother added, giving Angie a wink and sipping her martini.

"You need to go back inside, honey," her father said tenderly. "It's not time for you to be out here yet. It's way too soon."

"Yes, dear," Angie's mother said decisively. "Your father's right. Go back inside with David. We'll call you when it's time, okay?" She stabbed the olive in her drink with a pink plastic sword and ate it leisurely. "Deal, old man, and from the top, please."

"Yes, dear," he groaned, looked at Angie, grinned, rolled his eyes, and began reshuffling the cards.

Angie smiled and waved to them, a little confused. She saw a massive wolf just beyond her parents, lapping water from the lake with a long, bloodred tongue. She turned for the door wall. When she looked back, her parents, the wolf, the lake, and the blue sky were fading into darkness. Then they were gone altogether. She opened her eyes and found the little boy kneeling beside the bed, head bowed and hands clasped so tightly together that his knuckles were nearly white.

"Holy Mary, Mother of God, pray for our dinners, now and at

the hour of your death, amen. But don't let *this* be the hour, *please Jesus!*" Davie began to weep. The ambulance sirens were louder, very close.

"Don't cry, peanut. I'm still here," Angie said, her voice hoarse but a little stronger.

"Aunt Angie! Hold on, they're here!" Davie scurried off, and a few seconds later, Angie heard the front screen door swing open and bang against something. Davie hollered, "Hurry! Hurry! In here!"

What followed was a blur of commotion for Angie, the sounds of men and one woman calling out vital signs, shouting out for this and that, until finally they were carefully placing her on a gurney and carrying her outside. She saw two, maybe three men, Michigan State Police, in crisp blue-and-gray uniforms, moving through the house, room to room, guns drawn, already trying to piece together what had happened.

Angie didn't much care at that moment. She squeezed Davie's hand tightly as they toted her outside and toward the yawning back doors of a bright red ambulance, its lights flashing. "Honey, run inside and grab my purse, okay? Look on the kitchen counter." Davie spun and vanished, and a few moments later he returned, clutching the black leather shoulder bag that he was certain weighed at least two hundred pounds.

An IV started replenishing her blood, and a wave of tranquility soothed much of her pain, compliments of a dose of morphine. She pulled Davie close to her mouth with her good arm and kissed him on the lips. He smiled and kissed her back. The EMTs hoisted Angie into the ambulance, and Davie climbed in after her.

"You're my hero, baby." Tears began to roll down her cheeks. "Uncle Jack is gonna be so *proud* of you!" The boy blushed and looked at his feet, nearly falling on his butt when the ambulance heaved forward. Soon it found the road and sped off into the gray beginnings of another dawn, siren wailing.

"You're gonna make it, ma'am," a man in white shirt, dark blue pants, and black shoes said calmly. "We got to you just in time. *Just in time*. We're going to St. Mike's, and they'll take good care of you there."

The boy and woman held hands and soothed one another until morphine and exhaustion carried her away. The man in white rubbed the boy's back tenderly, but Davie never took his eyes from his aunt Angie. A female EMT squeezed by the man and pulled the two halves of Angie's T-shirt away and quickly checked for any wounds. Satisfied there were no injuries, she covered Angie with a blanket.

"There," she announced, satisfied. Davie nodded his thanks and continued his vigil until the racing ambulance reached its destination. He knew what a close call this had been, and he shuddered a little. He suddenly thought of his mother and wished he'd gotten to her sooner too. *Boy*, he thought, *what's Uncle Jack gonna say?*

They arrived at St. Mike's, and the medics quickly but carefully rolled Angie through a brightly lit emergency entrance, where a swarm of medical personnel converged on her, barking orders, calling out vital signs, swooping into action. They rush-rolled her down a long white hall as Davie jogged along beside the cart, still holding Angie's hand.

"Step aside, son," one of the orderlies commanded. "End of the road for you."

"No, sir," the boy announced. "I'm stayin' close!"

"Is this your son, ma'am?" a nurse asked Angie.

Angie looked lovingly into Davie's deep blue eyes and smiled sweetly. "Yes," she said. "Yes, he is." Woman and boy exchanged a pure love with their eyes that transcended everything in the room, everything in the world, a connection as untainted as there could be, beaming at each other under the fluorescent lights of the hospital hallway.

"Okay, but you gotta wait in the family room when we get to surgery," an orderly declared.

"Okay, mister," Davie said, squeezing Angie's hand and never letting their eyes part. When they'd reached their destination and the nurses and orderlies prepared to separate this new mother and child, Angie raised her right hand. "Just one second, okay?" Everyone stopped what they were doing and stood still.

"Davie," Angie said, her voice soft and calm, "I'm gonna be okay, thanks to you, so I want you to go take a nap in the waiting room." She looked at the ceiling and asked no one in particular, "Can he get something to eat?"

"Sure, ma'am. We'll take good care of him," a nurse said patiently, pleasantly.

"Davie," Angie whispered as her eyes moved back to the boy, "don't call Jack ... *Dad* ... just yet, okay? We'll do it together when they're done patching me up. Okay?"

"Sure, Mom, sure—okay," Davie said. It felt so good, so *right*, saying it, and he felt another rush swoop through his heart. "Just lay down and I'll be here when you need me." He stood on his tiptoes and kissed her on the lips.

"I know you will, baby. I know you will."

And with that, they were gone in a swirl of arms and beeping monitors and rushing footsteps, banging past the swinging doors— gone. Davie was alone, and he turned and looked around. He spotted a glass door with a sign, *Family Waiting Area*, and he walked in. It was empty and quiet, except for a TV up high in the corner, facing the vacant chairs and a few small couches. Bugs Bunny was running like hell from Elmer Fudd, who was toting a shotgun longer than he was tall. Uncle Jack loved Bugs Bunny, frequently impersonated that "cwazy wabbit," and so the boy smiled.

Davie padded to a couch and sat down, his feet dangling slowly back and forth above the gray carpeting. He was exhausted and had a headache, but he was relieved that Aunt Angie had been spared and he had helped save her. He was exhilarated, adrenaline still buzzing, as thoughts of Aunt Angie and his mother and Mr. Stan too all raced through his mind. With a measure of his innocence miraculously intact, Davie ignored the TV and sat alone, swinging his feet.

A few minutes later, a pretty nurse wearing a powder-blue cardigan sweater entered the room, toting two sandwiches, a bag of Lay's potato chips, an apple, and a can of Coca-Cola on a green plastic tray. "I hope you like peanut butter and jelly," she said with a sweet lilt in her voice. Davie looked over her shoulder and saw a policeman peeking through the glass. He nodded at Davie, smiled slightly, and then turned away.

"I sure do," Davie said enthusiastically. "Thanks, lady!" Davie carefully took the tray and tore into the plastic wrappings on one of the sandwiches. *Now this*, he decided, *this is a* sammich, *as Mr. Stan would say.* The pretty nurse popped open the can and poured some Coke into a paper cup. She put her hands on her knees and smiled at the boy. "My name is Wendy," she said. "Can I get you anything else, little man?"

"No. This is *great*," he mumbled through a mouthful full of sammich. "Thanks again!"

"Well, you let me know if you think of anything else, okay? I'll be just down the hall, to the left." She rubbed his head and whispered, "Your mom is gonna be fine, but she'll be in there for a little while, okay?" Davie nodded, devouring the meal with vigor. Wendy ripped open the bag of chips, set it on the tray, and started for the door. "You should take a nap," she suggested. "I'll come tell you as soon as we hear something."

Davie smiled and waved. He inhaled the second sammich around handfuls of salty chips and chugs of sweet Coke. When the tray held nothing but spent wrappers, a well-gnawed apple core, and an empty red can, he set it on a chair across from where he sat, belched wetly, giggled, and lay down on the couch. He used his folded arms as a pillow and absentmindedly watched Bugs Bunny mess with Elmer Fudd, who just never seemed to *get* it. Exhaustion finally took him, and Davie was fast asleep.

Chapter Fourteen

Jack awoke as morning's light filled the living room. He was sprawled on the couch now, with no recollection of moving there from the rocking chair. He dropped his feet to the floor and slowly sat up. A throbbing ache in his forehead spiked the misery meter to remind him of sins he'd committed the day before. *Fecking whiskey,* he thought, perhaps forgetting the twelve or so beers that also had gone along for the ride.

Curly waddled over to Jack, rose to two legs, and rested his forepaws on the man's left leg, his stub of a tail in full swing—a variation of it, anyway. Curly licked Jack's hand, and he returned the favor by scratching the top of the dog's head.

"You need to go out, bud?" Curly dropped to four on the floor, wagged his tail even more excitedly, and made a beeline to the front door. "Awright, awright, I'm comin', hold your water."

Jack went to the door, unlatched the hook from its hasp on

the screen door, and pushed it open. Curly dashed out, tail straight up, and began searching for a suitable spot to urinate. This could take anywhere from ten seconds to ten minutes, depending on whatever scents or distractions entered the equation. Jack watched for a moment and began to scan the neighborhood for anything that might have changed in the hours since he last looked. Bull Run Way looked the same to Jack, although the Japanese cherry tree by Stan Koski's porch had blossomed overnight. It was quite beautiful, a late bloomer, Jack thought, and its sweet scent wafted through the early morning air.

"Don't pee on the cherry tree, knothead," Jack advised Curly, who paid no heed, nose to the ground, before the dog settled on a small evergreen and hoisted a hind leg. "Atta boy, Curly," Jack said quietly. "Fart around for a minute and I'll be right back."

After a much-needed trip to the john, Jack walked into the kitchen and began to make coffee. He had done it many times, often before daylight, and he was sure he could do it blindfolded in the dark. This morning, however, he could not find the coffee can. He opened all the cupboards, even looked in the refrigerator, without success. He opened the double doors under the sink and looked in the trash to see if there was an empty can. Again, he found nothing.

"Sonofabitch. Son … of … a … *bitch!* Angie took the fecking coffee up north!" In the instant between frustration and revelation, anger welled and rose in him like the very brew he had hoped to percolate. *Fuck me silly,* he thought, *she'd rather leave me with no joe than make a quick stop at one of the hundred or so grocery or convenience stores or* fecking coffee shops *she would drive by on the way up north.*

He reopened the fridge and took a quick inventory: no milk, no orange juice, no half-and-half, lunchmeat gone, Coca-Cola gone. *You have got to be shitting me! Really? Great, now I have to go to the fecking market on a Saturday morning with a hangover. If she had said something,* Jack thought,

I would have said, "Yeah, go ahead, take whatever you need." Instead, Jack felt burgled, violated, and he was *pissed.*

And then, just as abruptly as it swelled within him and choked his heart, anger waned and then left him entirely. Jack felt spent and a little blue. "I guess that about says it all," he said softly. "Love is never having to say, 'I took the fecking coffee.'" Jack chuckled and shook his head, already over it, and then became aware that Curly was barking in the front yard, so he returned to the screen door.

"Curly," Jack called out in a loud whisper, "come here, dipstick, you're wakin' up the whole neighborhood!"

Curly continued to bark, so Jack stepped out onto the porch to investigate. He followed the sound of the dog's barks and looked to his left to see Curly in front of Stan Koski's house. The dog dropped his head on top of his forepaws, butt up in the air, short tail wagging slowly back and forth like a pendulum. The wag of a dog's tail expresses much more than "glad to see ya," depending on how it uses the gesture; Curly's wag said that he now faced something he didn't understand or recognize. Jack walked over to Curly in his bare feet, ignoring the cold grass, still wet with morning dew.

Jack reached down to rub Curly's butt and then looked up to follow the dog's line of sight. On the Koski porch sat Stan, and Jack started to offer an apology for his goofy dog. He stopped short when he took a harder look at the old man.

Stan Koski sat straight in the old wooden rocker, head back, eyes open, but they were pallid, almost colorless. Jack froze in his tracks. As he continued to stare, he noticed that Stan was *smiling.* "Jesus wept," Jack muttered. "Jesus." He climbed the porch steps and took the old man's hand. It was ice-cold.

Jack looked into those faded eyes and said softly, "So long, Stan. May you be in heaven an hour before the devil knows you're dead." This was one of Stan's toasts on those occasions when they shared a little Irish whiskey. "Always drink Jameson, Jack. Bushmills is for Protestants," Stan would say.

Jack felt a wave of sadness that found release as steady streams of tears streaked his cheeks. After several moments, he wiped them away and gently caressed Stan's face, once, with his right hand. Again without thought, Jack crossed himself and retreated down the steps to the lawn.

Jack picked Curly up in his arms and carried the dog home. Once inside his house, he set the dog down, walked to the phone in the kitchen, and dialed nine-one-one. His wet feet left a trail on the floor.

Within a few minutes, Jack heard a siren wailing as it progressed toward Bull Run Way, and he went outside to meet whoever showed up. Soon a police cruiser rolled up the street with an ambulance on its tail. Jack ran a finger across his throat and shook his head, and both vehicles shut off their sirens. Too late, Jack was sure; those who had still been asleep were by now making their way to their doors and windows to see what was going on.

The cop exited his cruiser and walked deliberately toward Jack. He was a tall white man, stocky, with ruddy cheeks and a blank expression behind reflective aviator sunglasses. *Guess that's the look you get when you've seen it all,* Jack speculated. What would it take to get a reaction from *this* dude? He thought of the Man with No Eyes who kept a stone-faced countenance while overseeing the chain gang in *Cool Hand Luke.*

"You the caller, sir?" The cop removed a notepad from a large pocket over his left breast.

"Yeah, my neighbor," Jack said as he pointed toward Stan. "Passed away on his porch sometime during the night."

The cop turned toward the Koski house, saw Stan, and gestured to the EMT guys in the ambulance. Two men got out of their rig and began the ritual of inspection and analysis.

"Did you know him, sir?" he said in a monotone, pencil poised above paper.

"Yeah, name's Stan," Jack said, watching the cop's pencil at work. "Stanley Koski, k-o-s-k-i. Lives alone; his wife died years ago. He's lived here since the twenties, I think. Nice guy ..." Emotion choked off his words, and he again felt grief for a friend now lost.

The cop stopped writing and looked up at Jack, then over to Stan, who was now being examined: checked for a pulse, a heartbeat, a breath. *Really,* Jack thought, *can't you tell by looking at the poor guy?* Behind him, Curly stood on two legs and looked out through the screen door, eyes wide. The dog's head was all that could be seen from outside the house.

"He's gone," the pudgy EMT declared. "Heart attack, I'd guess."

"Yeah, looks like it's been a while, too," the skinny black EMT chimed in. "A good ten hours, maybe more."

"I saw him about six last night; he waved to me and said hello," Jack said. "I was gonna go over and sit with him, but ..." *And here's another regret on the old scorecard,* Jack thought wistfully.

"Shit, lookie here! He's *smiling*, right? Smiling!" The black EMT placed his hands on his hips, leaned back, and shook his head. "Don't believe I've ever seen *that* before!"

The cop stepped a little closer, peering at Stan. "Yup," he said, "he sure is." The cop returned his attention to the notepad and wrote it all down. The morning sun gleamed from his reflective lenses. *Was he going to write in his report, "The old man died with a smile"?* Jack wondered.

"Hey, Jack!" Jack looked up to see Terry Ralls trotting across Bull Run Way in black sweatpants and a gray sweatshirt with "Property of My Wife" stenciled across its front in blue lettering. "What happened? You okay?"

Jack again motioned toward Stan with his left hand. Terry's eyes followed and took in the scene as he drew closer to Jack.

"Ah, shit, Stan, damn," Terry muttered. "Well, that's a shame." He scratched the top of his head, glanced at the cop, and then looked back to Jack. "I guess he had a good run," he said. "Eighty-five if he's a day. Katie's gonna have a hard cry over this one."

"She won't be the only one," Jack said softly, again perilously close to tears. He likewise dreaded telling Angie, and Davie especially.

"Any idea as to who we should call, like any family members, maybe?" The cop had returned from working his notebook.

"No family that I know of around here. He's got a daughter out West somewhere," Terry said as he walked a little closer to Stan. "Jesus, Jack, is he smiling?"

Jack had to laugh a little at that. How many guys went out with a big grin like the one on Stan's old puss? He thought of John Garfield, who supposedly had a heart attack and died while in the throes of making love. Or at the end, maybe, Jack deduced.

"My wife Katie cleans up ... *cleaned* and cooked a little for Stan, so she might know who to call," Terry said. "Lemme go ask her. Shit, I hate this duty." Terry turned and jogged for home. You could almost hear the wheels turning in his head, trying to think of a way to break the news to Katie. What do you say? *What do you say?*

The cop turned to face Stan Koski and announced, "I'm gonna radio this in; get a coroner out here." He turned to his car. Not two minutes later, the Rallses' front screen door flew open and Katie dashed through, clutching closed a pink, thigh-length, terry-cloth robe. In her early forties, blonde hair in flight behind her, wearing not a smudge of makeup, she was very beautiful, and always would be, Jack thought. She ran directly to Stan, ignoring all in her path. She knelt at his feet, took both of his hands in hers, and kissed each tenderly.

"Oh, Stosh, you old coot, what have you done?" Katie looked up into those pallid eyes and saw the smile that split the cracks in his ancient visage. Tears began to roll down her face, but she ignored them. "Why, Stan Koski, you old rascal! Did Hildie finally come for you, like you always said she would?" Katie began to laugh with a musical lilt, quietly at first and then louder, until the laughter turned to gentle sobs.

Terry made his way back and now bent down, wrapped an arm around Katie's waist, and slowly lifted her to her feet. He began to walk her toward their home, but then stopped and whispered in her ear. She spoke softly through her grief, and only Terry could hear or understand what she said. The cop exited his vehicle and walked back to Jack.

"Katie says there's a business card under the telephone in the front hall," Terry said. "It's from Stan's lawyer, Mr. Ritter, and Katie says he'll know what to do." He turned and led Katie tenderly, slowly home.

"Thank you, ma'am, and sir," said the cop to their backs, in full Joe Friday monotone.

"Are you through with me, Officer?" Jack asked.

"Looks that way," the cop said sharply as his glaring, reflective eyes turned to Jack. He closed the notebook, returned it to his shirt pocket, and began to look around the neighborhood, his neck on a swivel. "Which house is yours?" he asked when he'd finished his inspection. Jack turned and pointed to his house. "Okay," the cop said. "If we need you, we'll find you."

I have no doubt, Jack thought. He nodded to the cop and walked toward home, pausing to look at Stan for the last time. *Damned if he isn't* smiling! *Good for you, Stan, good for you. No better way to tell Death to fuck off than to smile when he or she comes for you!* But Katie was right. It wasn't Death who had come for Stosh, and so Jack smiled too.

Chapter Fifteen

Daylight advanced steadily from the east, delivering sunshine as last night's storm pushed off and crossed Lake Huron and Lake St. Clair, intent on pestering Canada and western New York. In Angie's bedroom on Lakewood Drive, samples were taken, various measurements recorded, and a very dead Peter Brookings searched. The Michigan State Police forensic team was on scene, and the medical examiner was en route.

A young investigator named Riley, with reddish hair and white latex gloves, frisked Peter. In the windbreaker's left side pocket, he found the motel key. "Looks like this guy was staying at Lake in the Woods, Sarge. No wallet on him, though." He stood, dropped the key into a plastic evidence bag, and wrote a brief note on its affixed white label. Sergeant Rick McDonnell took the key, examined it through the plastic, and turned to the middle-aged African American on his left flank. "Donny, head over to the Lake and see what you can turn up in number seven, but be careful what you move around, okay? Check with Sandy too. You know the drill."

Donny nodded, squeezed behind McDonnell, and was headed into the hallway when his sergeant stopped him. "Be cautious when you go in, Donny. We've got no idea what's goin' on here, or if this guy was alone. Okay?" Donny nodded again, turned, walked outside, got in his cruiser, and drove the mile or so to the motel, unhurried.

McDonnell, as ranking officer on site, began to formulate a theory. They were a long way from Detroit, some two hundred and fifty miles, and no team of detectives was at hand, so it fell to him to make an initial analysis. There would be more police and more support up here when the tourist season hit full speed Memorial Day weekend, but for now, they'd work with what they had. It was not his first bloody crime scene, nor was it the most horrific he'd seen, but the amount of blood in this small room left him feeling queasy. He was glad he'd not had his breakfast.

McDonnell took Riley by an elbow and steered him back a few steps to the doorway. "Okay, here's what I think. The perp," he pointed to dead Peter on the floor, "walks over here from the Lake in the Woods, breaks in, and attacks the woman in her bed. She manages to put up a fight, God love her," he squatted and pointed to Peter's face and battered nose with a pencil, "and somehow, even badly hurt, she won the day. We'll have to wait for an autopsy to know exactly what killed this asshole, that's anybody's guess at this point, but the only obvious weapon on scene is the knife." He pointed at the bagged and tagged Buck knife, lying near the foot of the bed where Angie had dropped it. "But he doesn't appear to have been stabbed.

"And there's this baseball bat," McDonnell said, gesturing toward the Louisville Slugger lying in the opposite corner, a black *Norman Cash* signature etched at the business end of the barrel. Jack had owned that bat since he was Davie's age; it was a family treasure, and now its legacy was forever secured.

"Yeah, maybe the bat." McDonnell scratched at his chin with his right hand. "The kid, maybe?" McDonnell squinted as the hamster in his head ran its little wheel at full speed. "The kid hears the struggle, wakes up, and the bat's in his room, so he grabs it, runs down the hall, clobbers numbnuts here," again pointing at Peter with a no. 2 pencil, "and he delivers the fatal blow?" More chin scratching. "Yeah, maybe. Maaaaaybeeee."

They had no idea how close to the truth they were. As in any case like this, where the perpetrator was dead and unavailable for questioning, they could never truly know the full story.

"Let's give the docs at St. Mike's a little time to sew up the lady of the house, and then we'll go have a chat with her and the kid. She'll be in surgery for a few hours, they tell me, and I've asked them to keep an eye on the little guy," the sergeant said. "We'll get somebody over there to keep watch, just in case. Meantime, let's keep snoopin' around here. Bag and tag *anything* that looks out of place, *capisce*?"

"Got it, Sarge," Riley said with a nod.

☆ ☆ ☆

Just down the road, Donny Mathews pulled his cruiser into the gravel parking lot at the Lake in the Woods Motel, and parked in front of number seven, next to a 1984 Firebird Trans Am, black, Michigan plate F63 29D. He climbed from the cruiser and checked the room door, but it was locked. Donny would wake up the manager, Sandy Lloyd, soon enough. For now, he unhooked a ring from his duty belt and fingered through twenty or so keys until he found the one he wanted. He inserted it into the lock and turned the knob.

The door swung open and Donny entered the room. He tugged on a pair of latex gloves and took mental notes as his eyes scanned clockwise, starting at the door. He spotted a Johnnie Walker bottle, two inches from empty; three empty cans of Bud; and a paper sack holding a bag of chips on the Formica table. There was a gym bag on the bed and a pile of clothing on the floor, next to a pair of brown dress shoes. Alligator, he noted, sweet. The bed appeared undisturbed, as did the shower; the commode had been used but not flushed.

Donny walked around the bed and, starting at its left head, stuck his right arm up to his elbow under the mattress. He probed counterclockwise around the bed until he found the wallet and car keys, which he extracted from concealment. Donny flipped the wallet open, read the driver's license, and got the skinny on Peter Oliver Brookings of Grosse Pointe. The picture *resembled* the dead guy on the floor up the road, he thought, precarnage. He counted fifteen twenty-dollar bills, a ten, and three ones, and returned the cash to the wallet before dropping it into an evidence bag and scribbling on its white label. After identifying the keys as belonging to the Firebird, he bagged and tagged them, and then placed both bags on the bed, directly above where he'd found them.

Donny continued to examine the room. When he was satisfied that he'd seen all there was to see with the naked eye, he exited the room and locked the door behind him. He peeled off the gloves, stuffed them in a pants pocket, and strolled to the manager's office. Daylight was in full bloom, and gravel squawked under his heavy footsteps. He couldn't shake the sights he'd seen in that bedroom up the road; it was the bloodiest scene he'd encountered in his eleven years in service, except maybe a couple of car wrecks on the interstate. He made a mental note to pick up a twelve-pack on his way home.

When he reached the manager's door, Donny tested the knob, certain it would be locked. It was, so he knocked on its wood frame four times and waited. Nothing stirred. He knocked four more times, harder now, and the door rattled in its frame. No reply. Donny pounded on the frame eight times and stepped back. A light flickered on inside the office.

"Hold yer goddamn horses, will ya? We ain't open! Can't ya see the friggin' sign ain't turned on?" Sandy Lloyd peered out, inches from the glass, and squinted at Donny, her blue-gray hair in disarray, a tattered green robe wrapped tight around her stocky frame.

"Fer cris'sakes, Donny, ya know what time it is?" she whined, unlatching and then opening the door.

Donny glanced at his wristwatch. "Yeah, Sandy, it's get-the-hell-up o'clock. You gonna sleep all day?" He stepped into the office as she turned and waddled behind the counter.

"Wha'sa matter, Donny," she croaked, "did yer old lady toss you out again? What'd you do, fart at the dinner table?"

"No." He sighed. "What can you tell me about the dude in number seven?" He pulled a notepad and pencil from his left shirt pocket, flipped the pad open, and held the pencil at the ready.

"City prick," she said, tugging on her left ear. "Pulled in just as I was closin' up, the snooty bastard, and he slammed the door on his way out, which pissed me off. He drove that black 'bird out there by seven." She pointed in the Firebird's direction.

"Lemme see his reg card, Sandy," Donny ordered. The woman pulled a gray metal file box from under the counter, opened it, and withdrew a five-by-eight-inch card from the back of the stack. She laid it on the counter, facing Donny, who spun it around until it was right-side up.

"Jack Thomas. That doesn't match the ID I found in the room, Sandy. Neither does this license plate number." He tapped the card with his pen three times and looked into her blue eyes, where a small spark still twinkled.

"Jayzus, copper," she whined, "it was rainin' like a sumbitch, and he didn't look like a crook. What'd he do, rob Louie's Donuts and steal your stash?" She gave him a wink, and he couldn't help but snicker. Things were different up here; he'd learned that seven years ago when he transferred to this post. Not exactly Mayberry, especially during summer's tourist and cottage season, but a long way from Detroit, that was for sure. Of course, that was safe to say about damn near anyplace in the state.

"I can't say right now, Sandy, but you can figure he won't be coming back to his room—ever. Don't go in there, understand? Stay out until the investigation team gets here and they give you the all clear. Dig?"

"Oh, fer shit sakes, Donny!" Sandy slapped the counter with her left hand. "It's Saturday! You know I'm gonna lose a bookin' in there tonight! Did he mess up the room?"

Donny shook his head as he placed the registration card in a plastic evidence baggie. "Nope, no mess, Sandy; it's very neat. Ask Sergeant Rick for a form and file a claim. I'm sure the governor will cut you a check."

"Oh yeah, I'll hold my friggin' breath waitin' for *that* one." She resigned herself to losing the eighteen bucks—twenty, if the sap forgot to reclaim the key deposit, like most of them did. "Tell Ricky, next time he comes here with that dopey broad with the bleached 'do from the bowling alley, he's gonna pay double! You wanna coffee, Donny? I can make us some lickity-split."

Donny couldn't help but laugh. This is what they call "local color." So was he, come to think of it. *Not too many brothers up here,* he mused, *but then again, nobody ever gave me any shit about what shade I am, either—other than this blue uniform, of course.*

"I wish I had time, doll, but I gotta roll. Can I get a rain check?"

"Yeah, sure, Donny, anytime," she said and waved her left hand dismissively through the air.

"Remember what I said about the room—do not touch any part

of it, in or out, okay?" said Donny, leaning slightly toward the old woman.

"Yeah, yeah, yeah," she muttered. "I get it, I get it, fer cris'sakes. Beat it, flatfoot. I got work to do and I need some java."

Donny smiled and shook his head again as he walked out of the office, careful not to slam the screen door. He knew from experience how much *that* set her off. He meandered back to the cruiser, sidestepped a good-size rain puddle, got in, and drove off, pulling out slowly to avoid kicking up any gravel. He made the brief but leisurely drive back to the crime scene by the lake. There was no hurry now.

Inside the house, the forensics crew finished up their evidence collecting, and the medical examiner had signed off on Peter Brookings, autopsy pending. He was bagged, tagged, and on his way to the morgue. Donny caught up with Rick McDonnell sitting at the kitchen table, smoking a cigarette, writing in his notebook.

"Well, what did you find at the motel?" Donny briefed McDonnell, occasionally glancing at his notebook. "Yeah, that fits," McDonnell said when Donny finished his report. "The name and address he used on the motel registration card belong to the lady's husband, who didn't make the trip up here, so far as we can tell."

"Do you think the husband was involved?" Donny asked.

"No, I don't think so, not at all. I think we'll talk to the missus at the hospital when we can, but we'll track down Jack Thomas, too, toot sweet." McDonnell set down his pencil and rubbed at his forehead with his right hand. "Thank Christ, they say she's gonna be okay, but I don't look forward to giving him the news."

McDonnell looked at his wristwatch. "Okay, I think we're squared away here, for now, anyways," he said. "Let's get some breakfast, and then we'll go to St. Mike's and see what's up, track Jack Thomas down, and give him the news."

Donny nodded and waited as the big man stood and pocketed his notepad. Together they walked outside. At McDonnell's suggestion, they strolled around the house to inspect the grounds one more time. At the foot of the short dock that jutted into the lake, both paused.

"Such a pretty spot," McDonnell muttered. "You just never know."

Chapter Sixteen

Jack Thomas waited and watched as the ambulance drove away from the Koski house, replaced by the coroner, who issued a medical certificate of death, declaring "natural causes" in the case of Stanley Koski, pending autopsy. The coroner and the cop went through their paces. Soon a black funeral hearse pulled up for Stan's trip to the mortuary, and, a few minutes later, a black Mercedes. Jack went outside and introduced himself to the man in the gray three-piece suit who climbed out of the car.

"Jackson Thomas," he said, offering his right hand. "I'm Stan's neighbor."

"Henry Ritter," said the elegant-looking gent as he accepted Jack's hand with a firmer grip than Jack anticipated. "Are you the gentleman who found Mr. Koski?"

"Yes, I did, at about nine this morning," Jack replied.

"Well, we thank you for your efforts," Henry Ritter said, looking

Jack in the eye. "I'll take care of everything from here, according to Mr. Koski's wishes."

With that, the lawyer turned for the Koski house. Jack said to his back, "Everyone on the street knew and loved Stan. If there's anything I can do, please don't hesitate to call on me."

"Thank you, Mr. Thomas," Henry said without turning. He ascended the porch steps. The funeral home's crew was waiting for the lawyer to take one last look at Stan. Henry Ritter put a hand on each hip and leaned back slightly. "By God, he's *smiling!*" After a moment or two, he waved a hand, and the two mortuary workers began the process of removing Stan for the last time.

Jack had seen enough, so he went home. The entire event took less than an hour, but it seemed like much longer to Jack. Curly, standing on hind legs and watching through the screen door, dropped to four on the floor, moved back as Jack entered, and took a seat in the living room entryway.

"Well, I guess that's that, Curly," Jack said. "Sorry you found that scene to start the day." He leaned down and grabbed Curly's head with both hands, massaging the dog's ears and jowls. Curly closed his eyes and wagged his tail briskly. His tongue dangled from the left side of his mouth. "I wish everyone was so easy to please, old pal." Curly fell to the floor and rolled onto his back, offering an ample belly to Jack, who obliged with a vigorous scratch.

Jack went into the kitchen and remembered the depleted supplies. He'd have to make a trip to the market, so he went upstairs, showered, and changed clothes, choosing a pair of well-worn jeans and a white T-shirt. Downstairs in the hall closet, he found a dark green, front-zippered sweatshirt with Eastern Michigan University's seal on its left breast, and he put this on, along with a pair of loafers. He grabbed his keys from the hook in the kitchen and headed for the entry door in the garage. "I'll be right back, old hoss."

Off the Path

Curly watched as Jack went out and then dropped his head for a nap.

Jack located his car, parked on an angle in the driveway. On his way out, he pulled down the garage door.

Kroger was busy, as it always was on Saturday mornings, so Jack patiently made his way through the aisles, avoiding the odd abandoned cart, screaming child, or ladies having a conversation in the middle of an aisle. "'S'cuse me, pardon me, behind you, 's'cuse me," on and on, until he finally reached the checkout line. *This is so tedious,* he thought. Women were better suited for this job; they had more patience and possessed an inherent shopping gene that men so clearly lacked, no matter what Gloria Steinem might think. *Hunters and gatherers, indeed,* Jack decided.

At last, Jack escaped Kroger's crowded confines, satisfied that he had everything he'd set out to buy. It was approaching noon and the skies were a dull gray. A cool breeze brought a sharp chill that recalled to Jack a basic tenet of life in Michigan: "If you don't like Michigan weather, just wait a minute."

Jack decided to pick up some lunch and headed for a McDonald's on Michigan Avenue. Driving felt good, helped clear his head, and before Jack knew it, he'd driven well past McDonald's and was in front of the Avenue Bar. He saw its bartender, Veronica, as she unlocked and opened the front door, so he beeped his car horn, but she didn't turn. He pulled up to the curb, parked, and got out of the car. Jack found the bar's dark-green front door unlocked. He entered with a bang when he shoved it open and slammed it into a chair.

"Jesus, Jack, you scared the hell outta me," Veronica exclaimed as she flipped on the lights behind the bar and then the dim overheads for the room itself.

"Sorry," Jack said. "I saw you going in, and I blew the horn, but I guess you didn't hear it. Are you open?"

Veronica was already busy performing the daily chores of opening a bar: wiping down the counters, aligning here and there, emptying this, refilling that. She did so quickly; it was a routine she'd repeated many, many times. "Always open for you, Jack," she said, pausing to smile at him. "Stroh's?"

"Sure, why not?" *Why not indeed*, he thought. Nothing in the grocery bags in the car would spoil or melt in this weather, and he felt no urgency to return to the empty house, without Angie and Davie, only the sad reminder of Stan's passing. At this moment, he wasn't sure where he belonged, and so this place would have to do.

Veronica pulled a longneck bottle of Stroh's Bohemian Style Beer—"America's Only Fire-Brewed Beer"—from the cooler, snapped its top off with an opener mounted to the back bar, and placed it on a napkin in front of Jack, along with a small beer glass. Jack poured the glass too full and admired its frothy head that overflowed onto the bar before he lifted the glass to his mouth and drained it.

"Thirsty, Jack?" she said, briskly wiping at the bar in front of the man.

"Yeah. I've had quite a time since the flower lady," Jack said softly, staring into the beer glass.

Veronica dropped her gaze to the floor and then closed her eyes altogether. She trembled slightly. "That was a rough one, all right," she mumbled. Jack could see that Veronica was fighting back her emotions. She'd applied her makeup that morning in an effort to hide the reddish reminders left on her pretty face by yesterday's sadness, but Jack wasn't fooled. He reached out and stroked her hair twice, and she smiled weakly.

"You know it wasn't your fault," he said gently. "There was nothing you could have done."

"The cops were here for a couple of hours, measuring this and that," she said, "but nobody stopped, and supposedly, nobody saw nothin', so the asshole that hit her got away clean."

"He's still gotta live with it, you know? Life has a way of evening out the score, sooner or later," Jack said with little conviction. "His karma is for shit, but maybe, you know, she just walked into the street. Who knows?"

Veronica shook her head and turned away. She resumed her work behind the bar, doing the little chores that she normally would have done at closing last night. She'd skipped these tasks in her haste to get away. Jack sat quietly and drank his beer. He pulled out his cigarettes, fired one up, and watched its bluish smoke fill the air above and about him. Veronica grabbed a clean ashtray from a stack near the sink under the bar, and set it in front of Jack.

"So, whatcha got goin' today, Jack? Don't usually see you here on Saturdays."

"I was in the neighborhood, as they say. Angie and Davie are up north for the weekend, and I just decided that it's too lousy outside to work in the yard," he said. He refilled the beer glass and continued to work on his smoke.

"Footloose and fancy-free, eh?" She shot Jack a coy smile before turning to grab another Stroh's from the cooler. She popped the top, set the bottle on the bar, and removed its empty predecessor. Jack nodded but did not speak. He thought for a moment of telling her about Stan Koski, smiling at Death on his porch, but thought better of it.

He watched Veronica as she finished her setup chores, finally opening the cash register and double-checking that she had the proper funds to handle the day's transactions. Satisfied, she grabbed her stool and set it on her side of the bar, across from Jack. "Okay, let the good times roll," she said.

"Can I buy you one, Ronnie?" Jack asked. "You know, an eye-opener, maybe?"

"Yeah, what the hell," she declared. "But these are on the house, Jack. I think the Avenue Bar owes us at least that much."

Jack smiled; Veronica *was* the Avenue Bar, ever since pancreatic cancer claimed her dad almost four years ago. She stood and walked to the middle of the long rows of bottles atop the back bar, her left hand extended and fingers wiggling, as if calling upon the bottled spirits to heed her beck and call. She'd been watching too much *I Dream of Jeannie*, Jack thought. If she nodded her head and blinked, he'd have to say something. At last she located her quarry and pulled a bottle of Jack Daniels from the formation. She grabbed two shot glasses and the bottle and returned to her perch.

Jack drank beer while Veronica poured out two shots. With glasses filled to their brims, she set the bottle on the back bar and turned to face Jack. "I wasn't gonna open today," she said, "but my place felt so empty, I decided what the hell. Ya know? Maybe I oughta get a dog."

They lifted their glasses carefully to their lips, poured the contents out in a rush, and simultaneously slammed their shot glasses down on the bar. Both grimaced, and the woman shivered a little before pronouncing breathlessly, "Holy shit, that's got it!"

"Smoooooooth," Jack said hoarsely, wincing. Veronica giggled and sat back on her stool. She pulled her long, mostly blonde hair back so that it rested on her upper back and shoulders. She was wearing a light blue V-neck sweater that struggled to contain its contents, and black jeans that complemented her figure nicely. When she leaned forward to take away the empty bottle, Jack again eyed the silver cross and chain that swung between her breasts. No bra attempted to harness what God had generously given her. When he looked up, her fetching hazel eyes were only a foot or so away from his gaze, and they gleamed affectionately above a comely smile.

Neither spoke as she leaned forward and pressed her lips against his, softly, sweetly, a taste of Jack Daniels, and then she began to caress his mouth with her tongue. He placed a hand on her back and stroked her, drawing her closer. She did not resist and placed her hands around his throat, fondling and massaging him. The kiss became more passionate, and they breathed through their noses with increased vigor.

She took his hand from her back and glided it up under her sweater. He felt her left breast and her heart, pounding and throbbing with life, and he heard his own heart, racing and hammering in his ears as blood rushed away from his brain, moving fast and surely away from logic and reason. She moaned hungrily in his ear. It was so easy, so thoughtless, that he did not notice as self-control ran off and desire moved in.

From behind them the front door creaked open slowly, and the man and the woman quickly separated and straightened on their bar stools. Veronica again collected her hair behind her and rose to her feet unsteadily, straightening her sweater and blushing. Gray light from the outer world entered and preceded a tall man into the bar. A pneumatic spring that occasionally functioned properly closed the door behind him with a soft cry, and he approached Jack and Veronica, who were looking very guilty if the man had noticed.

"Jesus, Dorsey, what're *you* doin' here?" Veronica said as she watched the tall man sit at the bar, leaving one empty stool between him and Jack.

"Just wanted to see if everybody was, you know, *okay*. I feel bad about yesterday, and I thought maybe if I came by, I could . . . Jesus, I don't know what I thought," he muttered.

"It's okay," Veronica said. She reached out and patted the back of Dorsey's hands, now folded together on the bar top. "You wanna drink?"

"Yeah, a Bud and a shot would be great, Ronnie, thanks," he said.

She rose to fetch his drinks and Dorsey turned to Jack. "What's up, Jackson?"

"Nothin' much, Dorse, nothin' much at all," Jack said, reaching out to shake Dorsey's extended hand.

"I guess it's true, misery loves company," Dorsey said.

Jack poured more beer and Veronica delivered a longneck Bud to Dorsey. *What the fuck was I thinking?* Jack thought. *What the fuck?* He looked at Veronica, who turned to him, smiled feebly, and shrugged her shoulders. She was still a little flushed, and it made her cheeks look rosy, which was a good thing. All three sat quietly for several minutes.

Finally, Dorsey cleared his throat, took a healthy drink from his bottle of beer, and said, "I guess you just never know. I didn't mean to be an asshole, but I guess I was." No one argued, so he continued, "I can't tell the old deaf lady I'm sorry, but I just wanted to tell you guys, you know, I didn't mean her no harm."

Jack could see that Dorsey was choking up and that he was genuinely upset. There was no point in putting a foot on the guy's throat now. What was done was done, and Jack reckoned that it probably would have happened anyway, with or without Dorsey's involvement. Dorsey was, at heart, a good guy, and in the years Jack had known him, he'd never seen him intentionally hurt anyone. Veronica, however, was still miffed with Dorsey for yesterday's antics and his overall lack of compassion.

"You didn't do anything to her. She didn't hear anything you said, and you weren't out there when she stepped out into the street, for whatever reason she did *that*," Jack stated. He reached over and patted Dorsey several times on his shoulder.

"I had a dream last night," Dorsey said, looking at his hands. "When I finally fell asleep, that is. There was a big wolf chasing me, fire in his eyes, growling like crazy. It was mad as all hell, and I tried to run away, but it was one of those dreams where it was like ... my feet were stuck in mud, or cement, and I couldn't move! *Slow fucking motion!*"

Jack watched Dorsey closely, his interest rising as the tall man's story continued. Jack felt an instant and shared connection to Dorsey's experience.

"I fell down and the fuckin' thing was on top of me," Dorsey continued, "growling, and drooling blood, and Jesus! I thought I was a goner, sure as shit, but the wolf just kinda stared at me, right *through* me, and then it laughed liked hell and just walked away. I woke up, drenched in cold sweat, shaking, and ab-so-fucking-lutely terrified. I didn't get any more sleep after that, ya know?"

Jack nodded his head; he knew. He also thought he knew the wolf.

Veronica walked away and returned to the corner of the bar with a third shot glass in hand, which she placed before Dorsey. She poured three shots and raised her glass toward the front door. She didn't say anything; she didn't need to. All three, at that moment, understood their precarious places in this world, and so they downed their shots and slammed the empty glasses on the bar.

After a few minutes, Dorsey stood, dropped a ten-dollar bill on the bar, and turned for the door. "See you 'round the campfire, kids," he said without enthusiasm. Jack and Veronica both gave him a wave as he walked into the street. Ronnie cleared the sawbuck, the Bud bottle, and the shot glass, then wiped down the bar and returned to her stool.

"So where were we, Jack? We could lock the door," she whispered, smiling seductively at Jack, an eyebrow arched.

Jack refilled and re-emptied his beer glass. He pulled another smoke from its pack and used his lighter's flame to give it life. He was not thinking about the woman in front of him, whose warm, thumping breast he'd held in his hand just moments ago. No; he thought of his wife and how foolish he'd just been. The interlude with Dorsey had given his blood ample time to meander back to his brain. If there was still any hope at all, however faint it seemed, he had to fight for his marriage and his wife.

"Ronnie, I've never cheated on my wife," he said finally, "and I just came pretty close, closer than I've ever been. If things were different, you know ..." His words dawdled off.

Veronica wrapped both of her hands around Jack's left hand, gave it a squeeze, and then twisted the simple gold band around on his left ring finger. She smiled, stood, leaned forward, and kissed Jack softly on his forehead.

"I know, Jackson, I know," she said. "You're a good guy. Don't give it another thought. Just think of it as a moment when we both needed a little *comfort*, okay? I'm glad you and me were together for that. *I* sure needed it!"

Jack grinned at her and finished off his beer and smoke. He reached for his wallet, and Veronica waved him off.

"Forget it, Jack," she declared. "Fuck it, you know? I'm gonna close up and go home. I think I need a day or two off, away from this joint, and I don't give a shit what anybody says! Will you give me a minute and walk me out?"

"Sure, Ronnie, you bet," Jack said. "Take your time." She moved quickly, and a few minutes later, they were on the sidewalk. Jack waited while she locked the door, and when she turned to go down the sidewalk, he walked beside her until they were next to a copper Oldsmobile Cutlass Calais—an '82, Jack noted.

"Well, this is me." She faced Jack and gave him a hug and a peck on the cheek. "I hope your wife knows how lucky she is, Jack."

Jack smiled as he pulled the car door open and watched Veronica settle in behind the steering wheel. "Be careful, Ronnie, okay?" She smiled up at Jack and winked an eye as he closed the door. A minute later she was gone, heading east down a largely deserted Michigan Avenue.

Jack walked back to his car and unlocked the door. In a few moments, he motored in the opposite direction on the same road.

Back at home, Curly was awakened for the third time by the ringing phone on the kitchen wall. He fought through a yawn, stretched his legs, and fell asleep again.

Chapter Seventeen

Jack pulled the Mustang into his driveway on Bull Run Way, got out, opened the garage door, and parked inside. He pulled the garage door down, retrieved the groceries from the trunk, and set them on the cement floor by the house door, save a twelve-pack of Stroh's that he put in the garage's corner fridge. He then unlocked the door, grabbed the groceries, and entered the house.

Curly's toenails clicked along the tile floor just inside the door. His tail and butt were in full swing. The sound followed Jack until the carpet of the kitchen proper muted the clicks and clacks. Jack deposited the groceries on the kitchen countertop.

"Hey, you old fart!" Jack gave Curly a thorough going-over, massaging here, scratching there. "Bet you could use a trip outside, huh?" Curly made a beeline for the glass door that opened to the backyard. Jack unlocked the latch, sliding the glass door open and then the outer screen door, and Curly bolted past him. "Make it a quickie, bud. Rain's pickin' up," Jack ordered.

The sky darkened above a steady drizzle as Curly circled about the yard, sniffing out the best spot to do his business. As Jack watched, the dog shook his butt a little and then dropped it low to the ground. "Atta boy. Green grass in that spot, anyway!" Curly finished his evacuation and continued to sniff around until he was at the tree line at the back edge of the Thomases' yard. He lifted his left hind leg and released a steady stream on the old oak tree as a flash of lightning burst in the western sky. A five count later, thunder resounded in response.

"Okay, bonehead, good boy. If you're done fertilizing, let's get inside."

Curly ignored Jack, frozen in his tracks, staring into the tall grass and weeds just beyond the oak. When the dog lowered his butt and began to growl, tail still, pointed straight up, Jack walked out into the misting air and called to the dog, now mesmerized by something in the woods.

"Jesus," Jack called out, "now what'd ya find? Come on, boy, come on! Curly, you flat-headed ape! Come here—*now!*"

Curly remained in place, not moving, a statue but for a low, guttural growl that rose from his belly. Jack moved forward until he stood directly behind Curly, raptly listening for something in the brush that caught the dog's attention. When Jack heard nothing, he reached down, patted Curly's arched back, and said soothingly, "It's okay, boy; there's nothing there. Let's go in the house. We can ..."

And then Jack heard it too, a deep, ominous grumbling, and he intuitively felt a rush of fear caused by this unidentified yet obvious threat to health and safety. "Curly," Jack whispered as he bent down and picked up the dog in both hands, "we need to get the feck out of here!"

He began to slowly back-step toward the house, careful not to repeat his fall-on-his-ass moment after Cheetah's funeral. He kept both eyes toward the edge of the small woods. The growl from the tall grass burst into the roar of an imminent danger, now let loose, and Jack hastened their retreat to double-time.

The sky went awash in a dazzling white burst. A split-second later, a deafening *crack* struck directly overhead. Jack held Curly tightly and quickened his pace toward the house. Both watched wide-eyed as lightning speared the oak tree and split its trunk, which then screeched with a sizzle as fire met rain and decades-old wood shrieked out a ripping death cry.

For what seemed like forever to the man and his dog, the tree wavered in the sky as though looking for a place to fall. At last, there was a loud tearing sound. The trunk began to sway and then topple, directly toward Jack and Curly.

"Ohhhhh, *ssshhhhiiiiiiiit!*" the man bellowed as he turned and ran for all he was worth toward the house. He looked over his shoulder just as the top half of the tree crashed to the earth, narrowly missing them and the house. It did, however, take down several overhead wires.

"Holy crap, Curly—that was fecking close!" He gave the dog a hug and said, "Are you okay?" Curly trembled and was not alone. Jack stood under the awning above the glass door wall for several moments as rain insistently drummed on the canopy above. He felt no inclination to put Curly down, and the dog was perfectly content in the man's arms. *That is gonna be quite a cleanup project,* Jack pondered. *But on the bright side, we're okay, and we should have firewood for the next ten years or so.*

"Well, thank God it missed us, right, Curly? That was *too* close," Jack said as he slid the screen door open, walked into the house, and set Curly down. He pulled shut the outer screen and then the inner glass door, and stepped out of his shoes. He returned to the groceries and mindlessly put everything away, including a second twelve-pack, thankful that the power was on and his beer would stay cold. Priorities! He plucked the phone from its cradle, just in case, but the line was dead. He could hear faint crackling sounds, like something heard off in the distance, far away, from the end of a tunnel.

"I need a drink," Jack decided. "How's about you, meathead? Are you thirsty too?" Curly sat in the doorway between the kitchen and the family room. The dog stood and shook his head and shoulders, and a light spray of rainwater flew into the air. He then sat down, tilted his head, and followed Jack's every move with full attention.

"That's an affirmative, old buddy," Jack said. He picked up Curly's water bowl and emptied it into the sink. He then grabbed a can of beer from the fridge, pulled the tab open, and poured enough to cover the bottom of the dish and a dash more. He set the bowl down, and Curly lapped up the contents greedily. "Not too fast, Bluto—you know how you get!" Curly paid no heed.

Jack poured the rest of the can's contents into a glass and took a long sip. *Jesus, I'm on some kind of a roll.* And what the hell was that *thing* growling in the woods? It occurred to Jack that maybe the lightning had been a good thing; happening when it did, maybe it scared off the growling beast. It didn't occur to him that perhaps it was the other way around; maybe the growling beast had forced their retreat *before* lightning struck, and had thus saved them from the falling tree.

Jack listened as thunder rolled off to the east, and he drank more beer. Curly licked his bowl clean and looked up to Jack, head tilted. Jack grabbed the bowl, rinsed it out, and refilled it with cold water. "That's enough for you, you old sow. I'll fix you some lunch."

Jack placed the water bowl in the hallway and grabbed Curly's empty food bowl, which he refilled with Purina Dog Chow and put back in its place. Curly waddled over, gave it a sniff, and then sauntered into the living room. Jack knew the routine well.

Daniel J. Wells

"A hunger strike, eh, Curly Q? You may be waiting awhile if you're looking for people-food scraps."

Jack peeled off the wet sweatshirt and hung it over the back of a chair at the kitchen table. He looked out the kitchen window, toward the back of his yard, where he could just see the outer edges of the fallen tree. Close call, all right. He grabbed another beer from the fridge, walked into the living room, and swung open the front door. The storm looked to have passed through, and the sky was beginning to lighten. In the western sky, Jack could see patches of faint blue. He dropped his sight line and spotted Terry Ralls sitting on the top step of his porch.

"Hey, Jack!" Terry called out with a wave. "You guys all right over there?"

Jack unlatched the screen door, pushed it open, and stepped out. "Yeah, just barely," Jack exclaimed. "Can you see that freakin' tree in the backyard? Curly and me were out there! Damn thing about got us!"

Jack stepped into his front yard and walked toward the Rallses' house. Terry stood and strolled in Jack's direction, crossed Bull Run Way, and walked up Jack's drive and around the garage. Jack followed. There they saw the wreckage.

"Wow," Terry said, shaking his head. "That the old oak tree from the woods? What did it take out?"

"Looks like phone, and cable, maybe," Jack said. "Still have power, thank Christ."

"You were in the yard when it fell? What were you doin', Jack?" Terry had a wry smile as he arched a brow.

"Curly was takin' a dump, and he started growling at something in the woods," Jack said. Then he stopped and looked at Terry. "Jesus, I'd forgotten about that. Have you ever seen anything . . . *wild* around here?"

Terry looked into the woods, beyond the fallen tree, and ambled toward the back end of Jack's yard. "No," he said. "I've seen rabbits and raccoons, a couple of possums, old lady Gibbons in a bathrobe with her hair in curlers, but nothing too out of the ordinary. Why, what did you see?" He turned and faced Jack.

"I didn't *see* anything, but I sure as shit *heard* something," Jack said. "And it wasn't any of those critters, that's for sure. It sounded big and mean and pissed off."

Terry shook his head slowly and then rubbed his chin. He had a two-day stubble going. Both men stared into the woods but said nothing for several moments. "So it wasn't old lady Gibbons?" Terry asked, peering toward the woods and then back at Jack.

Jack placed a hand on Terry's shoulder and said, "You want a beer, T?"

"Does a bear shit in the woods? Say, was it a bear, Jack, maybe takin' a shit in the woods?" Terry slapped Jack on the back, reached up, and mussed his hair.

"Gee, maybe so, maybe so," Jack said. "A couple of nights ago, Davie told me about a dream he'd had about a wolf. He said he thought it was out there," Jack pointed toward the woods. The two men stood quietly for a moment. "Ahh, maybe I just had that in my head. Probably just a dog," Jack said finally. "Let's pound a few Stroh's and think about it."

With that, the two men walked to the front of the garage. Jack pulled its door up and open. Terry grabbed two lawn chairs and unfolded them as Jack went to the corner fridge and extracted two beers. He finished off the open beer he'd carried from inside and dropped it into the very full tub of empties.

"You've got a small fortune in empties there, Jack," Terry observed. "Are you hoarding them to use as currency in the apocalypse?"

Jack sat in his chair with a creak and chuckled. "I'll be sitting pretty if the Russians drop the big one on us, you're damn skippy. You'd better be nice to me now, before it's too late."

The men sipped beer and looked at the western skies, now blossoming in blues of many hues and shades as the sun pushed its way through the clouds and dispersed them. Spring air responded warmly, carried on a light breeze. Jack threw his legs out before him and warmed his bare feet.

"Clearing up nicely," Terry said. "Just might turn out to be a nice day after all."

Jack nodded. "Yeah, I think so. I should probably go somewhere and call Ma Bell and the cable company."

"Our phone is out too," Terry said. "You took out the whole neighborhood, dumbass. Katie's gonna drive out and find a payphone and call it in, but you'd think they'd already know about it, wouldn't you?"

"I have no idea what they know, other than what I owe them every month," Jack said. "*That* they *always* know."

They clicked their beer cans together and resumed drinking. After a few minutes, Katie Ralls came out the front door, lovely as ever in a red flannel shirt and blue jean cutoffs. She shielded her eyes with her right hand, spotted the two loungers, and waved.

"Hi, Jack!" she called out.

"Katie, you look *great*, like always," Jack answered with a wave.

"Take it easy, Elvis," Terry said as he elbowed Jack in the ribs.

Katie cupped her hands to her mouth and shouted, "I'm gonna go find a phone. You guys want anything?"

"Don't ask for requests if you ain't prepared to deliver," Terry called back.

Katie giggled, threw her hands to her hips, and dramatically marched off with exaggerated side-to-side thrusts of her butt toward the burgundy Chevy Impala in their open garage. A moment later, the car roared to life, backed down the driveway, and churned up Bull Run Way. Katie thumbed her nose at Terry as she drove past. Jack rose and grabbed two more beers from the fridge, dropping two empties into the pile on his way.

"You are, without a doubt, the luckiest son of a bitch in the world, Ralls. What she sees in a wet end like you, I will never know. And shit can that Chevy and get yourself a *real* car." Jack pointed at the Mustang and sat back down. His chair, which only he dared sit in, moaned once again as it moved steadily toward its impending demise.

"You didn't do so bad yourself, Jackpot," Terry noted as he took the beer can from Jack. "What did a doll like Angie ever see in a mutt like you? We *both* know it ain't your charm or beauty that did it."

"I'm told I have 'rugged good looks,'" Jack said, puffing his chest out.

"If they were any more rugged, you'd be a permanent guest of the Detroit Zoo." Both men laughed as the sky cleared completely before them. The sun began to dry the wet lawns and warm the afternoon. A jumbo jet droned above, and the men leaned out and up to see it.

"Seven forty-seven," Terry said.

"American Airlines," Jack added. He'd left his smokes inside, so he went into the house, grabbed a pack and his lighter, and returned to the garage. Curly followed him out and plopped down on the floor behind Terry's lawn chair; the dog knew better than to lie behind Jack and that approaching disaster. Terry leaned back and scratched the top of Curly's head, and the dog licked his hand.

"Did you hear about Cheetah?" asked Jack, looking up as the plane faded from view.

"Yeah, Angie told Katie," Terry said with a sigh as he straightened in his chair. "That's a raw deal, poor thing. I bet Davie took it hard."

"Yes, he did," Jack muttered. "I didn't take it all that great either. Too much of that kinda shit going on lately." Jack stretched his long legs out in front of him, took a swig of beer, and told Terry about the old lady who died on the sidewalk outside the Avenue Bar less than twenty-four hours ago, and how he'd come to find Stan Koski just a few hours earlier.

"That was tough on everybody, losing Stan," Terry said, shaking his head. "Katie cried for a while, and then she was happy, like she somehow knew where he'd gone, and that he was okay." He lowered his head and stared at the concrete floor. "I learned a long time ago, man; never argue with Katie about such things. She's a lot smarter than me."

"Yeah. Stan was a great guy. And he was smiling, so maybe Katie's right. I'd sure like to think so." Jack returned to the fridge and made another Stroh's withdrawal.

"Wow." Terry spoke softly, shaking his head. "You are on a roll, and all that in just a few days? Who'd you piss off?"

"I don't know, T, but I hereby offer a broad apology to any and all concerned for every fecking thing I've ever done in my entire life." He started to tell Terry about his concerns over Angie, and their marriage, but decided against it. Jack sat back down and handed Terry a cold can of beer. Again his chair moaned. Curly's eyes opened wide, and its leg muscles tensed in preparation for a hasty retreat.

"What are you gonna do about the tree?" Terry shook a thumb toward the backyard.

"Well, I can pay somebody to clean it up, or I guess I can rent a chainsaw or something," Jack said. "Never used one, though, have you?"

"No, but I *saw* a *chain* in a hardware store once," Terry offered.

"Helpful, that's very helpful." Jack shook his head. "I forgot, Katie mows your lawn and fixes shit around the house. Guess I should ask *her* for advice, not her nitwit CPA husband."

"My advice, however unsolicited," Terry replied through a

chuckle, "is to hire somebody to do the deed for you. Maybe you can get a deal; that's gonna make great firewood, you know. Maybe you could use some of it in trade."

"We haven't used the fireplace in a long time, but it would be cool to get it going next fall," Jack said. "Well, guess I'll figure that out when the phones get fixed." He threw his feet out again and crossed his legs at his ankles. The sun felt good, the Stroh's was cold and tasty, and Jack enjoyed Terry's company. A warm buzz was moving in, a much-needed respite from recent events. He let his worries and dark thoughts drift away, knowing they'd return soon enough.

"Hey, maybe Ma Bell will clean it up!" Jack announced hopefully. "Ma Bell" was what Michigan natives called the Michigan Bell Telephone Company, which was now actually Ameritech, since Bell divested in January. The nickname would stick for years, however; that's just how it was, even as the phone service renamed itself several times.

"Man, you've had *way* too much Stroh's if you think *that's* gonna happen," Terry chortled. "Maybe you should go buy lottery tickets, or ..."

Both men stopped and turned to the left at the sound of a car coming up fast on Bull Run Way. It passed Jack's house, stopped abruptly, backed up, and then turned in to the Thomas driveway.

"State police," Terry said. "*Now what did you do, hombre?*"

Curly stood and barked twice before Jack shushed him. "It's okay, lard ass, sit down." Curly obeyed and sat, but remained at full attention.

Jack set his beer can down and walked slowly toward the cruiser. He stepped on a rock, stumbled, and damn near did a header into the lawn. The cop pulled something down from the visor, opened the door, got out of the car, and racked his trooper hat on his head. He nodded to Jack and then to Terry.

"What's up, Officer?" said Jack, regaining his balance, mostly.

"Hello, sirs. I am Officer Harrison of the Michigan State Police. Are either of you Mr. Jackson Thomas?"

"Yes, I am," Jack said. His stomach clenched and jumped to his throat. "What's wrong? Is it Angie or Davie? *What's wrong?*"

"Calm down, sir," the trooper said, but that ship had sailed. "There's been an incident up north, but both your wife and son are alive and okay. Why don't you sit down, and I'll tell you what I know." Jack returned to his lawn chair, and Terry reached over, put an arm around Jack's shoulder, and gave him a quick hug.

"We've been trying to phone you, but there was no answer," Harrison said.

"I was out this morning," Jack said, "and when I got home, lightning knocked down a tree out back and took out our phones."

The state policeman was dressed in a crisply creased blue shirt, dark gray pants, and a matching tie tugged tight to a perfect knot. He bent down to a squat and looked up at Jack, peering from under his hat's black visor, shined to military perfection. "Your wife was attacked last night at your cottage, apparently as she slept," he said. "She suffered a couple of knife wounds." The cop paused as Jack clenched in the chair and inhaled sharply.

"Oh Jesus wept," Jack sobbed softly. Terry tightened his squeeze on his friend's shoulders.

"She survived that assault; however, her assailant did not," Harrison continued. "She was taken to St. Michael's Hospital in Gaylord and is currently being treated there for her wounds."

"What about Davie?" Jack said slowly, fighting back fear, anger, frustration, and maybe a dozen other emotions.

"He's fine, no injuries at all. In fact, they think he might have saved your wife's life, although the investigation is ongoing. We do know that her attacker," the trooper paused, pulled a small notebook from his left shirt pocket, flipped it open, and read slowly, "Peter Oliver Brookings, was dead at the scene."

"That miserable motherfucker," Jack hissed, "that's Angie's boss. What was *he* doing up there?" Jack stood quickly, too quickly, and he teetered a little. Terry stood with him and held him steady.

"Mr. Thomas, would you please wait here for just a minute?"

"I gotta drive up there. I gotta leave *right now!*" Jack struggled to get free of Terry, but his friend and neighbor held tight. "Lemme go, T, lemme go!"

"No, Jack, hang on a second," Terry said as he nodded to the state trooper, who turned and got back into his cruiser, taking off his hat and tossing it carefully onto the passenger seat. The two men looked on as he brought the radio mouthpiece close to his face, but they could not hear him. Jack sat back down, and Curly walked around the chairs and sat at his feet. Jack, without thinking, reached down and scratched the dog's head.

"Jesus, what the fuck is going on?" Jack spoke to the blue skies and dazzling sun before him.

"It's gonna be okay, Jack," Terry whispered, trying to sound reassuring. "You heard the man—they're okay! That's all that matters, right?"

Jack buried his face in his hands for a moment and rubbed his eyes. "Yes, that's right; that's all that matters."

The man in blue got out of the car and walked toward the two men. He left his hat behind in the car. "Sir, we've come up with a plan," he said. "You can't drive up there on your own; you'd drive too fast, maybe recklessly, and you've been drinking, right?"

Jack nodded. "Not that much," he said, straightening. "If I've gotta get up there, I can do it."

"Listen for a second." The cop returned to a squatting position in front of Jack. "It seems that a Sergeant McDonnell up north is friends with my lieutenant at the Northville post. They've worked it out so that I'll drive you as far as Saginaw, where we'll meet another trooper who will take you to West Branch. From there, one of McDonnell's boys will take you the rest of the way. Okay?"

"You can't beat that, Jack," Terry said. "Who's gonna get you there faster than the state police? I'll sure drive you up, if that's what you want, but I gotta think they're gonna get you there a helluva lot sooner."

Jack looked in turn at both men. He stood slowly. "Okay, yes, that's great. Terry, will you take care of Curly for us?"

"I'd be delighted," Terry said as he gave the dog a chin rub. "Anything at all, Jack. All you've got to do is ask, and it's done—truly."

Jack turned to the cop, who also gave Curly the once-over. "Can I have a couple of minutes to get some things?" Jack asked.

"Take all the time you need, Mr. Thomas," Harrison said.

"It's Jack," said Jack as he offered his right hand.

"Tim Harrison," replied the cop as he shook Jack's hand. "I'll be ready when you are. They say your wife will be in the hospital for a few days, so get whatever you need."

"Don't forget your shoes, nature boy," said Terry.

Jack went into the house and used the bathroom, still in shock at the bad news, good news, and all points in between. He retrieved his shoes, gathered some clothes, smokes, and toiletries, and threw all into a large blue gym bag. He tugged on a gray sweater, grabbed his keys from the kitchen counter, and stepped out into the garage. He handed the keys to Terry.

"You know where everything is, right? Anything else you need, I'll cover when I ... we ... get back," Jack said, and the two friends shook hands warmly.

"Don't worry about a thing," Terry said. "It's taken care of. As soon as we get the phones back, I'll get ahold of you, or you can try

196

me anytime." Terry wrapped his arms around Jack and gave him a bracing hug, almost lifting the taller man from the ground. Jack grunted and hugged back.

"You take care of Angie and Davie, Jackson," Terry said, speaking softly into Jack's ear. "That's all you need to think about. Now get outta here, ya dopey bastard!" He clapped his hands against Jack's shoulders. "Keep an eye on him, Harrison!" The trooper smiled and nodded, and he and Jack walked into the afternoon sun.

"Thanks, Tim. I appreciate this," Jack said.

"No problem. Sit in the front seat, or you'll look like a perp." Harrison opened the passenger door, retrieving his hat, and Jack got in. A minute later, the cruiser rolled down Bull Run Way as Terry and Curly looked on. It was now very quiet.

When the car had vanished, Terry said, "Okay, Curls, let's go inside and grab your chow and stuff. You're gonna stay with Katie and me, okay?" Curly stood on two feet and licked Terry's hand. "Okay, that's a plan, then. But just so you know, and this is very important: *Katie is the boss.* At all times. Always." Curly licked Terry's hand again, and they entered the house.

Chapter Eighteen

As Angie was being wheeled from surgery to the recovery room, Davie slept on a small couch in the waiting room down the hall. A nurse looked in on the boy and decided he could sleep another hour or two while his mother did the same in recovery, just down the hall.

In his sleep, Davie floated through the sky like a kite, gliding silently and changing direction with the wave of an arm or the flap of a hand. He drifted effortlessly through white clouds on a powder-blue backdrop, with no destination, taking comfort in the ease by which he commanded the skies. He passed birds of all sizes and colors, and they seemed to smile and greet him as one of their own.

Eventually, the boy fluttered to earth and landed softly in tall, dark-green grass. The blades ran up his legs, tickled his knees, and smelled sweet and clean. Davie began to run, his arms straight out at his sides; he wanted to relaunch and again ascend to the heavens, but flight eluded him. He ran for what seemed like miles, stopping only when he came to a thick forest that rose above him like a tremendous wall of greens and browns.

There was no road or path here, just the tall grass that streamed to the forest wall and stopped. Davie turned around. The grass he had run through was now another dense forest, and he was surrounded. The blue sky had almost vanished, and it steadily got very dark. Where joy and wonder had frolicked only moments ago, fright and panic instantly moved in.

"Where has the world gone?" he called up to the tiny patch of blue above him. "Where has it gone?"

From behind, Davie heard a voice as tender as a warm breeze, as soothing as a splash of cool water, and he turned to face it. "You are standing in the very middle of the world, boy," the voice said. "It's all around you!"

Davie was stunned. He expected to see Aunt Angie, now his mother, with a loving smile and open arms. But it was something else, and it terrified him to his marrow.

"Don't be afraid of me, boy. You remember me, don't you?"

In a swirl of light and color, of music and magic, shadows and vapors, a lost memory returned to Davie—an encounter, just a few days old, one that seemed to have been lost for years. He walked toward the enormous wolf and looked into its flashing green-and-gold-specked eyes.

"Yes, I *do* remember you," Davie said. "You walked me out of the forest to safety, to my home. I thought you were God, but you're not, are you?"

"What if I told you that I was the devil?" The beast roared for effect and then sat down. It lifted a hind paw and scratched at its great neck.

"No, I don't think so," Davie decided. "If you were the devil, you woulda just eaten me."

"That's probably true," said the wolf. "But what I am, or am not, is unimportant. Do you know why you've come here again?"

Davie looked into the wolf's eyes and then down to his own feet. He closed his eyes and tried to think, but all he found was the image of an empty slate, black and wet, as though it had just been wiped clean with a damp sponge.

"No, I can't think of anything; there's nothing there anymore," Dave whispered. The beast rose to its feet and walked close to the boy. It looked into Davie's eyes, so deep and blue, and then bared its massive fangs.

"That's right," the wolf said. "There's nothing there anymore: nothing to fear, nothing to fret over, nothing to haunt you. The world is what you make of it, boy. What has gone before this *here and now*, let go, and you'll be free."

The beast pointed its snout toward the heavens and loosed a roar that shook the trees to the roof of sky above. Davie did not flinch, but reached out and placed his right hand on top of the wolf's great head. He stroked its fur toward its tail three times. The wolf put its huge black nose into Davie's stomach and pushed, and the boy fell back on his butt into the tall grass. He lay there and giggled for several moments, and then sat up and reached out for the beast. But it was gone.

Davie rose to his feet and looked about, spinning in a complete circle, but he was alone amid the tall grass and foreboding trees of the forest. Suddenly, the wind rushed in and grabbed the boy, taking him up and away again like a kite, and he soared above and beyond the trees, until everything was powder blue. He closed his eyes, blissful, content to soar forever, but he opened them and then he was awake.

The pretty nurse in the light blue cardigan sweater sat in a chair opposite the boy on the couch. She smiled and said, "Would you like to see your mom now?"

Davie jumped to his feet, eyes wide and bright. "Let's go," he cried out as he sprinted for the double swinging doors. The nurse followed, brought the boy to heel, and then led the way down the flat white halls. At one point, she held an index finger to her lips, and Davie slowed down until his gym shoes no longer slapped against the tiled floor.

Soon they entered a round room with a high ceiling and a circle of desks and monitors at its center. The air was filled with *beep*s and *blip*s and noises strange to the boy. It reminded him of the sounds heard inside a submarine in those old war movies he'd watched with Uncle Jack. Patient rooms surrounded the desks along the outer walls, sealed off by sliding curtains that served as partitions.

"This is ICU," the nurse whispered, "the intensive care unit. Your mom is gonna be here for a day or two, but you can see her now." She gestured to a curtained room on his right. She held the curtain aside as Davie rushed into the room.

Here he found Angie, tubes in her arms, an air line in each nostril, awash in a sea of white bandages. Her long, dark hair had been tied and wrapped behind her head, which was propped up by giant snow-white pillows. She looked like a saint to the boy, her pillows a halo.

"Davie, baby," she whispered hoarsely. "Sorry, my voice is little shot. How are you? Did you get something to eat?"

Davie carefully approached and took Angie's hand tenderly in his own, navigating through the tubes and wires. He bent over and kissed her hand, and excitedly but quietly said, "Yes, but how are *you*? What did the doctor say? What did they do? How long do you gotta stay here?"

Angie laughed a little and then stopped short. "Oh, it's true, it hurts when I laugh!" She reached down with her right hand and rubbed Davie's head, and then she collected his hand in hers. Her left arm had suffered the worst wound by Peter's knife and was now heavily wrapped and immobilized in a sling suspended from the ceiling.

"I've got a sore noggin, and those cuts you saw," Angie said. "The one on my arm is the deepest, and they may have to operate on it again, but I'll be okay. It's just gonna take time, pook."

"We've got lots of time on the clock, Mom, lots of time," the boy said, his eyes fixed on the woman's bruised face. She smiled again, looking to the white ceiling and all its little gray dots, a faraway universe, out of reach.

Another nurse entered the room, older, and looking much more official. "Would you like me to bring you a chair, young man?" she asked. "We've got a nice one that opens up like a lounger, so that you're almost lying down." She walked to Angie, took her patient's right wrist, and then studied her watch. After a few moments, she asked, "Can I get you anything, dear? How is the pain? Would you like something for the pain?"

"No, thanks, I'm okay for now. But," Angie winked at Davie, "I think we're a little hungry."

The nurse read Angie's chart and then replaced it at the end of the bed. "Yes, that's a good idea," she decided. "Let's check with the doctor, see what we can come up with, and I'll have an orderly bring in that chair." She rubbed Davie's head, which had seen quite a workout.

"Nurse," Angie said, and the woman in white stopped and turned to face her. "Has anyone been able to get ahold of my husband?"

"I don't think so, but they're working on it. The state police were here an hour or so ago," the nurse said as she glanced at her wristwatch, "and they said they'd be coming back. I'm sure they'll help with that." She gave Angie a quick smile and a nod, and left the room.

"You want me to call Uncle Jack ... *Dad*?" Davie asked.

Angie giggled a little and then groaned, "No, darlin'. Let's wait for the police; they should have gotten hold of him by now."

Off the Path

At about that time, Jack was being almost zapped by lightning, damned near crushed by a falling oak tree, and terrorized by some unseen monster in their backyard. A car accident might have seemed like a relief to him.

Someone rapped on the wall, just beyond the curtained partition.

"Yes," Angie asked the curtain, which then slid open to reveal a wall of blue and gray, highlighted by sharp creases. In stepped Sergeant Rick McDonnell, tall and white with ruddy cheeks and graying brown hair, and Trooper Donald Mathews, black, of average height, above-average width, and balding head. McDonnell made introductions and apologized for the intrusion.

"We're really sorry to barge in on you, ma'am, and we know you must be exhausted," McDonnell said, "but could you maybe answer a few questions, just to help us get a clearer picture of what happened?"

"Sure, Sergeant, okay," Angie said, her voice even and steady. "Davie, would you please go back to the waiting room and get me a Coke? There's money in my purse."

"Sure, Mom. I've got money. I'll be right back," Davie said. He excused himself and squeezed past the blue wall.

From beyond the curtain, an authoritative female voice called out, "No running in the halls, young man!"

After he'd left, Angie sat up a little and cleared her throat. "He doesn't need to hear *everything*," she declared. "Peter Brookings is ... was ... my boss. He was coming up to see me because," she paused, blushed slightly, but pushed on, "we were going to have an affair."

McDonnell and Mathews stood straight, stoically listening with no outward reaction. They'd both heard worse, Angie figured, and were pretty much beyond being shocked. "Go ahead, ma'am," McDonnell said as Mathews scribbled something in his notepad.

"Well, after I got up here," Angie said, "I started thinking about my husband, and Davie too, and I just realized I was making a *huge*

203

mistake, so I called it off. When Peter got here and I told him, he whined and pouted a little, but he left without much fuss—even asked if I'd be at work on Monday."

Angie used her good right arm to reach for a glass of water, which she sipped through a straw. Davie reappeared at the curtain, but the blue wall did not part. The troopers looked to Angie, who said, "It's okay, let him in." They stepped aside and Davie walked to Angie and handed her a can of Coke after he'd popped the tab. She took the straw from the water glass, dropped it into the can, and took a long draw. Each movement, however slight, brought burning pain to her upper chest and a throbbing ache to her head. She ignored it. She took another pull of Coke through the plastic straw, took a deep breath, and exhaled slowly.

"If you get too tired, this can wait, Mrs. Thomas," McDonnell said softly.

"No, that's okay," she said. "I can finish up. And please, it's Angie." She pointed her right index finger in turn at each of the cops, who nodded. Angie continued her account, sparing no details, exactly as she remembered it all.

Funny how clearly I can recall all of this now, she thought, and hoped to forget it just as easily, but she guessed that was very unlikely to happen anytime soon. The troopers studied her with admiration as her tale unfolded. Donny Mathews had become so intrigued by her tale that he forgot all about taking notes. He'd catch a little hell for that later, but he wasn't going to forget any part of her story anytime soon. Davie stood at the foot of the bed; he was already in love.

Angie continued, now nearing the climax. "That's when he sliced open my upper chest. They told me it took over a hundred stitches to close it." She wondered what Jack would think when he saw that slash, permanently emblazoned on her chest like Hawthorne's scarlet *A*. Angie looked at her audience. From Davie to McDonnell to Mathews, all stood staring, mouths agape, in awe.

She was almost done now, and so she pressed on. "I kind of blacked out for a second, and when I did look up, I was in a red fog. All I could see was blood. But I saw Peter at the foot of the bed, truly crazed, eyes bugging out of his head, holding that shiny knife over his head. I could only think of Jack and Davie, and hoped they could forgive me." She lowered her head and began to weep, the first time she'd allowed her tears to flow freely since the attack.

Davie dashed around the bed, took her hand, and asked, "You wanna stop, Mom? You tired?"

"No, baby," Angie said, shaking her head slowly. "Really, I'm done with *my* story, aren't I? Isn't this where you take over?"

Davie gently shook her hand and then turned to face the men in blue. "I was in bed sleepin', down the hall, when I heard screamin'," he said, his young voice steady. "I heard Angie ... I mean, my mom, yellin' at somebody, and him callin' her bad names. I just grabbed the bat from the corner and ran into her room. The man was bringing a knife back over his head, holding it with both hands." Davie mimicked the attack, using both arms, raised above his head. "So I took a swing and hit him in the middle of his back, here." He patted the left side of his chest. "I guess I got him in the right spot, 'cause he fell back and down to the floor. He didn't move much after that."

Sergeant McDonnell put a big hand on the boy's shoulder and gave him a quick massage. "No, he sure didn't," the big trooper said. "Coroner says he had a cracked rib, and the bat drove the bone into his heart, and that was all she wrote. Any idea how he broke his rib? Coroner doesn't think the bat swing alone, from such a little guy, could have caused both injuries."

Angie and Davie both shook their heads. "No," she said, "Maybe when he fell off the bed. I don't think I hit him there. Sure glad something did!"

Everyone in the room grinned again. McDonnell and Mathews

looked at each other. "Ever hear one like that, Donny?" McDonnell asked.

Donny stuck his notepad in his shirt pocket and said, "No, sir; that's one for the books, all right."

"Has anyone been able to locate my husband?" Angie asked.

"Oh, shoot, I almost forgot to tell you," McDonnell said. "We've been calling all morning, but there's no answer. I radioed a pal at the Northville post and he said a big storm knocked out power and phones all over your area, so he's gonna send a car to your house. We should get to your husband soon, and I'll get word to you just as soon as we do. Meanwhile, you two heroes get some rest, okay?"

Sergeant McDonnell then did something he'd never done in all his years on the force. He leaned down and kissed Angie gently on the forehead. He said softly in her ear, "We'll let you tell your husband how this started, however you see fit."

Angie whispered back, "I'll tell him the truth, but thanks. I'd like to tell him myself."

McDonnell straightened, smiled, and nodded to the woman and then the boy. Mathews said, "You get better, hear?" He winked, and both troopers left the room.

A few minutes later, an orderly delivered Davie's chair and placed it next to Angie's bed. This was soon followed by two lunches served on plastic trays. Before long, mother and son were sound asleep, waiting for their husband and father, now being rushed ever closer to them.

Chapter Nineteen

The trip up north was an agonizingly slow journey for Jack, but in fact it went as fast as could be hoped on four wheels. Weekend travelers who clogged this interstate on Friday afternoons and evenings could only dream of getting to getaway cabins, cottages, and campgrounds up north so quickly. He'd made the right call in accepting their transport, he now decided.

But Jack's mind was tormented by feelings of guilt and anger and helplessness. He should have been there with Angie; it was that simple. Instead, he'd been in a bar (twice), drinking too much, and to top it all off, necking and copping a feel with a virtual stranger while his wife suffered alone. If Dorsey hadn't wandered into the Avenue, how far would it have gone with Ronnie?

And what of Davie—what went through his young mind? What horrors had he seen or been party to? Wasn't he toting around enough baggage from his biological parents? Why was Peter Fecking Brookings in their cabin?

Jack wished he could shut it off, send it far away, but he figured he was one of those guys who swallowed feelings and emotions, locked them away in dark places, and was doomed to relive them ad nauseam. He only prayed he could somehow make it right by Angie and Davie, and he was prepared to do whatever it took to reach that end.

Just outside West Branch along I-75, Donny Mathews turned in to a McDonald's parking lot and stopped beside another blue goose, as the Michigan State Police affectionately nicknamed their cruisers. He gave a wave to the fellow trooper as Jack exited the car and walked around it to face Donny. They shook hands and introduced themselves.

"You want some coffee or something?" the trooper asked Jack.

"No. We got something at the last stop, but if you want something, go ahead," Jack said.

"No; let's get going. I know you're anxious to see your wife and boy."

They got in the cruiser and were soon sailing north. The radio occasionally squawked out cop speak, which Mathews appeared to ignore, but he heard every call and would have responded, had the situation so demanded.

"I saw your wife and boy just a few hours ago," Donny said, looking at Jack. "They're both okay, just so you know."

"Can you tell me what happened?" Jack sat straight and half-turned to face Donny, who scratched the back of his head and then gave Jack a condensed version of Angie's story, and Davie's too.

When he'd finished, Jack leaned back and sagged a little. "Jesus, I feel like a horse's ass." He sighed. "I should have been there, but I let petty bullshit and my goddamn pride stand in the way." He used both hands to rub his knees, his head bowed, on the verge of tears, in a mix of rage and sadness and anxiety.

"None of that matters anymore, man," Donny said. "You gotta let all that shit go! What's important now is that when we get you to St. Mike's, you are then and forever fully committed to your family. That's all that counts, Jack, and that's all they're gonna expect."

It was one of the longest speeches of Donny Mathews's life. He glanced over as Jack righted himself, kneaded his face, and turned toward Donny.

"You're right. Thanks. Thanks for everything," Jack said as he waved a hand toward the road ahead. "You guys have been great, and I won't forget it."

"Happy to help, Jack," Donny said, his eyes now on the road ahead. "I was proud to meet your wife and boy and hear their accounts of what happened. You should be so *proud*, man, seriously. We'll be there in just a little bit."

They continued to cruise north on I-75. Traffic was light, and Donny was making good time. The trooper stole another glance at Jack, who was staring out the side window, and asked, "Were you in the service, Jack?"

"Yeah, marines," Jack said as he turned in his seat to face Donny.

"I thought so. Semper fi, man," Donny said. It was a common greeting among marines, short for semper fidelis, or always faithful, the Marine Corps' motto. "You make it to Vietnam?"

"Yeah. The longest year of my life, bar none," Jack said softly. "You?"

"I was an MP in Saigon for fifteen months," Donny said.

"Jesus, I bet you saw more shit than I did," Jack muttered.

Donny chuckled. "I doubt it. I'm gonna guess that you were a grunt, just a hunch."

Donny cast a quick glance toward Jack, who nodded and mumbled, "Yeah, recon." Then Jack turned to look out the side window again.

Tall pines sped by in blurry bursts of green, and Jack read maybe the tenth billboard announcing, "Visit the Call of the Wild Museum in Gaylord!" Nothing else was said between the men until Donny Mathews pulled the blue goose up to the front entrance of St. Michael's Hospital.

Jack offered his hand and they shook heartily, until both men leaned into each other and exchanged a warm hug. There is, at times, a silent bond between men, forged by shared knowledge, shared experiences, or maybe just something they sense about one another. Jack now reflected, *In another life, in another time, we were once brothers.* Their eyes met for an instant. *Is this a guy I'd want in a foxhole with me when the shit starts and bullets are flying?* Donny, Jack was certain, was exactly that kind of man.

"I'm gonna go to your house, or cottage, right now, see if forensics and all of those cats are done snoopin' around. Here," Donny said as pulled a business card from his shirt pocket. "Take this and call me when you leave the hospital, whenever that is. Okay? You take care of yourself and your family, Jack. I'm gonna check up on you guys!" Donny pointed and shook an index finger.

Jack pocketed the card, got out of the car, and leaned in through the open door. "Anytime, Trooper Mathews, anytime at all. Thanks again."

Jack closed the door and walked toward the hospital. Donny rolled down his window and called out, "Turn left inside, take the elevator to three, then turn right and go to the end of the hall. She's in ICU—you can't miss it." Jack nodded and gave Donny a wave, walking briskly, and then in a full trot toward the hospital entrance.

Inside, Jack moved with purpose and followed Donny's instructions until he reached the double doors that opened automatically as he approached. He was greeted by the same sights and sounds and smells that Davie had experienced hours earlier. He walked quietly to the desks at the center of the round room. A tall, gaunt nurse with sharp features looked up over half-framed eyeglasses, her gray eyes widening and eyebrows arching as she anticipated an incoming question or request.

"Excuse me," Jack whispered. "Could you please direct me to Angela Thomas? I'm her husband, Jackson Thomas."

She smiled slightly and, without otherwise moving, pointed to a set of curtains with a black plastic nine affixed to the wall to the left. Jack nodded and mouthed a silent thank-you before turning toward the room. He paused before entering, took a deep breath, and braced himself for whatever awaited him within.

Davie slept on his side in a small lounger. Angie, connected to hanging bottles and beeping machines and lighted graphs, was covered in whites: sheets, bandages, gauze, blankets, and hospital gown. Flat on her back, save for an arm suspended in a ceiling sling, she slowly opened her eyes. She had always been the most beautiful woman he'd ever seen, and he began to cry. He had now officially cried more times in the three days just passed than he had in twenty years.

"Jackson," she whispered, and slowly raised her right hand.

"Oh, baby, I'm so sorry." He moved to her quickly and dropped to his knees. He took her right hand and began to kiss it. When he looked up, tears were streaming down his cheeks, and he bowed his head again, ashamed. "I'm so sorry," he murmured again and again. A deep well of emotions, the many feelings and fears he'd suppressed for so long, fought to leave him all at once.

Angie tenderly rubbed the back of his lowered head. When the heaves of his shoulders stopped, he looked up. She brought his hand to her lips and kissed it, pulling him up to her until his lips were upon hers, ignoring the shock waves of pain that surged throughout her body. She kissed him for all she was worth, and it *hurt* too, but she didn't care, not one damn bit; it felt too good and too *right*.

"Jack," she said delicately, carefully, sincerely, "you have nothing to be sorry about. Neither one of us must *ever* be sorry again, okay? Not between you and me. I love you, baby, and I always will. I've been stupid, Jack, and I know that now, but it doesn't matter anymore." She gingerly tugged him down again and they kissed, tenderly.

Jack stood and surveyed Angie from head to foot. In his eyes, no matter what happened to her or around her, she was always so enchanting that it melted his heart. He tried to keep to an analytical tack. He saw the bruises and cuts on her puffed face, her left arm heavily bandaged and in a sling, and heavy gauze covering her upper chest. He pushed down rage as it crept into his soul, already working to refill the emotional backlog he'd just depleted. He took a deep breath toward composure.

"What are the damages, sweet feets?" he finally asked.

She smiled and told him, saving the long gash across her chest for last. "Doctor says the scar should fade over time, but maybe never completely. For a while, years, maybe, it's gonna be pretty ... obvious." She winced a little and looked down at her feet.

"Baby, I don't care if it sings Christmas carols and has flashing lights! Every time I see it, and I hope that's a whole bunch, I'm gonna remember all of this," Jack said as he waved a free hand, "and how much I love you, and how close I came to losing you."

"Well, there are always turtlenecks!" She giggled and then cringed. "Jackson, it *does* hurt when I laugh! Those old gags are *true!*"

Jack leaned down and kissed her. He wanted to climb in the bed and hold her tightly, until he could feel her heart pounding against him, within him, in synch with his thumping heart, one throbbing, driving drumbeat. But that would have to wait. "I know you're tired, baby. I'm here now, and nothing could drag me away."

Davie yawned, stretched his arms and legs, rolled onto his other side with a grunt, and continued to sleep. "How's he doing?" Jack asked, shaking a thumb toward Davie. "The state police told me most of it, but not all of it, I don't think." He rubbed the back of his neck and looked at the boy.

"He's fine," Angie said, smiling. "He saved my life. I told the staff here that he was my son, so they'd let him come through with me, so now he's calling me Mom. Is that okay? Are you ready to be Dad?"

Jack flashed a big smile and vigorously nodded. "Yeah, yeah, I'm more than ready—Mom! Yeah, I think that's *great!*"

They shared the moment quietly, but both were beaming. Angie was blessed with another moment in love's truest, most precious glow, and she cherished it. She knew how close she'd come to the end of the line; she remembered seeing her parents playing cards and drinking martinis by the lake, and she was deeply thankful for this here and now. She did not want it to ever end.

Jack had seen death and despair in several forms over the past few days, and he basked in this instant of light and warmth, seizing it tightly for however long it lasted.

"Jack, I have a lot to tell you, but not now," Angie said softly after several moments had passed. "I'm too tired, too dopey, and baby, you look beat, too. But I want you to know that I love you with all my heart; I always will. When we do get clear of this, we're gonna live every day like it's our last and do all the things we've wanted to do—including a visit to those cabins in Virginia!"

Angie's green eyes twinkled in the darkened hospital room, and Jack dove into them blissfully. He knew in his heart that what she said was true. He believed her fully. Tons of stone crumbled to dust and fell from his back, and the walls he'd so carefully erected around his heart for years began to collapse.

"I love you too, honey," he said. "More than I can say, more than

I could ever hope to express. Nothing else matters. Go to sleep, and when you're rested, when you're ready, we'll talk. There's no rush for anything, not anymore." He kissed her again, her lips parting slightly to admit him, but his visit was brief by necessity and he backed off. *We'll have plenty of time for that later,* he thought. Angie closed her eyes, smiling sweetly, contentedly.

Jack walked around the bed to Davie and squatted down to his level. He reached out to the boy, but before he could make contact, Davie opened his eyes, slowly at first, and then as wide as his eyelids would allow. Jack threw an index finger up to his own lips.

"Uncle Jack!" Davie said in a loud whisper, and Angie didn't stir. "When did you get here? Did you talk to Mom?"

"Yes, yes, I did," Jack said. "How are you, porcupine? Okay? Is there room for my big butt on this thing?"

"There's always room for your big butt, horsefly!" an excited Davie declared.

Jack picked the boy up gently in his arms and then sat in the lounger, which sighed under the added weight. Jack had a curious relationship with furniture, chairs in particular, but amazingly, none had betrayed him thus far. He threw his legs up and over, then pulled the handle on the right side of the chair until the leg rest lifted and met the backs of his legs. He slid his butt to the far right side of the chair and then placed Davie into the new opening at his left side. Both stretched out, and the back rest went down until it was almost flat. The chair creaked faintly.

"Ahhhhh, that's the ticket. Hey, this ain't bad! So, I hear I'm your dad," Jack whispered.

"Is that okay with you?" Davie turned to face Jack, his left hand resting on the man's heart.

"I've felt like your dad for a long time, so I guess it's high time we made it official." Jack wrapped his arms around the boy and held him dear, a bond already struck and now set in stone, firmly in place. No more words were needed between them, so they held each other silently.

In a few minutes, they slept soundly as the bustling business of a hospital ICU ward carried on around them. Nurses popped in and out to record Angie's vital signs, check IVs, and issue meds, and everybody was called awake when dinner arrived, just as the day's last lights dimmed beyond the windowless walls.

They enjoyed hospital meat loaf, green beans, mashed potatoes, and red Jell-O, with small talk and some laughs. Jack was ravenous, and when Angie ate only a portion of her dinner, he eagerly polished it off. He chugged the last of his Coke, belching contentedly, and Davie followed suit. Everyone laughed, until Angie grimaced and moaned when her injuries barked back at her. Despite her pain, joy embraced them in this small cell they now shared as family.

Shortly after dinner, a doctor came by, and Jack and Davie were shooed from the room while he inspected Angie's wounds. Satisfied, he gave instructions to the nurse, who at once made preparations to change the dressing covering the cut on her chest. The doctor made a few notes on the chart and then moved closer to Angie.

The doctor was a handsome man in his late forties, Angie guessed, and now he smiled and gave her hand a kindly squeeze. *Jeez, she thought, those are some big, hairy paws for a surgeon!* He had a deep, full voice that called to mind Paul Carey, who shared Detroit Tiger radio broadcasts with Ernie Harwell and was known around Michigan as "The Voice of God."

"Maybe tomorrow," he continued, "we'll free you from the sling and let you take little walks, move around a bit. Your arm may never fully recover; there may be numbness, you may know the day before when it's going to rain, and you will *never* pitch for the Tigers. But there is nothing—absolutely *nothing*—that will stop you from living a full and happy life. Okay?"

Angie returned the smile and hand squeeze. She nodded as a couple of tears left home and wandered down her cheeks. They were not tears of sadness or self-pity, and the good doctor seemed to sense this. She wiped them away with her right hand.

"Thank you, Doctor, for everything," she said. "I truly appreciate it, and I am thankful for the care I've gotten here. My arm will be fine, and since I'm a righty, I just might pitch for the Tigers anyway!"

The doctor laughed out loud, a good, rich laugh that filled the room and let everyone who heard it know that it came from a warm place. He put the chart back and spoke softly with the nurse for a moment. She left, and the doctor returned to Angie's side.

"We're going to keep you in ICU, probably through tomorrow," he said, "and then I think for a day or three in a regular room. We'll play it by ear. I want you to keep still, let those wounds heal, and let your noggin settle down too. Then you can go home—if you'll promise to take it easy until your doctor back home gives you the word. Is it a deal?"

He offered his right hand, Angie grabbed it, and they shook on it. He placed her hand on the bed and turned to leave the room. He stopped short, stuck his head back around the curtain, and said, "Tell your menfolk to go home. I've given the nurse orders to knock you out for the night, so tell them to come back in the morning, say, after ten."

"Yes, sir," Angie said with a salute and a smile, and he left, for good this time.

Davie and his dad were lurking in the hall, just beyond the sensors that commanded the double doors. When the doctor came out, they came to attention. Jack walked toward him while Davie remained in place. The men conferred for a few minutes and shook hands. Jack thanked him profusely, and the doctor walked off through the auto-doors and into the hallway. Jack gestured to Davie, who came to his side, and together they reentered room nine.

Angie lit up when they came in and stuck her tongue out at Davie. "I'm gonna get ice cream before I go to bed!" she announced.

Davie sniggered and drew close to his mother. He took her hand, leaned in, and kissed her carefully on the lips. "I love you, Mom," the boy said. "Please take it easy, okay?"

"You betcha, babe," she said, beaming. "Doc says you two are gonna have to make like a banana and split."

"Yeah," Jack said. "He told us. But before I go, can I tap into your IV for a minute? I'd love to share that glow you've got going."

"Don't you dare make me laugh, Jackson Thomas!" But she couldn't help herself, and was pleased to discover that a recent jolt of fresh pain meds dulled the agony to a whisper. But that had very little to do with her glow. "Where are you guys gonna go?" she asked.

"The state trooper who brought me here—Donny—do you remember him?" Jack said, and Angie nodded. "He said to call him, that maybe the house would be clear by now."

"I don't know," Angie said slowly. "But if you do go there, stay out of our bedroom, okay? I think we should get a priest or something in there first." Their eyes met, and Jack understood just a tiny particle of the horrors she had survived.

"That's not a bad idea. I think we'll go to a motel tonight, maybe that new place over by Five Lakes."

Angie nodded, and Jack bowed and kissed her tenderly on the lips, lingering there for a moment as her warmth sped from her mouth to his heart. "I love you more than you will ever know, Angela Thomas," he whispered.

"One day real soon, I'm gonna make you back that up, big man!" She kissed him again, and he backed away, slowly.

"We'll see you bright and early," Jack said. "Is there anything I can bring you from the house?"

"Well, if you do go by there, will you grab me a flannel shirt and some warm socks? My feets get cold in here!" Angie wiggled her feet slightly under the blanket as Jack chuckled and nodded.

He took Davie by the shoulder and gently guided him past the curtains and into the center of the ICU. They stopped at the nurses' station, and Jack requested a pair of hospital socks for Angie. The nurse smiled and nodded, and Davie took Jack's hand. They walked out through the hall and into the elevator, down to ground level.

When they neared the main entrance, Jack suddenly realized he didn't have a car—Angie's LTD was still at the cottage. "I think we need to call a cab, hoser," Jack mumbled.

Davie pointed toward the walk outside, where a large man in blue and gray paced slowly in a small circle, puffing on a cigarette. "That's Sergeant McDonnell, Dad. He took our statements. I bet he'll help us!"

Father and son walked out of the hospital and into the evening, where a yellow moon captured and illuminated a cloudless sky. Up here, stars were plentiful, quite different from the sky anywhere near the city. Jack stopped and pointed to the heavens, where a magnificent show was on display, free of charge. All you had to do was look up. He and Davie enjoyed the view.

"Pretty, ain't it? Don't see that in Detroit, do you?" Rick McDonnell said as he strolled over and threw out an open right hand. Jack grabbed it, and the two men shook and exchanged nods. "You must be Mr. Thomas. I *know* this little big man." McDonnell gave Davie his umpteenth head rub of the day. Davie's cheeks blushed, and he smiled.

"Please, it's Jack. I want to tell you, I am forever in your debt. I can never repay the kindness and help you and the troopers gave me and my family today. All of your men were great, just outstanding, and I appreciate it."

Now it was the trooper's turn to blush, and he did, bowing

his head, taking a pull from his smoke. He blew a cloud into the night and snuffed the butt in a sand ashtray near the doorway. Two large glass doors slid open in separate directions, and closed when McDonnell stepped away. "It was my pleasure, Jack, believe me," he said. "Your wife is an amazing woman, do you know that?" He drew his face to a tight pinch and stared through Jack.

"Yes, sir, I sure do. I truly do. She's one of a kind, and I'm blessed to have her. She means the world to both of us," Jack pulled the boy against his leg, "and we're never gonna let her go."

"Good! If every guy had a lady like that, there'd be no need for flatfoots like me!" McDonnell reached into a pants pocket, pulled out a set of keys, and handed them to Jack, who recognized the goofy green rubber frog that dangled from the key ring: they were Angie's car keys. McDonnell pointed to his right, and there sat the silver LTD, directly under a light pole, awash in fluorescent white.

"Again, thank you!" said Jack, smiling at the big trooper. "Are they finished at the house? We were thinking of going to that new joint on Five Lakes."

"Yeah, do that," McDonnell said. "We're gonna need to keep the house closed for a couple more days. I had my female trooper remove your wife's clothes and what-nots, and that stuff's in the trunk. Leave the house to us for now, okay? I think it's gonna need more . . . attention."

"Yes. Angie already asked us not go in there, and thanks to you, it's now completely unnecessary." Jack stopped and slowly lowered and shook his head. Emotions surged through him with force, and he began to cry quietly. McDonnell took a shoulder in each hand and braced Jack slightly.

"That's okay, Jack. I know how tough this has been on all of you, and I admire you more than I can say. Go home, have a beer, hug each other, get a good night's sleep, and it's back at it tomorrow. Okay?"

Jack wiped at his cheeks and nodded. "Yes, we will. Thanks again, Sarge," Jack said, again shaking McDonnell's hand. "You guys are the best. From now on, whenever I see a blue goose on the side of the highway, I will think only good thoughts and never say anything rude."

McDonnell placed his hands on his hips, leaned back, and roared, laughing straight up to the heavens. "Get outta here, both o' ya, before I run youse two mugs in!" He dropped to one knee with a slight grunt and rested a hand on Davie's shoulder. "Sometimes," he said gently, looking into Davie's eyes, "bad things, or bad people, mess things up for the rest of us." Davie nodded. "Look up at the sky again, son. You just gotta believe there's more good than bad. Okay?"

Davie looked up to the heavens, where stars sparkled and the moon flushed the sky with a faint yellow gleam, for a long moment. He then dropped his gaze back to the trooper's eyes. "Okay, Sarge," he whispered with a warm smile. "You too. Okay?" McDonnell chuckled, stood straight, nodded to Jack, and continued to smile as he disappeared into the hospital.

Rick McDonnell would now check on the trooper he'd left on night watch, go home, kiss his girlfriend (the "dopey broad from the bowling alley") like he'd been at sea for six months, drink three beers, eat her pot roast with glee, and make love to her with tender care. He would then sleep like a very happy baby.

Jack and Davie went to a motel on Five Lakes, after stopping at a mom-and-pop grocery for some snacks and drinks. Jack turned on the television for Davie, fired up a smoke, and called the ICU desk at the hospital to let them know where he could be reached. He then phoned Terry Ralls. Just as he was about to hang up, he heard a click, and Katie Ralls said, "Hello?"

"Hi, Katie, it's Jack."

"Oh, thank God. I was hoping you'd call," she said anxiously. "How are Angie and Davie?"

"Davie is fine. He's with me; we're at a motel now. Angie is in ICU, but she's gonna be fine." Jack gave her a quick account of Angie's injuries and the doctor's prognosis.

"Terry is out walking Curly," Katie reported. "I think they're in your backyard, sniffing around. Those two are bonding; I swear they're starting to look alike!" She paused for several heartbeats while Jack snickered. "Are *you* okay, Jackson?"

"Yes, yes, I am now," he said. "Just tired, but *happy*, for the first time in a long time, you know? I guess that sounds weird, but ..." He lost his train of thought and his voice trailed off. *Oh Jesus, don't tell me I'm gonna start bawlin' again!*

"No, that isn't weird at all," Katie said. "I get it. Listen, they got the phones up and running an hour or so ago, cable back on tomorrow, they say, and Terry says the phone people dragged that fallen tree out of the way, so it can wait. Or he'll have somebody clear it out, if that's what you want."

"Tell him thanks, and I love him," Jack said. "And you, too, Kates, I truly do. We're gonna be up here for a few days, at least till the end of the week, I think. Okay? Are you okay with keeping Curly?"

"Are you kidding? We love that old knucklehead! Hey, what's one more old knucklehead in this house gonna matter?" Katie laughed, filling the phone line with a musical inflection. "I am a professional knucklehead handler from waaaaay back!"

Jack and Katie passed a few instructions, phone numbers, messages, and good wishes back and forth through the line. "Jack, take as much time as you need," she said. "We're here, so keep in touch. Anything you need, *anything*, just call, promise?"

"You know it," Jack said. "Tell that big ape you married we'll talk tomorrow, and don't worry about the tree. It ain't goin' anywhere, and neither are we. Maybe tomorrow, Angie will feel up to calling you guys, too."

"Oh, that would be so great! Please give her our love, and we'll talk soon. And Jack …" There was a short lull, and Jack heard her take in a deep breath. "You take care of yourself, okay? No beating yourself up over this one, *comprende?*"

"I read you loud and clear. Thanks, Katie."

They both hung up. Jack sat still for a moment and once again counted his blessings. He made a mental note to call his boss and good friend Tony at Ford's in the morning, and Davie's school, too. He also knew that he needed to tell Davie about Stan Koski, but decided this was not the time. It could wait until morning.

They ate turkey and cheese sandwiches, drank cold Coca-Colas, and topped it all off with a couple of Milky Ways. Jack and Davie crashed in the king-size bed in the motel room, and they, too, slept deeply, without dreams, without fear.

Outside, just down the road from the motel, under that vivid yellow moon and a field of sparkling stars, a massive wolf ambled deliberately around the house on Lakewood Drive, at each round stopping in the backyard to survey the lake. Flecks of dazzling gold twinkled in its great emerald eyes as it sat in the shadows, waiting, watching.

At dawn's first faint light, satisfied that all was well, the wolf broke into a trot and then a full sprint, across the road out front, into the dark depths of the forest. High above, in a nearby tree, a crow cawed loudly twice, and the sounds of a new day answered as the world once again came to life.

After another day in ICU, Angie was transferred to a private room on the fourth floor. It was much quieter there, and she enjoyed spending time with Jack and Davie when they came to visit. They arrived early in the morning and left after dinner, when weariness overtook Angie and she chased them out for the day. She was now free of the ceiling sling for her arm, and was allowed to take short walks and sit up in a chair.

On Friday morning, her doctor was satisfied that Angie had healed enough to be sent home, although her activities would be restricted for a few weeks until her wounds fully mended and her strength was restored. Jack and Angie decided the family would stay at the motel through the weekend, and then consider returning to their suburban Detroit home on Monday.

After Davie had gone to bed on Saturday night, Jack and Angela sat and talked at the table by a large window overlooking the lake. They eased into the conversation, beginning with their feelings for each other and for Davie. There was another subject brewing just beneath the surface, however, that now demanded expression.

"Angie," Jack said, reaching out and grasping her hand, "I'm sorry that you lost our baby, and I'm sorry that I wasn't there for you when you needed me. I was hurt because you didn't tell me. I just didn't understand, and I couldn't get the idea out of my head that you didn't want the baby."

Angie stroked his hand and then reached up to caress his face. His gaze was cast down to the tabletop, until he looked up and into her eyes. What he saw there, swimming in green and bits of gold, broke his heart. He began to cry.

"No, no, no, baby," she murmured. "I know, I know." She put her right hand on the back of his neck, pulled his head toward her, and tenderly kissed his forehead. "I should have told you right away, Jackson, but I was scared, terrified, that the baby might be ... *crazy*, or dangerous. That I had bad genes. My sister, my mother ... you know how it went for them. It was stupid of me, thinking like that." She put her fingers under Jack's chin, lifted his face, and stared into his eyes. He started to speak, but she pressed an index finger against his lips.

"No," she said softly, "let me finish. The day I lost him, I was crazy with fear and pain and sadness when you got to the hospital. You know, don't you, that I would have *never* done anything to hurt our baby. You *know* that, don't you?" She looked hard into his eyes, waiting for a curtain to rise, for the lights to come on, for a sign that he understood all that she'd said.

Jack smiled into Angie's emerald eyes through the tears that streaked his face. He cleared his throat, wiped at his cheeks and eyes, and then took her face in both hands. "Yeah, I *do* know that, honey." He paused and kissed her lips. "I was terrified when I got the call that you'd been rushed to the hospital, and I was hurt because you hadn't told me. I didn't handle it well, I guess."

"No shit, Sherlock," she said, lowering her voice as close to a baritone as she could get. They both began to laugh, nervously at first, until it reached a happy crescendo. They threw their arms around one another (one arm, in Angie's case), and held the embrace for long moments. After a while, Angie pulled back and kissed his ear, his cheek, and then planted one square on his lips.

"I need to tell you about Peter," she said, her voice hushed, her cheeks reddening. "I want you to know that I never slept with him, but it came close to that. I did invite him up here for the weekend. I did think about sleeping with him, before he got here, but I changed my mind." She again tenderly stroked his face. "You know why?" He looked into her eyes and shook his head.

"You," she whispered. "It was because of you. You called here, twice, and that did it. The way you sounded, what you said—*you* changed my mind. I knew if I did sleep with Peter, there would be no taking it back, and we'd be done." She began to cry.

Jack took her shoulders in his hands and delicately straightened her in the chair. "That's okay," he said softly. "Forget it; it's done. We're here now, right?" She nodded and wiped away the glistening wet lines from her cheeks. "And I've got to tell you something, honey," he said. "I came close to blowing it, too." Jack told her about his encounter with Veronica in the Avenue Bar. She listened, never taking her eyes from his face, as he told her what he had been doing as she was being wheeled into surgery.

Jack began to sob, his shame exiting in bursts and fits. Angie again raised his chin and gazed into his eyes. "Like you said, babe, we're *here now*," she said firmly. "We came close, but we came back to each other, and that's all that matters. So whattaya say, porcupine? Can we forgive ourselves and each other?"

"Yes," Jack said. He kissed her slowly and gently on the mouth, and held her in both arms. "I'm sorry if I'm manhandling you. I know you're sore," he said, leaning back a little to gaze into her emerald eyes. He knew he could get lost in there, safe and warm, loved.

"We had quite a week, didn't we?" Angie stated.

"I haven't told you all of it, but it started with Cheetah." Jack then told her about the old deaf woman who died in front of the bar. "And I told you about Stan Koski, how I found him, but at least he went out with a smile," Jack said wistfully. "Oh, and Curly and me nearly got crushed by the big oak tree in the backyard. It got hit by lightning while we were in the yard."

Angie began to giggle. "That would have been quite a sight, you two flattened in the backyard. I can see the headline: 'Bluto and Elmer Fudd Flattened by Oak Tree!'" She was laughing now, and Jack joined her. They laughed until they cried, but the sadness was gone, washed away.

When he'd composed himself, Jack leaned close to Angie and kissed her nose. "Did I tell you about the critter that growled at me, right before the oak tree fell?" he asked. "I heard it, just beyond the tree line, when I buried Cheetah, too. All I saw were these green eyes, glaring and glowing at me, but it growled like it was huge and pissed off. It scared the crap outta me, and Curly too."

Angie's jaw dropped. She turned and stared out the window and into the night. She stood, slowly, and with a slight limp and a low groan, padded around the table, pulled back the curtain, and tapped on the window. She thought she knew where their cottage was, and so she pointed into the night. Jack followed with his eyes, but remained in his chair.

"Jack, the night Peter came up here, before he ... you know, came back to do what he tried to do, I had a dream. I was sitting on the pier at the cottage," she turned to face Jack, "and I heard a growl and saw those green eyes too, glowing, and they were ... *ominous*. I tried to run inside, but I fell, and the *thing* told me to leave, to take Davie and leave." She lowered her chin to her chest and, dropping to her deepest voice, imitated the beast in the tall grass. "'*Take the boy and leave at once!*' it said."

Angie returned to her chair and sat down. She and Jack stared at each other for a long moment, and then Angie shivered as a chill ran up her spine. "You know," Jack said, "Davie told me that he had a dream about a wolf. In his dream, he thought that the wolf was God. Then he thought the wolf was outside, in our woods, when I was burying Cheetah. He asked me if the wolf killed Cheetah."

"Wow," Angie mumbled. "Weird. We're gonna have to think about this one. All I'm missing now is one of your Dylan songs." She pointed and wiggled an index finger at Jack, and then leaned forward and kissed him.

He returned the favor and whispered, "You know what Dylan would say about this?"

"No; please tell me," she purred in his ear.

"It takes a lot to laugh, it takes a train to cry," Jack said slowly, then kissed her cheek, stood, and carefully lifted her to her feet.

"What the hell does that mean?" she asked.

Jack shrugged and led Angie toward the bed. "You think about it, you know, and it'll come to you. Like any Dylan song," he said.

Jack and Angie climbed into bed and soon fell asleep, wrapped in each other's arms, as Davie slept soundly in a sleeping bag on a motel cot just a few feet away.

Outside it was cool and calm, but for an occasional breeze that quietly played among the pines and brushed against the windows. A pair of bright green eyes softened in the huge head of a beast that stood at ease at the edge of the lake and lapped up cold water with its tongue. It listened to the stars for a moment, then ambled without haste into the trees and was lost to the night.

Epilogue

O n Monday, the Thomas family made the drive south on I-75 for home. It was midafternoon, a bright and blue spring day, when Jack pulled the LTD into their driveway and parked outside the garage on Bull Run Way. The family was almost immediately swarmed by Katie and Terry Ralls and a jubilant bulldog named Curly.

Jack was stunned to see that the downed tree in their backyard was gone, reduced to a stack of firewood, placed neatly against the back wall of the garage. He gave Terry a hug, and when he finished it off with a kiss on the cheek, his friend blushed. "Ahhhhh, knock it off, ya mutt! I gave the guy about a third of the wood, so it didn't cost a dime. I hope that's okay," Terry explained.

"Beautiful, just beautiful," Jack said. "I really appreciate it, T. Help yourself to the stash whenever you want some firewood, all right?"

"You know what's funny?" Terry put a hand on Jack's shoulder and said, "That tree tore up a fair piece of ground back there, and so did Ma Bell's crew. But Cheetah's grave wasn't disturbed at all, and it should have been, for sure. It's right in the middle of the whole deal!" He looked at Jack and scratched his chin. "I know where you put the marker stick, and you can see the fresh ground. But it was and is totally undisturbed."

Jack shrugged, extended his arms outward, palms up, and grinned at his friend. This wasn't the first strange thing he'd seen or heard in the days just passed. They unloaded the car, and all reconvened in the house, where Curly excitedly made the rounds. He was very careful, almost delicate, around Angie; he went completely nuts with Davie, who fell to the floor and rolled around with his pal, giggling merrily.

"Curly is a real beaut." Katie chuckled. "He was a pleasure to have around the house—except for the farting contest he and Sgt. Schultz"—she pointed at Terry—"had one night. Lord, have *mercy* on me!" She waved both hands briskly through the air as everyone laughed.

"Hey, you're the one who made corned beef and cabbage!" said Terry. He and Curly exchanged glances, and everyone cracked up all over again.

They enjoyed the day and, after Angie went down for a quick nap, topped it off with a barbecue in the Rallses' backyard. Neighbors and friends wandered in and out, all expressing good wishes for the Thomas clan, sharing cold Stroh's, burgers, and Ball Park Franks. It was a good neighborhood, where people looked out for one another and shared in life's wins and losses. Stan Koski's death was a definite loss; Angie's safe return was a big win.

Life resumed its normal ebb and flow in the days and weeks that followed. One night, Henry Ritter, Stan Koski's lawyer, phoned and asked if he might pay a visit. An hour later, Jack poured this stylish man a glass of chardonnay. Angela and Davie joined the two men at the kitchen table, and Curly flopped at their feet, head resting on forepaws, eyes open and alert.

"I'm happy that you are doing so well, Mrs. Thomas," the lawyer said, his rich voice articulating each word like a Shakespearean actor, projecting to the last row of a packed theater.

"Thank you, but please call me Angie," she said with a smile.

"Fine, that's fine." Henry nodded and smiled and then opened a leather folder he'd carried in. He extracted several documents and set them on the tabletop. "Stanley was a very generous and considerate man, as I'm sure you are all aware," he said.

All three members of the Thomas family nodded, because it was true. Stan Koski had never been anything but kind to all of them. However gruff his demeanor occasionally seemed, he was a beloved curmudgeon, noted for his honesty and kindness by all of his neighbors. He would be greatly missed.

"He has left his home and the bulk of his estate to his daughter, Rose, who we are still in the process of locating. However ..." The lawyer paused and took a sip of wine. "My, this is quite good!" He lifted the glass, peered intently into its contents, as if he saw magic in there, and then took another sip. "It's really lovely, Jack. My compliments, truly. Won't you join me?"

Jack leaned over, grabbed the bottle, refilled Henry's glass, and poured one for Angie too. He went to the fridge, withdrew a Coke and a Stroh's, and returned to the table. Pull tabs snapped, two cans hissed, and Jack and Davie took healthy drinks as Angie and the lawyer enjoyed their wine.

"That's better," Henry declared. He returned his attention to the documents on the table, quickly scanning the papers until he found what he was looking for. "First, Mr. Koski has left a sum of $75,000 to be placed in trust for the college education of David William

Adams. With interest, it should be considerably more than that by the time the young man is ready to put it to use. Should he elect, or should circumstances dictate that David not attend college, the fund will remain in trust until he reaches the age of twenty-one, when the fund will be rendered to him in its entirety, at his direction, to use as he sees fit."

"Holy crap," Angie blurted.

Henry Ritter laughed out loud. "Holy crap indeed," he said with a chuckle.

"I had a dream about Mr. Stan the night he died," the boy said. "He told me not to worry, and that everything was gonna be okay, and then he sailed off with Missus Hildie in a big sailboat."

The three adults exchanged glances and raised eyebrows at the boy and then each other. Jack leaned over and gave Davie a hug. "You knew Mr. Stan had passed, son, before I told you about it?" Jack kept an arm around the boy's shoulder and stared into his bottomless blue eyes, which were beginning to fill with tears.

"No, not for sure," the boy said. "Not until you told me a couple days later, but I had a pretty good idea that he was, you know, gone."

"He loved you, Davie," Angie said, the waterworks active in her eyes, too. "He told me many times what a beautiful boy you are, and those were his exact words, baby."

"Let's continue, shall we?" the lawyer said, tapping his papers twice with a pen. "Mr. Koski has also left a sum of $50,000 to Jackson and Angela Thomas, to be shared jointly, at once."

"Holy crap!" Angie exclaimed. Again, the lawyer laughed out loud.

"We certainly didn't expect anything like that," Jack said. "Honestly, I feel funny taking it, you know? Do you think his daughter, or someone else in the family, will object or be upset?"

"No, no, not at all," Henry said, shaking his head. "She has been quite handsomely taken care of, assuming we do find her." Henry took a drink of wine. "Mr. Koski has also provided for your neighbor, Mrs. Katherine Ralls, of whom he was also quite endeared."

"Oh, that's just wonderful," Angie said, beaming. "Katie was a big help to Stan over the years, and we know how sad she was when he passed. But I'll tell you something." She paused and sipped at the chardonnay. "If I know Katie, she's not gonna want the money. She never did any of it for a reward. She loved Stan like a very dear grandfather."

"Oh, don't worry about that, Angela," Henry said as he reached out, took her hand, and gave it a gentle squeeze. "I'll see that she understands how important it was to Stan that she's provided for. He didn't leave *any* of this money as *payment*, absolutely not. He left this money to bring happiness, and some security, to the people he *loved*. You were all quite dear to him, I assure you; hence, this will." He tapped on the papers in front of him three times.

After Henry Ritter collected signatures from each member of the Thomas family, and provided a few hereby and wherefores and other legal jargon, he carefully placed the documents back in their leather folder. "Before I go, I would like to say something to you, Angela," the lawyer said.

Angie straightened in her chair, her left arm still in a cast from elbow to wrist. "Yes, Mr. Ritter?"

"I am aware of your ... *experiences* up north," he said, speaking slowly. "I am fully prepared to represent you in a suit against Peter Brookings's estate, which I'm told is considerable. You are clearly entitled to remuneration for your damages, hospital care—what you've had thus far, and any you may require in the future—as well as your pain and suffering."

Angie began to quietly cry. Jack walked to her, crouched, and wrapped an arm around her shoulders. Davie then followed suit, his arms around her waist.

"Hey, you two clowns, I'm okay, really," she said, but she did not struggle or resist. Henry Ritter could plainly see love in her green eyes, glowing behind a clear veil of shining tears.

"I would be honored to represent you pro bono, Angela." He extended his right hand to Angie, who warmly took it in both of her hands.

"Okay," she said, "but no pro bono, Mr. Ritter, please. We'll pay whatever fee you think is fair. I'm a legal secretary, you know. Maybe I can help you—after all, I'm unemployed!"

"Who's Pro Boner?" Davie asked, his head tilted slightly toward the lawyer.

Henry Ritter again laughed, his amusement let loose in a full-throated roll. It then struck Jack that the lawyer looked quite a bit like Frederic March, the actor. He carried a quiet but forceful dignity, and Jack would bet that played very well in a courtroom.

"Thank you, Mr. Ritter, you've been very kind, and we appreciate all that you've done," Angie said, leaning over the table, still holding Henry's hand and staring into his steel-gray eyes. "I accept your offer to represent me and my family from this day forward. We have other matters to handle for our future, and we'd love to entrust you with these too, if you're agreeable."

"Wonderful! Of course!" said the lawyer, clapping his hands. "Now, is there any more of this fine wine, Jackson?"

"Absolutely," said Jack, already pouring a fresh glassful. He smiled at Angie and gave her a conspiratorial wink; they'd been discussing how to go about the legal transition from their roles as Davie's guardians to permanent adoption, and now they had their answer.

After a little more chardonnay, Henry Ritter basked in a quiet moment they all shared in the Thomas family kitchen. It was a good feeling, a sense of togetherness, one that you'd wish could last forever, but you knew it would soon pass.

"You know," the lawyer said wistfully, "the poet William Blake once wrote, 'There is a moment in each day that Satan cannot find.'"

"That's lovely," Angie said softly. "This is *our* moment for today, isn't it?"

"Yes," Henry replied, gazing directly into her beautiful green eyes. "Yes, it is."

Henry raised his glass in a toast. They sat and talked into the evening, until the night's swathe was complete and the moon rose as a pale sliver. Henry Ritter drove away in his black Mercedes, no worse for wear, his faculties unimpeachable by wine or the vagaries of the law.

Angie's wounds healed almost entirely in time, although surgery was required to repair the damage done to her left arm, and it would remind her of the assault from time to time for the rest of her life. She was always the first to know when it was going to rain. Cat Stevens was right; the first cut *is* the deepest.

She fussed over the scar on her chest for a while, using the trickeries of makeup and neck-high blouses. But she simply let it go when it became quite obvious to her that Jack, and everyone else, cared not a whit about that thin pink line that ran from shoulder to shoulder. It would further fade away with each passing month until, one day, it was almost imperceptible.

Jack went back to work at Ford, and Davie returned to school, each cheerfully welcomed back by friends, coworkers, and classmates. When summer came at last and school bells chimed no more, the Thomas family spent every available hour together. Angie hired a local crew to completely gut the bedroom in which she had been attacked up north. They removed every piece of furniture, every yard of carpet, and every stitch of linen. They then repainted the room— three times, per Angie's orders, expense be damned. She was, after all, going to send the bill to Peter Brookings.

Emptied and refreshed, the room was refilled with simple furniture: a bed, a dresser, a small mirror, a nightstand, a chair, plain white curtains. When the Thomas family did return, they never used the room again, even after the local parish priest blessed the house and chased away evil with a Latin incantation.

Angie told Jack that she would have sold the place and gotten another one, maybe somewhere on the other side of the state, but she believed her parents were still hanging around, drinking martinis and playing gin rummy on the beach. Jack smiled at the notion and gave his wife a hug.

Davie dreamed of the wolf from time to time, often in advance of a life-changing event. When Curly seemed a little off later that summer, the wolf told Davie in a dream, "The dog is sick and needs help." So it was Davie who asked Jack to take the dog to their veterinarian, who found a grapefruit-sized tumor in Curly's stomach. It was surgically removed, and Curly soon returned to his chuckleheaded ways.

Jack fully appreciated his family, and was thankful that he and Angie were as close as they'd ever been. Sometimes, he wondered how or why their relationship had veered off the tracks, why they'd strayed from one another, but he was slowly learning it was pointless to waste time brooding about the past when so much of the present, the *now*, beckoned them to bask in the love they shared. Who knew when there would be no more tomorrows? That was the one true inevitability we all shared, Jack understood.

In early fall, Jack and Angie Thomas returned to Skyline Drive in Virginia, while Davie and Curly moved into the Rallses house to bring that couple a week of joy and laughter. Jack and Angie came home, absolutely blissful, and proclaimed their great love for the Old Dominion state and its bountiful, scenic splendors.

"So, where are the pictures?" Terry Ralls asked.

"Yeah, let's see a little bit of Old Virginny!" Katie Ralls demanded.

"Well, uh," said Jack, stammering, "we, uh, don't have any, uh, pictures."

"No. I think maybe we forgot the camera or film or something," Angie muttered.

Katie and Terry Ralls stared incredulously at the two lovers for a moment and then giggled like schoolkids. Jack and Angie turned a little red and joined in their goofy neighbors' amusement.

"Maybe it was raining, you ever think of that?" Jack protested weakly.

"That's okay, you two lovebirds. We did get a postcard, right, babe?" asked Katie, nodding to her husband.

"That's true," said Terry. "We sure did! It was a deer in the mountains, right? That was sure scenic!"

Everyone got more than a postcard a few weeks later, when Angela Thomas learned she was pregnant. Davie was as excited as anyone, wishing out loud for a little brother to play ball with, to take fishing, to do all of those things that brothers do together.

"What if it's a girl, wheezer?" his dad asked.

"Well, if it's a girl ..." The boy paused, letting that possibility sink in. "That's okay too. She can still go fishin' and play ball and stuff, right?"

Time would tell the tale, as it always does, and those who listen are slightly more prepared than the rest of us when its plans are at last revealed. Along Bull Run Way, there were still many stories to be told: some sad, some joyful, some extraordinary. But they would be shared or endured, suffered or cherished, however the cards fell. "It's not the hand you're dealt," Stan Koski often said. "It's how you play the cards. *That's* what counts. That's how we're judged, when all is said and done, so play 'em for all you're worth."

Early most evenings, as his family settled in for the night, Curly took his evening stroll, generally sticking to the backyard, where he waddled and sniffed and snooped until he found just the right spot and did what nature demanded. Sometimes he found himself at the back of the Thomas yard, where that old oak tree was felled, and where his friend Cheetah slept beneath earth and grass.

Sometimes, Curly heard grumblings beyond the tree line or snarls in the woods, and two or three times, he'd seen those glaring green eyes burning through the tall grass. But they no longer frightened him, no longer threatened him, and so he left them alone.

Credits

"Simple Twist of Fate," "Shelter from the Storm," "It Takes a Lot to Laugh, It Takes a Train to Cry" ~ Words and music by Bob Dylan

"Werewolves of London" ~ Words and music by LeRoy Marinell, Waddy Wachtel, and Warren Zevon

"Who Can It be Now" ~ Words and music by Colin James Hay

"(You've Lost) That Lovin' Feeling" ~ Words and music by Barry Mann, Phil Spector, and Cynthia Weil

"If Ever You're in My Arms Again" ~ Words and music by Cynthia Weil and Thomas R. Snow

"Ghost Riders in the Sky" ~ Words and music by Stan Jones

Piano Sonata No. 14 in C-sharp minor *"Quasi una fantasia"* ("Moonlight Sonata")

~ Composed by Ludwig van Beethoven

"Ghostbusters" ~ Words and music by Ray Parker

"The First Cut Is the Deepest" ~ Words and music by Cat Stevens

"The Man Against the Sky" ~ Edward Arlington Robinson

"The Rime of the Ancient Mariner" ~ Samuel Taylor Coleridge

"There Is a Moment" ~ William Blake

The Scarlet Letter ~ Nathaniel Hawthorne

As a four-year-old boy, Davie Adams finds his
mother in the bathtub, her wrists slashed with
a razor blade. Four years later, his father—a
murderer several times over—sits on death row.
Now eight, Davie is being raised by his aunt and
uncle, Angie and Jackson Thomas. Their marriage
is near collapse, the consequence of a shared
heartbreak that has been left unresolved.

Dreams and real-life drama interact and guide
them toward remaining together as an intimate
family, but if they should stray too far from the path,
danger and death awaits. Will the wolf that visits
Davie in his dreams devour their hope and tear the
family apart, or will it lead them back to one another
and the love they share?

A multi-layered novel, *Off the Path* weaves drama,
fantasy, horror, and humor to tell the story of eight-year-old
Davie, his aunt and uncle, and their struggles to overcome
threats to their family from within—and without. They must
be very careful to not stray from the path.

DANIEL J. WELLS has been a
sergeant in the US Marine Corps, bartender,
radio disc jockey, supervisor, and proofreader. He
earned a bachelor's degree with majors in written
communications and history from Eastern Michigan University and a
master's degree in history from Oakland University. Wells lives in Royal
Oak, Michigan.

iUniverse®
Editor's Choice